SONS

ALPHONSO MORGAN

D1247571

SONS

Published by:

Lane Street Press
399 Sterling Place
Brooklyn, New york, 11238

alphonsomorgan.com

Copyright © 2004 by Alphonso Morgan

ISBN 0-9748753-7-6

Cover design and Illustrations by:
Jason Mickle

Printed by adibooks.com United States of America

All rights reserved. No part of this book may be reproduced
In any form without written permission from the publisher,
Lane Street Press

For Marabelle…

But when they persecute you in this City, flee ye into another:

Matthew, 10:23

DAY

ONE

When the sun slipped into his room and cast a perfect white rectangle mask onto his eyes and forehead, Aaron didn't suspect a thing. The anticipation which had begun needling him from the moment he flickered his eyes open into the blindness of the light he attributed simply to the call of summer, which began, officially, on that day. Not officially, in the haphazard manner with which the months and years are delineated by the stars or by the angle of the earth tilting toward the sun, but o-ficially, because the New York public schools commissioner had said that it was so. It was June 17th.

Aaron sat up and rubbed his eyes, angled out of bed and into a pair of rubber sandals parked beside it. The room was dark except for the finger of light that pointed down at him from the paned square of glass at the top corner of the room. He wiggled his feet in the sandals and stood, took three familiar steps to the little mirror leaning against the wall of his small square of a room in the basement. Normally, after a few seconds in the dark, he would reach for the switch to the right of the mirror and pour a hundred watts of hard light into the situation to get a clearer picture. But today he felt somehow unprepared for what he might find in the harsh reality of light, so he stared into the shadowy

1

reflection of the mirror, faintly recalling the way his waistline curved down into his too-loose boxers, unable to make out the ridges of his stomach or the outline of his still broadening shoulders.

At sixteen Aaron was small—compact, it could be said—but unmistakably reminiscent of a man. His brown body had yet to take on the full flavor of manhood, but the promise of it wafted from every pore, mixed subtly with the colognes and aftershaves which, he thought, masked his adolescence. His muscles, though not fully developed, were sinewy and lean and pulsed under his skin. His thin arms and legs curved out at the biceps and calves just enough to say that the little boy who had inhabited that body months before was gone, and that a full-blown man might just come pounding out at any minute.

To Aaron's eyes, though, peeking through the darkness, he was the same skinny kid he had been years before, except for the shadow which gathered now above his lip and trailed imperceptibly down his jaw. He no longer wanted to be that skinny kid, no longer wanted to weigh a hundred twenty pounds or wear two pairs of sweat pants beneath his jeans to disguise his little waist. He wanted to be six feet tall and look down into the eyes of other sixteen-year-olds instead of up. He turned away from the mirror and lifted an abandoned T-shirt from the foot of his bed, pulled it on and went out of his room, down the hall, toward the creaking staircase, leaving the fading white rectangle on the bed near his pillow.

In the kitchen his mother stomped frantically around sipping and choking into a broken coffee cup, inserting items into a black leather bag. Aaron recognized this: her effort not to be late for the third time in one week to the bright tiny cubicle under the clocktower of the Republic National Bank where she worked.

"What you doin' up so early?" she said and looked

at him. "Forget you ain't have school today?"

"Sun woke me up," he said quietly, sitting down at the table.

"The sun?" she said, and stood for a moment in front of him. "I guess you think you too old for me to slap you 'cross your mouth?" They stared at each other.

"I ain't got time to play with you," she said after a moment. "I am late for work." She went out of the kitchen, and from the front hallway said: "Your Uncle Jack is dropping Anise off at 5:30. You better be here to let her in, or you going to be in trouble. You hear me?" The front door opened. "And stay out of the streets!" It slammed shut and Aaron could hear her scuffed black pumps clomp away down Newkirk toward the D train.

Anise was his sister. She was nine years old. She had the exact round head her brother had, and his exact color, with exact black hair twisted into geometric configuration by her mother on Sundays. The style, whatever it was, was intended to last all week, until the following Sunday when she would again get her creative juices flowing and invent a totally new series of flips and twists for her little daughter's hair. But Anise had her own ideas, and had usually, by Tuesday or Wednesday, reduced her mother's weekly ritual into a lone unicorn twist down her back. Anise liked the *idea* of getting her hair done, and would sit in front of the mirror those Sunday nights admiring and examining that week's creation. But a head full of ribbons and whatnot was unconducive to a week's romping and Tom-boying.

Aaron liked his sister. The amount of control she seemed to have over her little life infuriated him. But he forgave her because he realized there was something of it in him too—a basic ability to handle almost anything life dished up, maneuver in whatever predicament. But there were times when he doubted himself, when adolescent uncertainty crept in to blur his vision and put a choke hold on his confidence. A neat combination of aloofness and brand-name clothes was

3

Aaron's cool camouflage, his very effective way of projecting a more perfect version of himself onto the world.

But today Aaron felt only anticipation, a prickly urgency to step out into the world and feel against his skin whatever was in the air. Quickly he showered and dressed and stepped coolly out onto the stoop. He could hear the jingle and chimes of the ice cream truck dissolving odd into the morning. He breathed the Brooklyn air, considered his mother's admonition, and dropped off the steps, kicking his black and brown Gore-Tex boots down Newkirk toward Flatbush Avenue.

TWO

At 9:45 in the morning, Sha sat on gray cement steps squeezing a spark into the tip of a Newport. By that time he had already pulled three cherry embers down the white shafts of three previous Newport cigarettes, pushing his jaw forward and pressing the smoke out of his lungs in short, forceful breaths. Everything Sha did, he did exactly in this manner: Forcefully. Quickly. Decisively. All of the daily processes of life being done with force and decision to mask the limpness of life in its greater scheme.

The steps he sat on were attached to a row of brick apartments. The owner of the steps, Mrs. Barbara Beckford, left for work by eight-o'clock each morning and he would plant himself on her stoop, which was closest to the Avenue, and sit for hours smoking weed and cigarettes, watching the brown bodies move through the sun up and down Flatbush Avenue.

Sha took a last pull of his cigarette and flicked it to the ground. His eyes scanned the Avenue, past the old Jamaican ladies in their printed hats and dresses, and the young men in their blue and gray uniforms delivering produce and Coca-Cola and cigarettes. Down the block, past the blue and white ice cream truck with its sunny jingle and chimes sounding before any cones or sundaes or bombpops would be wanted in the day, a familiar stride was making its way down the Avenue in his direction. He had seen Aaron before, carrying himself through the neighborhood on his manicured teenage gait, going to the store or back and forth to school.

They had collided one afternoon that winter. Aaron was coming out of the bodega with a carton of milk for his mother. His headphones pounded against his ears and he hadn't noticed Sha stepping into the store as he was stepping out. Their bodies came together, and startled Aaron dropped the bag containing his mother's milk and started to fall back into the store himself. Sha had instinctively put his arm around Aaron just at his waist to steady him until he felt the hard little body regain its balance and stoop to pick up the dropped package.

"You alright, son?" Sha had said, looking at him.

"I'm cool," Aaron blurted too loudly over the head-phones. He slipped past Sha and flew around the corner toward his house.

Sha had stepped backward out of the store and watched through the clouds of breath for a second before Aaron disappeared around the corner. It was his first glimpse of the boy. He had liked his small, purposeful hump-walk, a slight variation of that employed by every Brooklyn boy alive in the decade. Later he thought about the boy, visualized his face and triangle nose, big eyes and round head and low haircut, the small tight body hiding and the layers of clothes. *Perfect*, he had thought.

Fuckin perfect, he thought again as Aaron came closer, the jingle and chimes whisking up from the ice cream truck, the combination making his mouth water. But Sha was surprised to detect something else creeping in along with the attraction he felt for the boy. There was a thin innocence

6

with which the boy lifted and lowered his eyelids to take in the world, something about him Sha wanted in his life.

He was fifteen or sixteen, Sha guessed. There was nothing overt in the boy's demeanor that should have made Sha think he messed around. There was nothing there that showed. But there was something: the way Aaron's eyes lingered a second too long on certain young men on the Avenue and not at all on others. The familiar resigned solitude in those eyes when they looked. Something caught Sha's eye, something not altogether quantifiable that danced slightly and incongruously in his ever-discriminating peripheral.

It had not occurred to him immediately. But Sha, who, at twenty, had not yet accustomed himself to the traditional types of employment, had had plenty of occasions in the months he had been staying in Flatbush with his sister to observe Aaron from the Beckford stoop. Most of the time, Aaron would avoid his pregnant glances—too hard, Sha thought. One more clue, according to his impeccable logic, not only that the boy had it in him, but that whatever it was, was bubbling closer and closer now to the surface. Maybe he didn't know it yet, or understand it; but he felt it, Sha bet.

To Sha it seemed that the ones seeming *not* to pay attention were generally the ones paying the utmost attention. A nigga with nothing to hide would just nod and say *what's up* and go on about his business. No big deal. But the ones who doubted themselves, who read too much into the casual exchanges which occurred between men a million times a day on avenues all over Brooklyn, those were the ones who were suspect. Those were the ones you could shake down and assault and unmask, which was usually the way he thought about the whole process—as a tactical maneuver, an exercise in strategy. Sometimes he didn't even want the boys. But he wanted to say to them *I see you, you're not gettin over on me, I could get you if I wanted to.*

But he didn't regard Aaron in this way for some reason; an unfamiliar impulse was stirring in him. Right there,

with the taste of nicotine swirling in his mouth, Sha swore
that if he ever got hold of the little boy, he would never let
him go. Shocked as he was by this, he had said it and he
guessed he meant it.

THREE

Anise got down out of her Uncle Jack's black El Dorado, twirling her jacket string around her finger and thinking of stupid Keisha Armstrong who lived across the street from her Aunt Jesse's apartment on Kosciusko. She had gone to the fourth grade at P.S. 126 with Keisha and had hated every minute of it. Not school. Just Keisha. But Keisha had figured so prominently in the scholastic experience of the preceding nine months that it was hard for Anise to think of one without the other.

Standing on the corner of Kosciusko with one foot planted in the mother-approved sidewalk and the other thrust rebelliously into the forbidden cement of the street, Keisha had put her hand on her hip and yelled: "If you let a boy put his thing on you, you'll have a baby!"

CeCe Miller, age eight, immediately dropped the red plastic handle of her jump rope with a click onto the cracked cement. "Keisha, my mother said for me to come home if you start talkin bout that kinda stuff."

"Don't listen to her, CeCe," Anise had said. "She don't even know what she's talkin about anyway."

9

"For your information I do know what I'm talkin bout, Anise. You always think you know everything." Keisha threw her hand out in front of her. "Anyways, my cousin Trina let this boy rub up on top of her and she bout to have a baby in two more months. And *she* only fifteen." The last point she added vehemently, as if it strengthened her argument.

"He has to do more than that, Keisha," said Anise. "The boy has to put it *inside* of her for the girl to have a baby."

CeCe whined. "Ya'll nasty."

"Least I know what I'm talkin about, CeCe. Keisha's confused."

"I *do* know what I'm talkin about I *told* you!" Keisha moved her head on her neck. "The boy, Anthony, did it on her leg and they just went in, and now she's gonna have the baby in two more months." She formed a V with her fingers.

"Keisha, that's the dumbest…that's not even …" But secretly she wondered; and she admitted to herself, substituting certain of Keisha's laymen's terms for technical ones, her inability to disprove any of it. Now all the secret books she had read and all the piecemeal information she had amassed seemed useless.

"Anise," Keisha said then, tilting her head thoughtfully, "you need to try to find out something for yourself sometimes. Some people is smart in school but don't have no *common* sense cause all they do is read books all day. That's what my mother says."

That's why your mother works the cash register at Caldor's, Anise thought. *And if she had any common sense…* But tactful Anise kept this to herself, knowing it would be wasted on Keisha, and not forgetting that Keisha was eleven and had repeated the fourth grade twice already and would pound her if she did not. Anise said nothing, just raised her eyebrows in glib acceptance of her status as one of the smart, no-common-sense people.

10

"Dummy," she now said lightly to herself, making long circles in the air with the string of her jacket, raveling and unraveling it into the air. She climbed the stairs and pulled at the heavy outside door of the house. Locked. She slammed her little thumb into the doorbell. *Ding.* Waited a moment and let go. *Dong.* She heard nothing from inside, rose to her tiptoes, tried to peep through the glass. *Ding...Dong. DingDongDingDongDingDong.* Anise sighed, exhausted from her long series of debates with Keisha Armstrong, and the ominous negotiations she engaged in always with her Aunt Jesse for what privileges were allowed her. She sat down on the steps. The jingling chimes of the ice cream truck trickled up from somewhere and the new summer sun slanted into the street through the trees. Her uncle Jack had already accelerated the big El Dorado down the street. She was not worried—not *afraid.* But she was irritated now, and wondered where her brother could be. He didn't have *friends.* There was the set of girls that called giggling on the phone but were never seen. There was the vague occasional teenage boy for whatever period of time, each identical to the next and identical to her brother, seen at some point, but vanished thereafter. But not now—there wasn't one now, and she knew in her heart he was walking aimlessly to spite her and remind her he was free.

Then the bolt clicked behind her and she turned and squinted into his eyes. "What took you so long?"

"Sorry," he said.

"You're not sorry. You did it on purpose," she said. "Just to be mean."

"I did not," he said weakly. "I didn't even hear the bell."

"What do you mean you didn't hear it," she said, lifting herself off the step.

"I said sorry, Anise."

"I rang a million times. And, if you didn't hear it why did you answer the door?"

"Because it's five-thirty."

"Shut up." She shoved through the door past him and punched him in the stomach. "What's *wrong* with you?"

Anise slammed her bright book bag into one of the chairs at the table and began tearing her arms out of her jacket. She dragged the jacket half-on through the apartment and slung it into her room in the back. She came back into the kitchen, pulled out one of the chairs. Aaron stood at the sink, his back to her.

"What happened?" She sat down at the table.

"What do you mean 'what happened,'" he said and glared over his shoulder at her.

"I mean," she said very slowly, mocking, "what did you *do* today?"

"Well then why did you say 'what happened'"?

"A lot of people say that."

"Well, it sounds stupid."

"Not to me."

Aaron stared menacingly at her for another moment and turned away. The dishes clanged in the sink. Anise smiled to herself.

"So, what did you—"

"Don't worry about what I do, Anise," he said, without turning. "I do what I want to do. I'm grown."

"You think you are," she said under her breath.

He turned on her then. "Get out!" He came toward her, pulled her out of the chair by her arm. "Get out of here!"

"Let go!"

He shoved her out of the kitchen then and she turned and screamed at him. "I'm telling!" she said.

"Tell, I don't care."

"I didn't even *do* anything. I was just asking a question."

"So what."

"That's why I'm gonna tell, and you're gonna get in trouble. It's not my fault. You probably got beat up."

He lunged at her then and hit her hard in the arm. She screamed and ran wailing to her room, slamming the thin door behind her.

A wave of guilt knocked into Aaron at that moment, swirled and frothed with the other things that bubbled inside him. He wanted to redeem himself but the swirl in his head distracted him and he knew it would be insincere. He felt sorry for Anise, but the most significant event in sixteen years had transpired that afternoon, ending not ten minutes before with the back door closing behind Sha's lean silhouette even as Anise punched her little finger into the bell at the front. All he wanted was to be alone and reflect, mull excitedly over the images of the day's events crystallized in his mind. He was giddy with excitement, but racked with fear and uncertainty at the same time. He couldn't fit the square peg of what had happened into the sphere of context he understood. He didn't have time to be sensitive.

Aaron had learned to guard his feelings viciously and always. Every indication from the world suggested that whatever he felt really at whatever significant moment was the exact wrong thing at the wrong time. His affinity for his sister was all wrong, he knew, knew without ever being told or warned or chastised. So he did what he could to disguise the truth. He taunted and tricked and insulted her, hit her with snowballs in the winter and stripped leaves off mulberry branches in the summer, switching her little legs until she screamed. But whatever he did and however she screamed or hit back or told her mother, there was always, below the noise and confusion, some little gleam in her eye, faint but unmistakable, that said that she knew. She knew that her brother was crazy about her and was laughing at him all the time. She understood—this was the fear. And the threat. Because he had never allowed anyone to understand. His grandmother and aunts who doted over him. His friends who praised his cool and whom he allowed to be drawn into his world briefly. The girls who laughed and smiled. He never

13

once doted back—on any of them. He rarely even acknowledged their praise of him, because to do so would require him to affirm some feeling within himself. He could no more easily admit to believing he was cool or smart or cute than he could admit believing he was not. Either way, he thought, would open him up to ridicule. If he thought he was okay he could be picked apart by those who might suspect that he was not; if he did not, he would be eaten alive by the vultures who lived on self-doubters, or pitied to death by those who felt sorry for them. Better to remain aloof, never to reveal his exact feelings on *any* matter to anyone. Always hold on to just a little piece for himself.

Aaron finished in the kitchen and the stairs creaked as he dropped quickly down them to the basement. He wanted to be out of sight before his mother appeared to compose himself and wipe away whatever trace was left of it all on his face. His mother did not come down the steep stairs and he knew he would be safe until dinnertime.

In his room he closed the door and snapped on the light, changed his mind—snapped it off. The television was on, and he lay back on his bed under its glow. As the participants of the program taunted and screamed, Aaron floated back to Flatbush Avenue.

The sun had felt good on his back. Even at nine forty-five in the morning it was warm enough to send tiny beads of moisture onto his forehead and into the small of his back. The anticipation he had felt since the sun first seeped into his eyes and woke him that morning was still alive and poking around furiously in his stomach. He felt the sun and the light breeze in the air and wondered why it felt like Christmas morning or his birthday. There was something in this day for him, in this summer that was just beginning, but he did not know what. Life was calling and he meant to answer. That's all he knew.

He had come around the corner onto Flatbush and walked for some time breathing the Avenue's early air before he saw Sha squatting ahead on the stoop. He knew who he was. He remembered the bodega and his mother's milk and Sha's arm around his waist. And something about the way the boy had looked at him with those dark eyes that shook him.

Later, he had seen Sha around the neighborhood; there on the stoop, on Church Avenue, near his school. He would be on Church with the slim vocationless boys who were always there, talking with their hands and shifting their weight on their feet. He had never spoken to Sha. He had nodded at him once when it was unavoidable but always said nothing and evaded the dark eyes. He didn't want Sha to think he was looking. Didn't want him to think he noticed. But he *had* noticed of course, and when Sha wasn't watching, let his eyes follow Sha's body down the block or rest on him there on the stoop. He was taller only a bit than Aaron, but sturdier, he could see, even under his clothes. He was dark, with those almost black eyes and quarter inch of perfectly unkempt hair.

Sha was good-looking, yes, but he had never said this to himself. He had never thought this thought. And even if he had *thought*, Booklyn swarmed with them—with brown boy wonders like Sha. He had only ever to look around. But there was something else about the way he moved, the way he placed one foot swiftly and solidly in front of the other when he walked, cocked his head and showed his white teeth when he talked, that drew Aaron in. Sha seemed so comfortable in his world, so in command of it. Everything drawn to taut perfection.

Aaron moved down the block closer to Sha. He did not look at him. He wanted to know Sha, but his awareness of the fact made it impossible. He couldn't speak to the boy because he wanted to speak to him too much, and for Aaron, and for the mind trained never to take any thing out of its box, here was the problem. The most he could do was admire the boy's clothes. And in his mind he left it at that.

As he passed the bakery shop and the corner store and the blue and white ice cream truck with its happy jingle and chimes his eyes were cast downward or out, but he sensed Sha there on the stoop.

"Son." He heard the voice.

Aaron did not stop walking. He heard the voice (the gravelly tenor) and knew it must be Sha, but he couldn't be talking to *him*. The tingle in his stomach grew out of control. He thought he missed a step.

"Yo, son," the voice came again. Aaron hesitated, instinctively wiped all trace of expression from his face and turned with vacant eyes toward Sha. From the stoop Sha peered into him, motioned Aaron toward him with a single quick flick of the wrist. Aaron took the careful steps back toward the stoop, concentrating to keep his balance. He raised his eyebrows with easy disinterest. He could feel his heart beat the blood into his ears. The sun got hotter and the shine on his forehead got brighter. He could hear the ice cream truck. What could the boy have to say to him? What had he done?

Aaron looked at him. He kept his eyes steady.

"Eh. Let me ask you something, " Sha said.

Aaron panicked. *Why would he want to ask—*

"You know who got trees on this block?"

Trees? Oh. Aaron thought for a minute. He knew where the weed spot was; he didn't understand how Sha didn't.

"Yeah," he said. "You know that little store down on the next block across the street? With the yellow sign? That's a spot right there."

"Yeah?" he looked vaguely out at the avenue. "They got nicks?"

"Just dimes, I think."

"That won't do me no good today," he said and stopped. He sat there calmly. Aaron squirmed in the silence. Sha tilted his head then and looked at him again,

16

showed the white tips of his teeth. "You live around here, right?"

"I live on Newkirk," Aaron said.

"Yeah. I thought you look familiar," Sha said. "What's your name again?"

"My name's Aaron."

Sha nodded and moved his hand through the air. He said his name.

Aaron stretched his arm, cupped his hand into Sha's. He relaxed. Sha had spoken to *him*. He had not noticed anything, then.

"You got a light?" Sha shook a cigarette up out of the pack and took it between his teeth. Aaron shook his head.

"Don't smoke, huh? Don't start. It's a pain in the ass." He grinned up at Aaron, the cigarette between his teeth. His hand shot down into the pocket of his jeans then, came back with a silver lighter, squeezed a spark into the tip of the cigarette.

Aaron looked strangely at him.

"It don't work sometimes," Sha said, and laughed.

Aaron showed his teeth. He liked Sha's voice, the way his words clipped together when he spoke. "You live here?" Aaron motioned toward the building.

"My sister lives right there," he said, tilted his head. "I stay with her."

"What school you go to? I never seen you at Erasmus."

Sha laughed. "I'm grown. I'm out of school."

"Oh."

Sha pulled on the cigarette. "I'm twenty-one. " He blew the smoke out hard. "You bout, what? Nineteen?"

"Be seventeen next month. I'm graduating next year."

"Yeah? You look older," Sha lied. "I thought you were nineteen or twenty at least. But you just a young buck, huh?"

Aaron stifled his smile.

Sha looked him up and down. "Why ain't you in school right now?"

"Yesterday was our last day."

"Oh, so you just chillin now."

"Basically."

Aaron felt fine now. There was always that surge at the spring of a new friendship. And it was happening already. He could feel it.

Aaron had had a long series of what could be called best friends, all of whom had eventually been cast by the wayside of his somewhat twisted emotional path through the teen ages. It began in the eighth grade. Tony Bias was light brown with squinted cat eyes and a curly taper haircut stuck under a blue Knicks cap. He was the first boy in the eighth grade with that year's ultimate Air Jordans. Navy blue and black. Shipped direct from the factory. The Jordans, and the fact that he was easily the cutest boy in the eighth grade had made him infinitely popular at J.H.S 137. Aaron could not keep his eyes off Tony. He had spent the first semester of the school year staring at him secretly, watching the way he moved and acted. He wanted to be *like* Tony. But he knew it was more than that; somewhere, below the fear and confusion, he knew. By the time he was in the eighth grade, he had been aware of his problem for some time.

When he was five, he had heard one of the older kids at school say faggot on the playground, and when he asked one of the other kindergartners what it was, his little classmate answered confidently that it was a bug. When he asked his mother she told him that it was a very bad word for a boy who likes other boys and that he never should say it. He thought he understood, but a boy who liked other boys seemed unworthy of its own cussword.

By the time he was ten he knew just what a faggot was and knew *he* wasn't going to be one. They were those men with women's ways, punks, sissies. Disfiguring and distorting the mannerisms and speech that made women so fluid into something else. Something that everyone hated. And he hated them too.

Eventually he learned that men who were fags slept with other men. He was sure he was opposed to this. All the faggots having sex together—this was a crime, certainly. Or did they do it with other, *regular* men? And if they did, he wondered, what were those other men? Fags too, or something else? And what did any of them *do*, exactly? Suck each other's dicks? It seemed nasty, but he did find the bodies of men...interesting.

By the time he was thirteen and found himself sitting next to Tony Bias in Civics class he had realized the severity of his addiction. He thought about boys all the time. And men. He had masturbated looking at the men's underwear section of a Montgomery Wards catalog that had been delivered to the house for his mother. The symmetry of the lines stamped into those stomachs and the lean power of those tan legs jutting out of the white briefs and boxers had kept his attention for hours. He kept the catalog under his bed for weeks, until the recurring nightmare that it would be found there became too much. He threw the thing away rather than take the chance that his mother would notice it creased open to that page. He knew he could never unmask himself, never tell how he felt, but his attraction to boys was becoming so integral to his existing, to his feeling *anything*, he thought. It was so much of what he felt in total. At first he didn't want the feeling to go away. It felt good: the passion, the infatuation he felt for boys, the desire to see and to touch their bodies. But he just did not see how he could ever work these feelings into his reality. He had never had sex with a girl. Women hypnotized him with their grace and femininity, and he liked the sensibilities of girls, but he didn't want to *sleep* with them. But then, he wasn't sure he wanted to have sex, *per se,* with other boys either. He had heard, by this time, that gay boys fucked each other in the ass: and the idea made his stomach turn. And he decided at this point that the men who did this were all like the fags he had learned to hate. Pussies. And something changed in him. A part of him disappeared. Or he pushed it down so hard and so far, so deep into the dark recesses of himself that it was unrecognizable. He raised a dark wall in himself, blocked his thoughts and blanked his mind and he was numb. He resigned himself to a life of celibacy and clandestine masturbation. But he was sitting there three feet away from the best-looking boy in the eighth grade.

When Mr. Thomas had told the class that they needed to copy the information he had written on the board, Tony had leaned over and asked Aaron if he could borrow a piece of paper. Naturally, Aaron had obliged, and they started cracking jokes on Mr. Thomas' too-tight clothes and long bald spot. Over the course of the weeks that followed the two became inseparable, Tony evidently not realizing that his new best friend, though good-looking and well-dressed, was nowhere near his own social stratosphere. Aaron wasn't a geek, exactly. He was a loner, and for the most part didn't participate in the mandatory grouping patterns of J.H.S 137. But Tony loved Aaron for his wit and quiet ways, the few words he said always cutting right to the chase of things, and always said over an ambiguous half-grin. Aaron was cool and reserved, and somehow seemed above the fray of teenage angst. In reality, he was far from above it, and went home from school every day dizzy with thoughts of Tony's dash and charisma. He ruled over the rest of the kids and was by all accounts, and perhaps by some fluke of fate, his. *His.* Everyone knew that Tony was his, and the special clenched-fist pound they gave each other every time they met or parted company sealed their status as *boys* to the rest of the world. They would talk on the phone and go to dances and play basketball after school, and when Tony spent the night at his house, he would sneak looks at his smooth, hairless body. In private, he would fantasize about Tony—not sexual

20

fantasies exactly, but he would visualize the bronzed tan skin and slanted eyes and imagine what it would be like to touch him. Not the way they touched each other usually—hands on each other's backs and shoulders, patting each other's stomachs, speaking into each other's ears. He wanted to really touch Tony, to feel his skin next to his own, but he had resigned himself that this could never, ever happen—not under any circumstances he could imagine. So he satisfied himself with being Tony's friend and confidant and spent every possible waking moment with him, patting and playing in the only way boys were allowed to.

But Aaron was not dissatisfied with his relationship with Tony. He loved Tony, and the oaths Tony repeated to Aaron that they should always remain together, as boys, reached deep in and touched a new part of him. He was experiencing the profoundest joy he could conceive of at the time.

But eventually, much to Aaron's surprise, he began to lose interest in Tony, and by that summer, the infatuation he had felt at first had wilted into a pile of discarded feelings, and a mountain of regret for having shared even the tip of his own iceberg of emotions with Tony. He was as confused at his sudden change of heart as was poor Tony, whose own feelings had evidently continued on the same course as before. He had sensed a chill in Aaron's demeanor toward him as the jokes and hand smacks in Civics class came less and less frequently, but he had kept trying until summer came, and when Aaron hadn't returned any of his phone calls for two weeks he gave up, finally, heartbroken.

By the time he stood there on Flatbush Avenue, shooting the shit with Sha, Aaron had repeated this sequence half a dozen times with unsuspecting boys he met at school or around the neighborhood. He would fall madly under the spell of some precious, good-looking brown Brooklyn boy, and they under his; and then, with sometimes as little as a few hours notice, the magic would disintegrate and the boy would be left to make whatever sense of the situation he could. Aaron would be characteristically non-communicative. But what could he say, really? That he'd fallen out of love with them? He didn't even think of it in these terms himself. And it was usually something relatively insignificant that sent his emotions spiraling imminently downward: something they had worn or said, a new friend or girlfriend he didn't approve of, a quirk or imperfection that suddenly became a glaring annoyance. He couldn't point these things out to them the way teenage couples cruelly pointed them out to each other when they broke up, so he just disappeared as quietly as possible and told his mother to tell whoever called on the phone that he wasn't home.

But he had learned to value these relationships for all they were worth. They gave him joy while they lasted, and each time he would swear he had found his new best friend for life.

"You smoke trees?" Sha asked, shooting ash off the tip of his cigarette onto the ground. "You don't really look like the type."

"Sometimes," he said gloomily. *What did he mean he didn't look like the type?*

"So, what? You want to get a bag? If you got five bucks on it I got five."

Aaron did not want to spend his precious five dollars on weed. He knew how his mother was, how unrealistic about the money she gave him, but he wanted to stay with Sha and five dollars seemed a small price at the moment. "It's whatever man," Aaron said casually. "Shit, I ain't got nothin else to do—I'm free!" He raised his arms above his head like a victorious prizefighter and laughed.

They walked down the block side by side, talking and laughing, weaving in and out of the people on the Avenue. They stepped into the tiny store where weed was peddled at all hours of day and night. The dirty yellow sign above the door said **GROCERY**, but a few faded boxes of Brillo pads and Kraft macaroni and cheese were all that were on the shelves, and they had been there as long as the spot had, attracting dust, and not attracting, conspicuously, the attention of the protectors and servers of New York law enforcement. No one ever came out of the place with anything even vaguely resembling groceries, only tiny plastic bags of weed with pictures of marijuana leaves or chocolate kisses on them. No one seemed to notice, or they didn't care, or had decided long ago that there was nothing they could do about it, so the steady flow of tiny plastic bags, and nothing else, continued from behind the filthy, bullet-proof glass inside.

On a rusty aluminum stool inside the store, a tall man with matted hair and worn clothes sat fingering his hair with one hand. When he saw Sha he pounded his fist against Sha's familiarly. "Peace," he said, monotone.

"What ya'll working with?" Sha said.

"We got the chocolate back there now," the man said slowly, without intonation, and motioned toward the glass.

Sha stepped to the glass and tapped on it with his knuckles, slid his five-dollar bill and the one Aaron had slapped into his palm on the way up the street through the little window. He bent down to speak into the opening and Aaron could not hear what he said. Old lotto tickets and candy wrappers were pasted up around the opening in the bullet-proof glass, and the person behind it could not be seen. A weathered brown hand came down on the bills and slid back inside, came back pushing one of the decorated plastic bags.

Aaron watched the exchange from the door. Sha seemed to know them. Or maybe his apparent familiarity was only directness, an exact understanding of his role in the scenario. He didn't think Sha had hustled him for the five dollars; he didn't seem that petty.

"Now what, little man?" Sha had said to him as they stepped back out onto the Avenue. "You don't have nothin to do, right?"

23

Aaron shrugged and shook his head.

"Well, you with me today, then," he said. "Let's go down by the courts and blaze." He pulled a Dutch Master from somewhere, tapped it on Aaron's chest.

Again they weaved through the sunny streets, moving slowly toward the courts on Ocean. When they arrived, Sha threw himself up onto the back of one of the benches facing the court; his feet rested on the seat. Five young men ran back and forth on the half court in a breathless game of twenty-one. They wore the names of five different superstars on their feet. Three others stood near a second bench, talking loudly to each other and glancing occasionally toward the court. Sha expertly broke open the Dutch Master and spilled the tobacco out onto the ground. He emptied the brownish crumbled contents of the bag into the cigar.

"You ever wonder why they let them sell these little bags," Aaron asked, taking the clear empty bag from Sha. "You can buy em at the Chinese store in packs of a hundred. The only thing they good for is to sell weed."

"Jewelry," Sha said, not lifting his eyes from his task. "Earrings and shit—that's what they supposed to be for."

"With weed plants on the side?"

Sha laughed. "Yeah, well, they ain't tryin too hard to keep *this* shit off the streets, let alone the bags. Jakes go by that spot ten times a day, man, you think they don't know what's goin on? They pay them niggas off. Why you think they never busted that spot? It ain't like they don't see it. Shit, half of them be gettin smoked out *inside* the squad car, eatin donuts all fuckin day. They don't want to get rid of it. Too many people makin money off it." Sha licked the blunt. "Giuliani probably got a cut of this bag."

Aaron nodded and made a face. Sha finished the blunt, licked it a final time and set it on his lap, took his lighter and ran the blunt through the flame to dry. He lifted it to his lips and lit the end, pulling the weed and tobacco smoke deep into his lungs. He puffed several more times

24

and passed it to Aaron.

They sat and smoked silently, watching the men on the court dip and pivot in strong graceful movements. Aaron blinked. The drugs swam in his bloodstream. Things seemed surreal. He wondered how was he even sitting there talking to Sha, whom he had seen and thought about so often, and whether their meeting was as simple as it seemed. Sha had to know about the weedspot, he thought. It must have been the five dollars. Whatever it was, he didn't care. He liked Sha. He was glad to be with him.

"You want to play?" Sha motioned toward the court.

"In these?" Aaron lifted one of his brown and black boots off the bench.

"Man, what? You afraid to get em scuffed? Those Gore-Tex old as hell already. Look what I got on."

Sha dropped off the bench, called to the next bench. "Can we hold your ball?"

They played alone at the other end of the court, both of them stomping in their boots, touching each other too often. Sha had taken off his shirt and sweat gathered at the nape of his neck and trickled down his dark body in a thin stream, over the ridged stomach and into his white boxer shorts. Aaron tried not to look at Sha's body, but there it was, twisting and glistening in the sun right before him, jumping and bumping into his own. He looked like a boxer, Aaron thought, a bouncing brown featherweight floating past his opponents, sticking and moving with fearless precision. Aaron had already been attracted to him. But now, with Sha's half-naked body slamming into him every few seconds, and his senses heightened by the weed and the heat, he was excited beyond comfort. The blunt had made him paranoid. He was afraid something might show.

"Let's go, man," Aaron said gasping. "The weed is makin me tired."

"So what you want to do, little man? Anybody at your house right now?"

25

"Nah. My mom's at work."

"So we can chill at your house? You got cable?" Sha grinned.

"Yeah, we got cable." He laughed. "Come on."

For the third time that day, they wound through the crowded Brooklyn streets in their boots and jeans and T-shirts. The afternoon sun was hotter now and they walked more slowly than before. When they reached the house, Aaron unlocked the door and led Sha into the dark hallway.

"This whole house yours?" Sha asked. They descended the creaking dark staircase to Aaron's room in the basement.

"Nah. We just have the first floor and the basement. Somebody else lives upstairs." Aaron led Sha into his small room, turned on the light and closed the door, punched the little button on the remote.

Sha sat down on the bed, one booted foot hanging off the corner of it. His eyes changed; they were different now, looking up at Aaron as he emptied his pockets of change and lint and dollar bills. Sha grabbed the crotch of his pants and pulled it toward him—a gesture familiar to Aaron, but one which now took a foreign flavor over Sha's obscure accomplice eyes.

Aaron had just averted his own eyes nervously. Sha broke the silence. "So what's up with you, Aaron?"

Aaron lifted his brows as if to say, *huh?* Sha licked his lips. "I'm sayin. What's up?"

That was it. Those few words, carefully phrased and intoned so that Aaron could disregard them if he needed to and whatever happened could not claim later in some moment of desperation or denial that Sha had made a move on him, were his sole proposition. They rang in Aaron's ears. It was a simple phrase, one which Aaron had heard a thousand times, and which typically required only a stock response, if any. But a real question, with all the urgency and precision of wanting to know floated in those words the

26

way Sha looked at him and said them. And Aaron, who would never have dreamed of divulging even the most trivial piece of who he was or how he felt to anyone, was terrified by this; and there was a pertinence in Sha's voice that went right to the very heart of it, that asked Aaron to tell exactly who and what he was, and that said *I already know; I see you.* But at the same time, he seemed to be offering up something of himself, to be saying *here I am, if you want to look.*

Aaron smiled nervously. "I don't know," he said, keeping his voice steady but averting his eyes. "You tell me."

"I was about to in a minute. I just wanted to know how you felt." Sha spoke slowly and kept his eyes fixed hard on Aaron's. He could see the hopeful panic come into his face. When Aaron did not answer, Sha lay back on the bed and cradled his head in the crook of his arm.

"Why don't you turn the light off," Sha almost whispered, still keeping his eyes on him. Aaron still hesitated, standing there looking down at Sha lying there looking back at him, one hand behind his head and the other under his loose T-shirt stroking his stomach. Aaron's own stomach twinged; he sensed something strange and familiar, something he knew instinctively, but had never experienced. A familiar melody played in his head; he knew the rhythm and feel of it, the runs and rifs and mighty crescendo of it, but not the words, and not the moves that went with it. It was something he understood, but could not express, and certainly had no way to respond to.

Aaron had never had a boy come on to him before. He had never flirted with a boy, never winked and smiled at one in math class. He had never, when he was younger, gotten a card from or passed a note to a boy that said *I like you, do you like me? Circle yes or no.* He had never hung up the phone with a boy and said *alright baby, talk to you tomorrow.* And he had never, ever, and would never in a million years have thought that he ever could like someone and possibly have them like him back in the same way. It simply could not happen, and he had given up on the idea a long time ago.

And still he could not believe it. Sha could not be lying there on his bed stroking his perfect stomach, looking up at him with those black eyes, meaning what he could not be meaning, telling him to turn off the light. So he stood there hesitating by the door until Sha spoke again in that rough, reassuring whisper: "Turn the light off. It's mad bright."

Well, it *was* bright, he thought, as he flipped the switch, and moved through the darkness and uncertainty toward Sha. Aaron's feet moved on their own, his mind still frantically evaluating, weighing every possibility, so that he did not notice them becoming entangled in the wires of his video game, stereo, television, he only felt himself falling and his knees coming down on the floor. Sha sat up to catch him, and as Aaron came down between his legs, their mouths came together and, against the light of the television, they kissed, as it were, by accident.

***

Aaron lay there listening to Sha's steady breaths, wondering what he would say to him when he awakened. He watched his chest move up and down under the gentle radiance of the television, which neither of them had bothered to turn off. Aaron had lost track of the rest of the world, and at first could not place what should have been the very familiar sound of the doorbell ringing.

"Oh my god," he gasped when the sharp *Ding-Dong, Ding-Dong, Ding-Dong* of the bell finally forced itself upon him. "It's 5:30! Sha, get up! It's my sister! Come on, my sister's home, shit! Shit!"

Sha rose with an initial start, then very calmly, very quickly, stood and began to reassemble himself. For the split second Sha stood there with his nakedness illuminated by the television, Aaron did not believe that his sister was at the door, or that he even had a sister, or that anything he had ever known existed. Sha continued to dress, quickly and calmly, like someone participating in a routine fire drill. Aaron struggled and twisted hopelessly. When they were finally dressed, Aaron led Sha quickly into the dark hallway toward the door in the back. Neither of them spoke. Aaron unlocked the door and pulled it open. He focused his eyes on the handle of the door. He was dumb. He could not speak. Sha slipped past him and patted his ribs. "Alright, son. Talk to you later," he said, and disappeared.

***

Even now, Aaron could hardly believe it. He lay on his bed, smelling Sha all around him, wondering what to do, what to say when he saw him. He didn't know if Sha would speak to him now. But however confused or terrified he was, however much his brain sloshed in his skull, Aaron knew that he *wanted* Sha. He wasn't sure how he wanted him, precisely, or what it would mean, even, to have him. But he knew what he had felt lying there with Sha and, for now, that was enough.

On the television two huge drag queens tugged each other's hair in front of a studio audience. Aaron sighed and lay back on his bed; he hit the button on the remote and the room became dark. There was a glow from the tiny window near the ceiling. He could see the brown brick of the house next door, and wondered how the sun had shined so brightly that morning.

FOUR

When Flatbush Avenue was a dusty trail and the City itself a speck of blunt wilderness in the minds of a drizzle-soaked Civilization, the Dutch Governor, Stuyvesant, in his eternal wisdom, commanded the building of a church, that there be morality on the settlements of Long Island. So the church was built on the old Indian road, in the form of a cross, and surrounded by a stockade to guard against attack. Inside, the parishioners heard sermons for a New World in a language that could hardly comprehend it, and as they prayed and shivered in their skins from cold and fear, the Indians looked on curiously from the road and shivered in theirs, fevered with the pox and choleras which were their only gifts from the Continent.

In time, the Indians succumbed, the wilderness receded, and the happy little village of Flatbush flourished on its own merits. The church was torn down and rebuilt and torn down and rebuilt again, but always on the same foundation, and with only as much attention to detail as the prevailing religious winds required. The stockade gave way eventually to a series of bright picket fences which were themselves replaced in time by elegant wrought iron that enclosed the sprawling churchyard and the tiny cemetery that had been established there, and pointed its spiked railings heavenward as the sun rose and set.

Centuries later, when the modern world had whirred

into existence and Civilization redistributed itself along the banks of the Hudson River, the Reformed Protestant Dutch Church stood still, its white bell tower rising monumentally over Flatbush, its heavenly spikes still pointing toward the sky. In the shadow of the church, yards from the dead Ditmases and Duryees, heads move back and forth across the fence. They are not like the old pink faces of the Dutch going stiffly up and down, or the old copper ones of the Indians moving slow and exact. They bob and dip and beneath them shoulders swing pendulum-like, buttocks and thighs move together in rhythm.

"Fuck them." Sparks pushed his palm over thick rows of hair and looked sideways at the three asses shaking away down Church.

The Haitian, Claude, threw his head back and laughed.

"I can't stand these bitches." Sparks said.

"They don't like you, either."

Jay Toriace leaned into the payphone. He said over his shoulder: "Can ya'll shut the hell up?"

Sha passed the trio of girls as they jingled and swished down the block. He had lifted his eyes to them only for a second, but all their heads turned to look, and when they turned back the girls erupted into moving hair and hands. Sha approached, smacked his hand into Sparks' and into the Haitian's. "What you still doin out here, Sparks?" he said.

Sparks shook his head, looked sideways down the block.

Sha said: "What's wrong with him?"

Jay Toriace slammed the phone down. "He's a dumb-ass, that's what's wrong with him."

"Who the hell is you talking to?" Sparks looked at him.

"You, asshole."

"I'm tired of your shit," Sparks said through his teeth.

"Come on, now." Sha put his hand on Sparks.

"Don't get mad at *me*," Toriace said. "You the—"

"You just watch your fuckin mouth, Torious."

"He don't know how to talk to females," said the Haitian then in his accent.

Sparks looked at him. "I wasn't even sayin it like that. I was sayin it as a compliment, son. I wasn't sayin, like, '*Ill*, you got a fat ass, bitch.' I was sayin, like, '*Damn*, you got a FAT ASS, bitch!'"

They all screamed at this, and the gold in Sparks' mouth flashed between his lips. "That's my word," Sparks said. "Anyway, she know what she got and what she don't. I'm supposed to act like I don't know nothin? Like I don't see nothin? Am I blind?"

"You supposed to not say shit," Sha said. "You supposed to shut the hell up sometimes."

Sparks shook his head, squinting disbelief. "They like it. Look how they dress. Then want to get mad if somebody speak on it. I mean, really. *I* don't get mad if a bitch tell me she like my ass. I don't *give* a fuck."

Jay Toriace looked at him. "Ain't no female told you she like your ass."

"You shut the fuck up," Sparks screamed.

"Calm down," Sha said.

"I *am* calm." He looked at Sha and raised his palms, turned to Jay Toriace. "You think your ugly ass be mad if a girl told you you had a big *dick*? Hell no, you wouldn't be mad. You might be *surprised* as hell," he said, "but you damn sure wouldn't be mad."

They shook their heads.

"Anyway," Sparks said. "I don't care about these bum bitches."

"You ain't got to care about em," Sha said. "You got to figure em out."

"Oh, no. Don't start that shit with me. I ain't got time to be psychoanalyzing these bitches. All I want is some ass."

33

"It ain't about ass, strictly," Sha said. "Figure em out, you get whatever you want."

Sha knew what he was talking about. His life had become a series of calculations, an ongoing process of figuring people out, deciding what they needed in their lives, and what he had or could create, to exchange for what was lacking in his own. What they needed (passion, protection) and who they needed it from (friend, father-figure, little brother; lover, thug, or whatever combination) he provided in return for the smallest tokens of appreciation: a new pair of Jordans or Tims, buds of green hydroponic, tickets to destinations out of state. Cash, checks, money orders. Whatever they could contribute. And if they wanted pain, and the misery of loving, or worse, being infatuated with someone capable of perhaps half the range of human emotions, then he would give them that too, at no extra cost. Most of the time he would give them this whether they asked for it or not, assuming, perhaps correctly, that no matter what else they wanted, they wanted the pain. Because he believed this: that whatever pain suffered was precious to those suffering it, and because he had allowed himself to feel so little for such a long time, he felt no guilt or remorse for the things he did. And in truth it was the things he *didn't* do, and the things he didn't *feel*, that had wreaked havoc over the lives of so many of them. Sha was not mean-spirited. He did not do things just to hurt them, just because he could. But he needed things and so did they, and what they got, they got very cheaply the way he saw it, so if they had to squirm a little during the exchange, that was alright by him.

"Ah, shut up and spark it," Sparks said finally and sucked his teeth.

Clouds of smoke rose above them as they puffed and laughed the minutes and the hours of their lives eagerly away. The sun moved westward over their heads. As far as any of them were concerned it set over Red Hook and plunged violently into the East River. The streetlights that worked began to flicker on and the traffic on Church Avenue slowed. Sha said his goodbyes and took his slow way back along Flatbush Avenue toward his sister's apartment.

As he walked he thought of Aaron. He wondered what he was feeling right now, if he was hating himself for what he had done, hating Sha for what he had done to him. It was his first time, Sha knew. The slight and constant trembling that had come over Aaron as he pushed his tongue into the boy's mouth and pulled him to his feet had said everything that Aaron, in his state of shock and disbelief, could not. Aaron had kept his eyes shut tight all the time, even as Sha pulled the shirt over Aaron's head and lay him down on the bed. He lay on top of him, both of them with only their shirts off for a time, kissing Aaron and letting Aaron kiss back, which he did timidly, slowly moving his head to the rhythm Sha set. He lifted his body, moved his head down and kissed Aaron's stomach, one arm around his little waist, like in the bodega, the other reaching down to unlace his boots. Aaron kept his hands clenched at his sides, brushing Sha's neck or shoulders only occasionally, as if by chance. He had not, at this point, been able to bring himself to any level of intimacy that would have allowed him to actually open his hands and move his palms over Sha's neck or shoulders as he wanted to, to actually grasp him in any meaningful way. But as tightly balled as they were, he kept them always brushing Sha's skin, and to Sha, this meant something.

Sha knew boys who wanted to appear so detached that they would contribute nothing to the lovemaking process except their screaming erections, would just lie there with their rock-hard dicks trying to look disinterested. These boys Sha despised, and he would reverse their shit on them so fast they would not know what hit them. As soon as he saw it, he turned instantly cold. He would not put his lips on them or touch them unnecessarily; he would only drop his pants down around his ankles and grind his dick on them as they lay there, or jerk off over them, dropping cum on their sheets or clothes, and on their hands—always on their hands, so they could really feel what he had done to them, feel his sticky loathing seep through their knuckles and into their palms. He would never fuck them, since he knew this was probably all they wanted anyway, and he had no intention of allowing them even one thing out of the transaction. After, he would pull his clothes back into position, cock his camouflage cap to one side, sniff hard once for effect, and say *alright man* under his breath and leave. They'd still be lying there naked (or half-naked) dumbfounded and destroyed before Sha's semen had yet even begun to crystallize on their skin. It wasn't that he was so sensitive or needed so much from them that he did this, but he would be damned if he would let any of them act like they weren't with it, like he was the only one lying there wanting sex from another man.

But Sha knew that innocence and anxiety and nothing else had slammed Aaron's eyes shut and clenched his fists into those little balls, and once he had slipped Aaron's jeans off, along with his own, he kissed the fists open and breathed into the hands. He held Aaron's hands open a long time, pressing their palms together as he rocked up and down over him. He finally released them, nearly laughed out loud at the way Aaron moved them furtively over his body, not knowing how to hold Sha, at his waist or his shoulders, not knowing where to put his hands.

The absolute tenderness of the boy moving under him touched him, but at the same time, threw his own existence into stark relief. What had happened to *his* innocence, and his tenderness? He did not remember having them.

He had been dragged around, as a child, to every imaginable decaying section of Brooklyn. Dragged by his mother, a woman more likely to pay the neighborhood bootlegger or drug dealer what he was owed than to pay rent. She would use fake names and social security numbers and could usually come up with a money order for the deposit, but they

36

could stay only as long as it took their new landlord to throw them out. They never lived anywhere more than a few months, but they lived always in Brooklyn, never the Bronx or Harlem or Queens, always Brooklyn because, his mother said, anyplace else would have been too far. Too far from *what* Sha had not been able to assess, since his mother did not go to work or to school or to anyplace else, except to his grandmother's house on the first of each month to collect the tiny check sent from the state to that address.

They never had any furniture, just clothes and the dingy, nappy blankets they all slept on. Finally, when he was six, his mother bought a tiny black and white television from the Salvation Army, and after that when they were evicted they would tote it, along with the other things, in plastic bags, to the next residence.

His brother, four years older, spent time in screaming rages at his mother, and hitting Sha over the head with clenched fists, telling him to be tough and not to cry, telling him to be a man. His sister, the oldest, was sweet to Sha, as she was to all men, and made love to whoever looked at her.

On his tenth birthday his mother had stumbled into their apartment with a package of Devil Dogs and a loose candle for him, a fifth of Bacardi and a bottle of Coke for herself. Sha had not bothered with the candle, but choked down the whole box of cupcakes before his brother could get home and rob him of them. As he held his stomach his mother sat against the wall behind him and drank and ranted: *"Oh, baby. Happy birthday, baby! I can't believe my little one is all grown up—ten years old. I remember the day you was born. Hell, can't forget it. You hurt me way more than Shavar. Sheena too. You was turned the wrong way and bigger than them. Six pounds almost. But you grown now, baby. All grown up."*

Then, for some reason she had begun to cry, quietly at first, then in long heaving sobs. Sha had not even looked back at her, just kept his eyes fixed on the fuzzy television screen, not wanting to comfort the woman who had provided him with so little comfort in life, and not understanding or caring what it was all about anyway. After a few moments she had poured what was left of the liquor into the bottle of Coke and went back out of the apartment as she had come in, leaving the empty rum bottle sitting against the filthy wall. He never saw his mother again after that and he always assumed the reason had something to do with what she told him that night. She had simply fulfilled her responsibility, he guessed, raised her last child up to be a man, which was how he always considered himself after that, and left. Maybe what she had said was her way of saying goodbye.

A few weeks later, his brother was placed in juvenile detention for some reason Sha had never understood, and within a month, had beat another fourteen-year-old to death with his bare hands. Actually he had kicked him to death, planting his foot square in the boy's windpipe. Sha had heard that the boy had called him a faggot.

Sha and his sister stayed with their grandmother briefly after their mother's disappearance, until Sheena's pregnancy became too obvious and she kicked them out as she had their mother years before. A god-fearing woman, their grandmother could not abide any children with sins of this nature, though some light boosting or drug trafficking had always been accepted as long as it brought dollars into the house. So while their grandmother lamented the fate of their brother, Sha and his sister went to a tiny room in Bushwick which Sha always thought of as a kitchen—a ten by ten linoleum square with a stove and sink and nothing else—and lived off the check that began to come every month from the State of New York for Sheena and her baby. Meanwhile, their grandmother lived off the one that still came for Sha and his mother, finding a storeowner who would cash it for her for a fee, and never reported her daughter's disappearance.

Sha and his sister continued their migration, at a

much slower rate, but still always in Brooklyn, holding on to the tradition as if it were some precious family heirloom handed down to them by their mother. In a strange way, Sha began to enjoy life. There was a vague depression surrounding his mother and brother, but a new freedom came over him at the same time. He came and went now with relative ease, free of the looming emotional dangers he had always to dodge with his mother and the physical threat of his brother.

He began to learn the lessons of life at an accelerated rate. He learned, for example, that if you bought your sneakers a half size too small, they stayed crisp longer. He learned that if you missed the whole fifth grade, nothing happened. He learned that summertime in Brooklyn barely lasted a hundred days and was precious, not to be wasted. He learned that money made him happy, and that he could get a hundred dollars just for walking a few blocks with a brown paper package under his arm and handing it to the red-eyed man who came to the door. And once he had enough to buy the new Cannondale Racer, the run only took two minutes anyway. He learned that he could get almost anything he wanted from people were he just bold enough to ask. He learned that people didn't trust each other, and that this was usually a good policy. He learned, somewhat conversely, that if you said something, and stood by it, nine times out of ten, people believed it, no matter what it was.

So when Sha told Michael Stringfellow that he was sixteen years old, he was surprised at the expression on his face. Mike was twenty-five and used to boys lying to him about their age. The boys who ran his shit in Brooklyn always wanted to be older, to appear stronger than their little limbs said they were. When Sha said he was sixteen Mike had just laughed and kept talking. He knew a thirteen-year-old when he saw one.

Sha said that he had run it before. For two years. For Richie in East New York.

"Jamaican Richie?" Mike said. He knew all the guys

who still used kids to run the packages. There weren't many left. Mike still thought it was worth it. They cost less, and they were more loyal. Or more afraid. "So I guess you know how this works."

"Yeah. I know." Sha answered, puffing out his chest.

"No stops and no detours. Don't talk to nobody while you working—not your boys, not your little girlfriends. Nobody. I don't care if your momma's callin you. And I don't want to hear about no *emergency*. Don't say shit to nobody til the work gets where it's goin. Understand?"

Sha nodded.

"And I'll give you a pager number and a code for you to confirm. You don't get paid til the next day, so don't come back here when you're done. Just go home and come through the next day." Mike paused and leaned down with his elbows on his knees and clasped his ringed fingers together. "And you know how to deal with the Jakes, right?"

"If I get caught, just say I picked it up off the ground, and I don't know what it is."

Mike smiled. "And if they take you downtown, don't get scared. No matter what they tell you, they can't do shit to you. You just a kid. So don't say nothin but that you found the package. Nothin else. If they ask you who your friends are, don't answer. I'll make sure you're out the same day, all right?"

Sha nodded.

"And I hate to say this, but I have to," Mike said, walking Sha to the door of the empty Brownsville apartment that was his office. "If you fuck up... It's gon be problems. You understand what I'm sayin?"

Sha understood. None of the boys ever got hurt because none of them was ever stupid enough to talk to the cops or run off with the product. So Sha ran Mike's work around Brownsville on his silver Cannondale, and before long, Mike was running Sha around the City in his black Infiniti. They would sail down Atlantic toward the Bridge, floating on perfect suspension above the grit and grime of the city.

Sha admired Mike. In actuality Mike was a simple, garden variety ghetto Prince with everything money could buy—everything, culminating for him, in the black Infiniti, one of the first Q45s ever sold in Brooklyn, purchased with cash, and the silver-dollar-size medallion that glistened at his throat—fourteen karats with the image of Apollo in his chariot pressed into the gold. But to Sha Mike was a king, a brown Vito Corleone, but good-looking and six feet tall. Mike was strong, but he was fair. He never hurt anyone unnecessarily, but he made his position clear: he was *not* to be fucked with. And he had taken a special interest in Sha. He never rode any of the other boys around in his car, or took them to the movies on their birthdays, or to see the woman he called his wife and their little girl in their mirror-decked, shag-rugged apartment near the projects. He never told any of *them* they were like his little brother, or that he would take care of them if they stuck with him, or called any of them *little man* the way he did Sha.

One motionless night after Labor Day, as they were sliding over the Bridge toward Manhattan, Mike reached over and lay his hand across the back of Sha's neck. He had pressed his thumb back and forth across its base, massaging his spine, holding Sha's neck firmly with his fingers. As he did, a tingle began to form under the folds of Sha's sweat pants. Not the bland perfunctory event that comes over a fourteen-year-old for no reason sometimes. Or the inconsequential one that is there to greet him when he awakes. It was the real thing: that creeps carefully over you and is connected to something.

Sha was surprised by this, and confused. He was as in touch with his sexuality as he was with the rest of his feelings, which is to say that he was hardly in touch with it at all. But he had assumed, at least, that the things he felt were the normal things all boys his age felt. The bootleg pornography which had circulated through the hands of Mike's pubescent runners had excited Sha thoroughly enough—the brown bodies jerking and groaning under the bad lights. And he had not a doubt that the stream of electric droplets which fell out of him at the sight of the virile young porn star slamming himself into a perhaps not-so-lovely lady was exactly the correct response to such an event. He had followed this particular male actor through a series of ill-titled flicks, cast opposite various energetic leading ladies, not finding his affinity for the man strange or discomforting at all. These were heterosexual scenes, after all, and Sha had come to think of the actor as a kind of hero for his prowess and for his *style. That nigga can fuck,* he had thought to himself. *He really knows how to fuck.* The man was handsome, well-built—the more reason, as Sha saw it, to admire him. Since women were always present in some capacity in these films, the men never being left by themselves in the scenes, it had never occurred to Sha that he might be attracted to this man in particular, and not just the act of sex itself being portrayed so terribly on the screen. As for the lesbian scenes, he had never quite understood the excitement of his little colleagues at the sight of two women fucking—licking and kneading each other's huge silicon tits. Still, that was no reason for him to think he liked men.

So when Mike touched him like that, holding him firmly about his neck and pressing his thumb into the back of it, Sha had no way to process the situation or his prominent physical reaction to it. But then, Sha had never been in the habit of *feeling,* let alone processing anything he might have felt. So he just stared out the window over the water, with the tingle in his sweats, trembling under Mike's touch, as Aaron would tremble under his centuries later.

Mike felt the trembling, but kept stroking Sha's neck under the midnight tint of the Infiniti. When they had finished their run and slipped back over the Bridge into Brooklyn, Mike had said, slouched down in his seat, with just his wrist on the wheel, tooling the big car through the streets: "Why don't you come by the house for a minute. Josette's in Jersey with her mom. We can chill."

Sha just shrugged and said, "Alright." They had not spoken since they had been in the car. The speakers in the back banged loudly, so there was no uncomfortable silence, only the conflicted lyrics filling up the space between them:

Street dreams are made of these
Shorties on their knees for niggas wit big Gs

When they pulled up to the falling-down apartment building where Mike lived with his girlfriend and daughter, Sha was still staring out the window, pushing what he had felt going over the Bridge to the very edge of his consciousness.

Who am I to disagree
Everybody's lookin for somethin

Mike unlocked the half-dozen locks on the dented aluminum door to his apartment and stepped in out of the filthy hallway. When he flipped the switch to the right of the door the small apartment came alive, assaulting them with color: burgundy curtains, black leather and lacquer shining, gold and silver trimmed mirrors with black cats silhouetted in the glass. Phlegm-beige carpet wall to wall. Long dyed plumes with dusty tips in various dusty vases. Sha liked the apartment, but he sometimes wondered why Mike still lived in Brownsville in that same ratty apartment building. He knew there were nice buildings in Brooklyn, places where people who were different from them lived, people who went to work in suits and skirts, and picked their kids up from school every day. He had never lived any of these places, but he knew they were there.

Mike had given him a beer and they both sat drinking and watching television for a long time, not speaking. After a moment, Mike got up and went into the room in the back. He called to Sha. Sha got up and moved toward the back of the apartment, dragging his heels in the carpet. He hovered at the door of the bedroom. He wondered why the light was off.

"Come here, little man," he heard Mike say from inside the room. He could see Mike's dark outline against the wall. It looked like his shirt was off. As Sha stepped into the room, Mike put his hands on his shoulders and pulled Sha to him. A certain excited terror ripped through him then, and the trembling started again, harder now than before. But for all his terror, the fire that raced through him as Mike pushed against him was the realest thing he had felt in his life. Mike stood with his hands on Sha, moving against him, pulling Sha's clothes off with his own. Sha hadn't resisted, succumbing to the fire and the darkness, and Mike's hands, until the hands moved to pull off Sha's underwear.

"Uh-uh," Sha had said, shaking his head in the dark, holding on tight to the elastic of his briefs. Somehow, the thin strip of cotton and elastic that barely even covered him was the difference between an experience to thrill and excite, one he could live with, endure, enjoy, and one that would consume him and demolish him as a man.

"Alright, Sha," Mike had whispered, feeling Sha's body tense. "Alright," and moved his hand. Mike had never wanted to hurt any of them. But he knew he had, knew he had wrecked the worlds of many of the thirteen and fourteen-year-olds who had worked for him over the years, had damaged them more than they had already been damaged by the shit their lives had dropped on them. But he hadn't wanted to, and he didn't want to now, especially with Sha, who had an intensity and a boldness he had rarely seen in boy or man. He hadn't wanted to crush the light out of Sha's eyes the way he had crushed it out of so many others, hadn't wanted to crush Sha's little limbs with his own heavy ones the way

44

he had crushed many before. So he stood there with Sha and made a kind of love to him, both of them standing, in their underwear, grinding against each other in the dark.

Sha never did take his underwear off, even after they were soaked from the inside and sticking to his skin. He just pulled his clothes on over them and told Mike he had to go. Mike had offered to take him, but Sha said he could take the train and was out the door before Mike could protest. While Sha waited at Saratoga Avenue for the 3 Train, shifting uncomfortably in his clothes, Mike shifted in his, hoping Sha was all right. He had thought, for a minute, as they stood in the dark room together in their underwear, that Sha had enjoyed it, that he had actually made himself a part of it. But he had told himself that before, even when he knew it was a lie.

Mike would have preferred to sleep with men. But that, of course, was impossible. Getting into bed with another man would have compromised too seriously his status in life. And if any of his peers, any one of his associates in business ever found out, they would have had him killed immediately. They would have to. They certainly could not allow anyone (or themselves) to believe that a faggot could do what *they* did. And Mike knew that no self-respecting Brooklyn boy would ever tell that Mike had messed around with him, so he continued his assaults, despite his guilt, and bought his wife gaudy and expensive jewelry in place of sex.

But Sha was not destroyed by Mike, not at this point anyway, and the two of them continued their unsophisticated sessions for weeks, Sha always in his underwear, and Mike becoming increasingly impatient. One day when Sha came by the office to pick up a package, Mike said to him: "I want you to go somewhere with me tonight, little man. A spot I found in the City."

Sha had begun to look forward to their times together; his heart had begun to open to Mike. The intimacy that was physical, such as it was, had engaged a greater, even

45

more unfamiliar intimacy between them. They never kissed, which seemed sensible to Sha, but they held and stroked each other, and Mike always took Sha's head in his arms the times they slept together, and held it against his chest until he was asleep. Sometimes they went to hotels, but not very nice ones, and never in Manhattan. He wondered what it was all about.

Frost formed on the windows as they pulled into the garage on Forty-Fourth Street. Stepping up the stairs to the Algonquin Inn, Sha looked over his shoulder and saw a long black Lincoln pulling up to another hotel across the street. A white-haired, pink-skinned gentleman hurried out of the driver's seat, and around the car to open the door. Two young men and a woman with straight auburn hair falling around a small auburn face rose out of the car, all in dark sunglasses, all dressed in black like assassins. One of the men placed several folded bills into the driver's hand, who bowed graciously and handed his passengers off to the black-suited doormen. They were escorted then, with all their accoutrements, through the huge mahogany doors, under the stone engraving that said 'ROYALTON,' onto the royal blue carpet inside. The limousine moved away into traffic, emptied of its contents, and Sha turned, unescorted, into the Algonquin to meet Mike, who was already standing at the counter inside.

The room was nicer than the ones before, with green and beige wallpaper that looked to Sha like something he had seen on television. Still, he could not stop wondering about the threesome he had seen outside. Who were they? Were they famous? *They were something*, he thought. *They were something.* Mike had not noticed, and so continued his special night as planned, twisting the tops off two twenty-two ounce bottles of beer and lying down next to Sha on the polyester blend bedspread. Soon they were standing in the dim room, naked except for Sha's underwear, moving their bodies familiarly against each other. Mike moved his hands under the elastic and over Sha's body, but when he tried to pull him

46

out of the little briefs, as he had each time since that first time in the apartment, Sha just laughed nervously, as had become his habit, and shook his head.

"Uh-uh," he said, smiling tensely and holding on to his drawers.

"Come on, man," Mike said. "It ain't gon kill you to take em off. You supposed to be my boy. Why you still act like you scared of me?"

"I ain't scared of nothin," Sha said. "I just ain't goin out like that."

Mike frowned. "Like what, man? Why you always act like this? I thought we was cool."

"We *are* cool."

"Then, why? Why every time I get close to you, you pull this shit on me? Like you don't fuckin know me or somethin. It's me, Sha," he said, hitting his palm against his chest. "You know what I'm sayin? It's just me."

Sha was silent, his eyes on the floor. Mike's voice had always moved him. Sometimes he didn't even hear the words Mike said, but he watched the way he moved when he said them and listened to the bass go up and down in his voice. When he saw Mike pat his chest like that he knew he was claiming him somehow, being sweet and demanding in some way, but Sha could simply not give him what he knew he must be asking for. Was not ready for whatever it was Mike wanted to do to him once he came out from under the cover of his protective cotton briefs.

Mike blew out a long, exasperated breath and sat down on the bed, pulling Sha between his legs. He held him around his waist and spoke in a low voice: "Why we always got to go through this, huh? All I do is treat you nice, run you all over fuckin New York with me...I treat you like family and this is what I get? This is bullshit. Don't I do shit for you? Buy you shit? Don't I give your sister money and the whole nine? What the fuck? And you still cry like a little fuckin kid every time I touch you."

Sha narrowed his eyes and pulled away from Mike. "I ain't no fuckin kid," he said. "I just don't want to do it."

"Well you need to grow the fuck up, okay?" Mike turned away from him and snatched his boxers off the floor. He shot his legs into them and lay back on the bed, aiming the remote and pressing the buttons furiously.

Sha hated Mike at that moment, and he hated himself for caring, for giving a *fuck* about Mike and what he wanted, and what he thought. Instinct told him to strike back, hard— to clamp down on the man's jugular for dear life. "I never asked you for nothing," he said. "And I never wanted to *do* nothin either. You the one pulled this faggot shit."

Mike's eyes narrowed then too, and his teeth came together. "Oh, it's faggot shit now? I should fuck you up, little boy. I should bust you in the fuckin mouth for talkin to me like that."

They stared at each other with hooded eyes full of contempt. Sha sighed through his teeth in disgust. "Whatever, man," he said, and began pulling pieces of his wrinkled clothing from the floor.

"Yeah, whatever," Mike said back, looking away. "I ain't gon be puttin up with this shit much longer, either."

Sha just shook his head and continued gathering his clothes. As he pulled on his jeans he spit venom under his breath. He would make Mike feel him this time; he would make it count. He spoke slowly and carefully, pronouncing the words just loud enough for Mike to hear them, with just enough force for him to feel them. "Fuckin trick," he said, and cut his eyes.

"What?" Mike shouted, the rage coming. "What did you say?"

He sprang up and grabbed Sha's arm, pulling his little body toward him so that Sha's face was almost touching his own. "What the fuck did you say?" he screamed into Sha's face, shaking him hard with both hands.

"Get off me, son," Sha shouted back at him, trying to

pull free.

"Shut the fuck up," Mike shouted, catching Sha's shoulders and shoving him hard against the wall. "You think this is a game, little boy? You think I couldn't kill your little ass right now?" He slammed him against the wall again, grabbed him around the throat with one hand, held him there against the wall.

"And do you really think I had to ask," he said, and with his free hand began yanking Sha's clothes off again. Sha struggled harder as the denim fell down around his ankles, but Mike just tightened his grip around the little neck in his hand. Sha choked and coughed, gagging on the lining of his own throat. His kicking and hitting only made it worse, but he could not stop.

"Did you really think I couldn't take the shit, nigga," Mike growled, punctuating his words with a light knocking of Sha's head against the wall. He reached down and took the elastic band of Sha's underwear in his fist and Sha heard the cotton tear: "You think I couldn't have done anything I fuckin wanted to all this time? Huh!" he screamed. "Huh?"

Sha still struggled pointlessly against Mike's strong arms and hands, jerking his head back and forth as if to say no, no. Mike kept pulling at the underwear, so hard that when they finally ripped apart at the seams, welts raised on Sha's waist and thighs where they had bit into his skin. Mike held him there against the wall with just his one hand around Sha's neck, waiting for the tears to come dropping out of his eyes. He looked into them, but the tears did not come. Only a nauseated disgust came into them, a poisonous disdain that left the taste of lead in Mike's mouth and the image of himself reflected in them burned into the corner of his soul forever.

"Get the fuck out," he almost whispered, and let go of Sha's neck. Sha wasted not a second on drama. He did not drop to his knees, pant or gag or put his little hands to his neck and cry. He just got quickly into his clothes, except for the tattered underwear lying lifeless on the floor, and slipped out the door without saying another word.

An hour later, when he walked through the door of the small basement apartment that had served as their residence for the few months he and his sister had stayed in Brownsville, Sheena knew immediately that it was time to go. She could tell by the look in her little brother's eyes that their time there was up. She did not even bother to ask why; it didn't matter, and she had never expected to stay long anyway. She just followed Sha's lead, silently stuffing clothes into plastic bags and digging the folded wad of twenty-dollar bills Sha had given her to hold out from under the corner of the tattered green carpet. She woke her little son and they were all gone in less than an hour, leaving nothing but the vaguest memories and a few discarded and unimportant possessions behind.

Even now, as Sha marched through the night toward the apartment on Flatbush, thinking about Aaron, he remembered how Mike's hand had felt around his neck. He remembered how it felt not to breathe. He knew something else had been choked out of him that night too, that some part of him had been torn apart and mangled like the lifeless little briefs lying on the floor of the Algonquin. He would never do that to Aaron, he thought. Never rob Aaron of the things that had been robbed of him: his hope and sincerity, the light in his eyes. In Aaron, he had found what he believed he was looking for: a clean slate, a blank canvas, a shiny new penny unmarked by filthy fingerprints. He knew he could make Aaron what he was going to be, and that through Aaron's eyes he too could appear unstained, unexploited, ungroped by heavy hands. And this he wanted more than anything else—to be something other than what he had become.

As he passed the bodega where he had seen Aaron that first time, months ago, a melody hovered in the air.

My sweet morning dew
I took one look at you

A shriveled little woman stood at the corner of the little store, shaking a plastic change cup and smelling of rum. She was singing strangely, almost whining the little melody as she banged the cup against her hand like a tamborine:

And it was plain to see
You are my destiny

Sha reached into his pocket and pulled out a handful of change. The dirty coins clanged noisily together as they fell into the yellow cup. Sha walked on never bothering to look at the woman's face.

FIVE

Anise fingered the yellowed last pages of the book and closed it. The girl on the cover didn't look anything like the girl in the book, looking up over those heart-shaped glasses. She would have been prettier, she thought, and tanner—more whitegirlish. The picture was what prompted her to pick up the ragged little paperback in the first place, thinking it would be one of those stories about a sassy young whitegirl who was smarter than everyone around her, who saved the world or solved some great mystery or just learned to be happy. She had always loved those little girls: the ones from the books she read, but this one was different. She was beautiful, yes, and smart; but conniving too.

The man behind the counter at the library had looked strangely at her over his wire-rimmed glasses. "Is this for you, young lady?" he had asked, leaning closer and holding the book up to her.

Anise looked at the little whitegirl looking up over her glasses, at the balding little white man looking over his. She nodded.

"Well," the man said, shifting in his seat and tensing the muscles in his face, "this is not a *children's* book, you know."

Anise did not blink; just looked at him straight and said: "I read at the twelfth grade level." She always liked the feel of those words flipping over her tongue. Never would she utter them unprovoked, never wanting to be obnoxious, but she kept them in her personal repository with the rest of her artillery, to drop when the opportunity presented itself.

The series of standardized tests administered at the beginning of the year had yielded the surprising results, and the school counselors had arranged a special meeting to discuss possibilities with her mother. They suggested skipping Anise ahead a grade or sending her to a special school, but Anise's mother would not hear of any of it.

"No," she had said, shaking her head at them suspiciously, "I don't think so."

"But Ms. Roycrist," they said, and told her what a shame, what a real pity and a shame it would be to waste the child's natural ability, told her there were hundreds of programs for children like Anise, dozens of schools that would love to have her.

"I *know* Anise is smart." She said. "Her brother taught her to read when she was three. But I just...I just don't think so. I don't think all this is right for Anise. These kids grow up too fast as it is these days, and I just don't want all kind of confusion." She sighed. "No. No, I don't think so."

"But Ms. Roycrist, wouldn't you—"

No she wouldn't. And Anise was furious. The elegant boarding school she had imagined with the stone walls and the vine up the façade, and all the skipping around on bottle-green lawns in perfect starched uniform and stockings, and the lovely luscious kissing on the cheeks by all the wonderful whitegirls vanished immediately behind a blast of exhaust and car horns. And when she heard all those *nos* and *I-don't-think-sos* and understood that it would be her mother who would keep her from this setting miles and miles from Flatbush Avenue—it was then that she knew finally that her mother had never loved her. Her mother had never loved her, and all the tricks and deceptions she had attempted over the years to disguise it now stood out stark and outrageous against the dull backdrop of her life.

But something else happened at the same second, and Anise did something strange and unwitting: She stopped loving her mother. She felt something close down inside her, and though she had not understood at that moment, she understood after, that it was she who had closed it and that she had done it with one easy stroke. She had seen her brother do this, of course—flip his mysterious inner switches off and on. But it was only now that she had accomplished it herself and understood the force of it. She no longer cared what her mother did or thought, or anything about her. All her mother's offenses she dismissed now only as stupidity.

There were times, certainly, when she was weak, would slip or forget, awaken almost from a trance to find those switches thrown up again on their own, some inexplicable surging emotion suddenly present again for her mother. Those Sunday nights especially, with her mother's hands in her hair and steady voice in her ear, going on, sounding like a recital—especially then she would waver until her brother would look at her dirty or something else would remind her of Ms. Roycrists's criminal lack of mother-love. She would calm herself, catch herself quickly before she slid down again into her mother's trickery and deceit.

But she was not angry, not mad at her mother for long, after the initial shock at the school, and she did not deny her the basic courtesies of a child toward her mother. She smiled at times and said please and thank you and in her heart did not *blame* her mother. She had by this time begun to formulate certain ideas about *race,* and based on her conclusions, had decided that it was the very fact of her mother's blackness that caused her to think and act the way she did. Anise did not know any white people. She had never had a whitegirl for a friend. But she had a television in her room, and books on her shelves and she knew good and well that white people did not act the way her mother acted and that the mothers of all the little whitegirls did certainly not treat them the way her mother treated her.

Anise had spoken to a whitegirl once. The girl had worn the same blue winter coat Anise had and held her mother's hand like Anise did when she got on the train. The girls had just stared at each other for a moment standing there side by side with their mothers and their identical quilted coats until one of them giggled and the other laughed and their mothers looked at them both and smiled. But her mother's smile was different than the other mother's and Anise saw it in an instant. The girls chatted on for a moment about coats and snow and what books they read until Ms. Roycrist turned a nervous smile and said "Alright, Anise." Anise had just stared at her mother for a moment in disgust and disbelief and when she smiled at the little girl again her mother just pinched her arm quietly and took her off the train. She would always remember that nervous smile and unequivocal *alright* of her mother's as sure evidence that the little whitegirl in the puff-blue coat had or knew something that her mother did not and that she was right: white women loved their daughters and their little sons too, and this was what her mother was afraid she would find out. This was why white children sang and danced on T.V. This was why the pale little cubs were always allowed to do precisely what their happy hearts desired: go off to train for the Olympics or become ballerinas or away to grassy green schools. She had once seen on channel 13 a boy whose mother was sending him to Tibet to become a Buddhist priest. He was only five, but a high priest of some apparent spiritual prominence had pronounced it the little bugger's destiny, so off he went to Lhasa to fulfill it. His mother had just waved and dabbed a tear from the corner of her eye with a silk handkerchief as the big Mercedes carried her son away to greatness.

And here Anise was, all but being told she was a

genius, in no uncertain terms, by people whose job it presumably was to know, and her mother wouldn't even think of letting her skip a stupid grade. Her mother did *not* love her.

Anise looked at the tattered book again and the whitegirl on the cover who looked nothing like the girl inside and knew there were things she didn't understand. She knew the words, most of them, and looked the ones she didn't up in the dictionary. And she wrapped her mind around all her little plots and subplots with ease. But what interested her more than the words, or all the little things that were said and done between the long pages of the books she read, were the things that were *felt* there, and she said to herself that in her life she would feel things too, all the things she had ever wanted to, because she would not be afraid. She would not be like her brother or like her mother. She would find out what it was like to be alive.

She practiced. She kissed the mirror and put on her mother's lipstick and said *yes, yes, oh yes, I love you too.* And when she went to bed at night she would touch her panties and whisper *oh yes, I do. I love you too. I love you too.*

She left the book on her bed and went into the kitchen, pulled open the refrigerator door and let the cool air spill out onto her shins. Jesse was at the doctor and Anise was glad to escape her for the day. But Jesse, at least, had potato chips and grape soda and all the things she had grown fat on at her house. She wished her brother would hurry. She reached into the refrigerator, grabbed the scratched plastic container and swallowed right from the spout. She tilted her head back and let the last cool drops fall onto her purple tongue.

The doorbell rang and Anise banged the pitcher back down onto the refrigerator shelf and slammed the door. *Finally,* she said to herself running, giant-stepping into the hallway. She pulled open the heavy door, standing behind to let her brother through with the bags from the store. "Come on," she said to Aaron from behind the door. "I'm hungry."

A second passed, and she peeked around the door to ask what he was waiting for.

But it wasn't Aaron. She looked at Sha standing there on the stoop, his arms hanging loosely at his sides. She came out from behind the door. She wrapped her fingers around the doorknob, hung her body out over the stoop, looked down the block toward the Avenue. "Aaron's not here," she said.

Sha laughed. "Who said I want to see Aaron?"

Anise looked up at his coarse hair and black eyes, down at the denim falling down around his boots. "You look like it," she said.

"I look like it?"

"You all look the same." Anise stepped back then and motioned into the house. "You can wait for him if you want. He went to the store."

Sha shook his head. "No. I'll come back." He looked at her. "You not supposed to let strangers in the house, you know. I know your mom told you that before. "

She sighed. "She always tells me stuff like that. But you're not a *stranger*, really."

"Well you not supposed to let anybody in the house. Especially not a man."

"Man?"

Sha stared at her.

"I mean you just look like a regular...boy. Are you over twenty-one?"

Sha smiled. "Don't I look like it?"

"Not really," she said.

"Well, be careful. People ain't always how they look."

"I know. Well, do you want me to tell him you came over? What's your name?"

"Don't worry about it," he said. "I'll come back later."

"Okay." Anise shrugged. "But it doesn't make sense

58

not to tell him you were here. Don't you want him to know you came?"

Neither of them had noticed Aaron coming up the block, so when Sha turned to leave, distracted by his exchange with Anise, and found Aaron staring up at him nervously from the sidewalk, Sha was taken by surprise, and a brief look of uncertainty passed quickly over his face and disappeared. It was the only look like it Aaron would ever see breaking that constant calm face of Sha's but Aaron was too far engulfed in his own fear and apprehension to notice. But Anise noticed. Saw the way Sha's body stiffened when he looked at Aaron, saw Aaron's eyes not quite looking into Sha's.

Aaron, who had seen Sha there on the stoop and braced himself, spoke first: "What's up," he said, eyes steady but low.

"Sup, little man," Sha said, swinging his arm back. "I was just comin to check you."

He looked, to Sha, more like a little boy than ever, despite the flex and shine of his bare brown arm under the weight of their handshake. The gray nylon basketball jersey he wore fell lightly over his chest and the fitted blue cap on his head made his eyes huge, and the sun shone through them.

"I had to go to the store." He tilted his head toward Anise then. "My sister," he said.

Anise frowned, came down the stairs for the bags. "Took long enough," she said and went back up into the house.

Sha's eyes moved up following Anise, came slowly down again to Aaron. He said finally: "You been alright?"

"Yeah," Aaron said, nodding vaguely and moving his feet up the stairs. "I been cool." Then, with unsure footing: "You want to come inside?"

Sha glanced up at the doorway. "You sure it's cool?"

"It's cool."

"I ain't seen you around." Sha said, his fast words snapping close to Aaron's ear as he moved past Sha on the stairs. "Thought you forgot about me."

Aaron laughed nervously and kept up the stairs. Sha sent his fist gently into Aaron's ribs. Aaron started, but hoped Sha was coming up the stairs behind him. Aaron still could not look Sha exactly in his eye, and to Sha he seemed almost cold. But Sha didn't worry, and went up the stairs as light as air.

Sha shut the door behind him. He followed Aaron down the creaking staircase into the little room in the basement.

Aaron felt sick sitting on the bed next to Sha, the bed he imagined still smelled of Sha, the sheets he buried his face in and moved up and down under nights since he had been with Sha, imagining it was Sha's hands on him instead of his own. Sha knew all this somehow, Aaron was sure. He could see it in his eyes.

"I didn't know your sister was here," Sha said leaning forward, his elbows on his knees. "I wouldn't a just came by."

Aaron nodded, stared at the television.

"Well look, man," Sha said then, "I can't stay. I got some things I got to do. I just wanted to make sure everything was alright."

"What you mean?" Aaron sounded calm, but he did not look at Sha.

"I mean I ain't see you on the block like I usually do, so I thought maybe you was goin through something." He kept his heavy eyes on Aaron. "Like maybe you was feelin a certain way about everything. About how everything went down with us, and maybe that's why you ain't been around. Cause you ain't want to see me. Me—I feel like we got something. Know what I mean?"

Adrenaline rushed into Aaron's veins. His heart beat. His face burned. He had no words to respond, no way to answer without telling everything, so he sat there, mad and silent, staring blindly, unable to think.

Sha watched him, fingered the heavy Cuban link around his wrist. "Well, I guess you ain't got nothin to say," he said finally. "It's cool. I just wanted to make sure you was straight."

"Look, man, I'm not..." Aaron stumbled. "I ain't like that." He hadn't meant to say it. He hadn't meant to. But Sha sitting there looking at him, seeing everything, knowing it all—he could not stand it, and the words had slipped out on their own.

Sha sat calmly with his eyebrows raised, watching time take its toll on Aaron; he smelled the fear, anticipated the pain, knew he would need to inflict both over time, lovingly, the way a parent hits a child, devotedly, for its own good. He glanced around the tiny room. The small frameless bed in the corner. A beaten metal footlocker across from it where the television sat, a dozen video games and their boxes splayed around it. The familiar dresser on the opposite wall—wood grain and aluminum handles painted gold. Above it, Buckshot gritted his teeth ferociously at them in the dark.

Aaron looked at him. He was baffled. Infuriated. Had he not heard? How could he just sit there like that?

Finally Sha looked back at him blankly, acknowledging nothing. Just looked at him. Silent.

"Did you hear me?" Aaron said again weakly. "I dont...I don't get down like—"

Sha shrugged and moved his head slightly. "Me neither," he said. "And anyway, me and you is cool no matter what."

They sat there for another moment until Sha brushed his hands over his pant-legs and got up to leave. "Look, I gotta go. I'm a come through tomorrow, see what you doin."

Aaron heard his own voice. "Come in the afternoon," it said. "I got to go to the City in the morning."

SIX

The D train rattled and shook as it pulled itself over the rusty blue bridge. An old man stared gently at him with pale green eyes. Aaron looked out the window, watched the drab Brooklyn warehouses sink slowly out of view. In the distance, tiny cars moved back and forth over the Bridge in a constant, furious stream. A little yellow man with straight black hair slid open the door at the front of the car, came through with a huge box of trinkets, a rope anchoring dozens of tiny stuffed animals and key chains, other things Aaron could not recognize or make out. "One dollar," was all he said. "One dollar."

The steel girders of the blue bridge threw bright shadows into the car and onto the faces of the passengers as the train moved closer to the City. Out the window, Aaron thought he could make out the bouncing heads of joggers and cyclists on the Bridge. He remembered holding his mother's hand going over, the stone and metal heart of the thing peeking through the wooden slats under his feet. The City had glistened and shined, the towers of Lower Manhattan jutting up out of the cement—crystal giants skirted by the mercury surface of water. Even then, the sparkle of it had seemed deceptive; the filth he knew instinctively was there somehow inaccessible from that height and angle—his first view from the Bridge.

In the distance, a horned statue stabbed menacingly at the air. His mother had made him repeat the name, which he knew but did not understand, and sat down on a wooden bench rubbing her big stomach. Anise kicked all the time; her mother was walking the Bridge hoping she would come. She told Aaron that the Bridge was built in 1869 and stood him in front of the sign that said so. And she told him New York was the biggest city in the world. It looked like it, he thought.

In time, Aaron learned that New York *was* the world for all practical purposes, and attached an unaffected yet totally self-conscious arrogance to that fact. New York made sense. Brooklyn mattered. When white kids in California and Belgium and places he saw on TV started wearing camouflage and Wu Tang hoodies he knew that what he did mattered, knew that somewhere, everywhere, there were people watching him, taking careful note of how he walked, talked, looked, danced, dressed. And he thought this was exactly right.

Instinctively, Aaron knew that Sha could only have occurred on Brooklyn cement. He reeked of Brooklyn, down to the socks. Boys from Brooklyn were a different breed from the ones from Queens or Jersey or the Island. Uptown had flavor of its own—Harlemworld, the Puerto Rican boys from the Bronx; but Brooklyn style was calmer, cleaner, more natural, its flash slightly more restrained and confident. Brooklyn boys moved with a singular sense of ownership as they navigated through the City, putting feet to pavement with the easy knowledge that it belonged to them, in ways perhaps more even than to the people who lived there, high above Central Park or the Village or Times Square. And Sha had all of it—the style and assurance, the candor, the guts and audacity that belonged to Brooklyn boys, but with an easy and virile warmth, a way of making everything seem right and okay.

But how could he? It was still a mystery to Aaron—how Sha could possess himself so fully, how he had moved into Aaron's world with the exact same boldness with which he moved through his own, with the exact same confidence with which he had looked into Aaron's eyes afterward and acted as if nothing at all unusual had happened, had raked his black eyes over him and made no apologies for any of it. He seemed completely unhampered, unaffected by what should, in Aaron's estimation, have been the deepest, darkest, most shameful secret of his life. Maybe there was something he didn't understand. Maybe what had happened between him and Sha was something other than what it seemed, fell into some category he was not yet aware of.

He remembered an old talk show episode, between the fights, with a young woman in dramatic confrontation with her boyfriend. The boyfriend was handsome, young, masculine, brown, and had vehemently denied the allegations being thrust at him, fidgeting and bouncing his long legs nervously as the plot thickened around him. The girlfriend had ranted and waved her ruby airbrushed nails in his face while her friend, a roaring but beautiful dyke, and the obvious instigator of the scenario, had shouted and announced that she knew for a fact—*for a fact*—that the nigga was fuckin around, and that she had proof. The proof shortly pranced itself onto the stage in the form of an extremely handsome, unmistakably effeminate young man whom the boyfriend, from the look of shock and desperation on his face, had had some unseemly relation with. Finally, with Aaron's eyes glued tight to the screen, the boy had admitted reluctantly, that he *might* be bisexual, that he had been to some clubs and whatnot, had messed around, but was definitely *nobody's* faggot. His girlfriend evidently disagreed, and screamed every vicious epithet, every bitch, cunt, faggot, every punk, pussy, queer and queen she could think of at the top of her lungs, egged on by her hard little girlfriend who at that point slung a word of her own. *Why are you doing this to me*, he had pleaded over the audience's boos and hisses. *Why?*

The boy had looked so beautiful at that moment, so unlike a faggot, in fact, that Aaron would have believed he was an actor, had it not been for the indisputable grief and terror in the boy's eyes as his world came crashing down around him. Aaron had wanted to call the show, wanted to find him somehow, to touch him to see if he was real, to say *me too, man, I'm here too,* but he knew he could not, and his only hope had rolled away with the credits off the screen. His only hope until now.

But Sha was different. He was Aaron's only hope certainly, but he was his greatest terror too. He could not imagine Sha being afraid of anything, could not imagine him fidgeting or avoiding eyes, or cowering or pleading the way the boy had. He didn't know what Sha would have done, but it wouldn't have been this, he was sure. And this was what terrified him.

The train slowed slightly then, accelerated and threw itself into Manhattan, plunging into the darkness beneath grim Chinatown. He watched the people getting on and off the train, the composition of the car changing slightly at every stop. At West 4th a man carrying too many bags sat down in the seat next to him. Aaron was irritated by his clothes—black leather boots and too many buckles—and by the sheet of cellophane around his white huddling flowers. Aaron looked at him out of the corner of his eye. Lines formed at the corners of the man's eyes and around his mouth. Aaron wondered how old he was. A young man, black, in sneakers and exaggerated clothes got on at the next stop and sat across from him diagonally. He tossed a blue handball from fist to fist, squeezing the rubber in his palms, and looked at Aaron. Aaron had worn his khaki pants and blue button down shirt, as his mother had said, and he now wished he had on his jeans and boots and baseball cap. He

66

hated to look that way, and didn't see the point; it was just a movie theater and his mother knew the manager anyway. She had wanted him to wear a tie, and they had argued for several minutes about it, but that was where Aaron drew the line. She had left the house before him and slammed the door, saying loudly in defeat: "Wear the damn tie, Aaron."

At Columbus Circle he transferred to the local, and as he stepped off the train he could feel the eyes of the young handballer staring through the closing doors behind him. He walked across the platform to the B Train just pulling in and stepped in through the doors. At 86th Street he stepped off, past the token booth, up the stairs, into the Upper West Side sun.

The theater faced Broadway and people swarmed continuously out and in. Velvet ropes dammed the floating crowds, pouring them through at regular intervals. The manager was a tall, wiry black man named Walter Linnen; he wore a tattered gray suit, with a tie and bent black wingtips. "Well," he said, and shook Aaron's hand. "Your mom tells me you want to get into the movie business." He grinned and tapped Aaron jovially on the arm. Aaron hated him immediately.

"So why do you want to work here, Eric?" Walter asked as he sat Aaron down at a desk in the little cubicled office.

"Aaron."

"Oh yes, that's right. Aaron. Why do you want to work here, Aaron?"

Aaron stared blankly. *Why you think?* he thought. *My mother's makin me get this fuckin job and you know it.* He breathed. "This is a nice theater. And I like this part of the City." He forced a terrible smile. "Plus my mom told me you was cool...I think it'd be a good job... For the summer."

Walter looked strangely at him. "I started out as a usher, man. I been here almost eight years. I'm assistant manager now."

Assistant manager, Aaron thought.

"It's a good business, man. You just got to know how to deal with people, you know what I mean?" Walter leaned grandly back in his tiny plastic swivel chair.

Aaron raised his eyebrows and frowned and nodded.

"Well, anyway. You got the job if you want it. You can start next week. It's from eight to twelve."

He didn't want it, particularly. But he would take it.

Aaron eased out onto Broadway, the violent titles spilling off the marquis behind him as he walked back toward the subway. He exhaled and let his eyes roll briefly and wearily into his head. Walter was going to terrorize him, he knew, in that polite and sheepish way the sweet and respectable morons of the world have of terrorizing. *Eight years*, he thought, *and that mufucka's assistant manager?* He shook his head. *Fuck that.*

Aaron had thought vaguely about college, but he had never been able to see his future precisely, had never had a clear vision of who exactly he was and what, exactly, he was supposed to *do*. People seemed to like him, seemed to think he was smart or funny, so he had taken to substituting all these fuzzy messages for a plan, had simply decided that there must be something out there waiting to happen. He hated school, and he had no reason to believe this would change, but he had to do *something*. But Anise was the smart one; let her be the doctor or whatever, let her bear that burden; Aaron would wait and see what happened.

He had gotten to the subway station, and come down several steps before he finally decided to walk. He had been preoccupied and moved almost subconsciously toward the train. *How had he known?* he had been thinking. *How had Sha known?* This more than anything troubled him now. And angered him. And this subtle rushing home he was doing now angered him too. When he stopped on the third step, a large shopping bag carried by a tiny old woman with ashen face and pale unnatural hair, crushed against his back.

The old woman, irritated, sighed and waited for Aaron to move. But the stairway was crowded with people coming up the other side and for a moment he was trapped there with the old woman's breath coming down against his neck. When finally he could move, he jumped across to the other side, scaled the few stairs, saying *Scuse me* as he did, and walked back down Broadway toward the Seventies.

It was his favorite part of the City—his favorite part to look at anyway, and his head tilted slightly up, as he walked, to the buildings rising up like two crystal walls on either side of wide Broadway. Life up here was different, he thought, locked behind those high walls. Not like Brooklyn where it occurred at street level, or just a few steps up on the stoop, or hung out of fourth floor windows with a dishtowel in its hand screaming down on you at the top of its lungs. Up here, life happened far, far above the street, as wide as it was, its true clicking and clanking masked by the artificial clamor below. You would never see people here cry or scream or laugh too loud, never see them struggle or start or doubled in grief or joy. It wasn't that they didn't do these things or didn't feel them, but they didn't do them down here on the street like people in Brooklyn did, and they sure didn't feel them on the six o'clock news the way people in Brooklyn did either. Life up here was quieter, he suspected, more planned and predictable, but he had never really believed it was happier. In fact, he had never really believed white people to be happy at all. He was sure they didn't have problems, not real ones, not the ones who lived up here anyway. He knew they had money and cars and apartments that covered whole floors practically, but he imagined them, still, to be locked in a constant state of boredom and monotony—which was why they did the things they did, why they sky dived and bungy jumped and ran marathons, why their kids mimicked everything they saw black people do on T.V. These walls were supposed to lock people out, he knew, but they locked them in too, it seemed.

As he made his way down Broadway, inching, threading in and out of the crowds, no one looked strangely at him, no one looked at him as if he were out of place, or even looked at him at all that he could tell. And he hadn't expected them to. New York, after all, belonged to him as much as to any of them, and he felt himself a necessary participant and contributor, a requisite observer of it all, the absence of whom would somehow render the whole scene absurd and meaningless.

Aaron had always had something of a hard time mustering up the anger and resentment he knew he was supposed to harbor toward white people. They had very little to do with *his* life, as far as he could see, and were a source more of amusement than contempt or hostility. The few white kids who had been sprinkled through the schools he had attended over the years—and they were very few—had raised no particular suspicions in him. They were generally either isolated skater types or white kids sunk so deep in hip-hop that they scarcely seemed white at all. Both cases he found somewhat strange, comical, but not significant in his social world. Certainly there were situations in the City, on the train, in department stores, where he had been regarded with fear or suspicion or uncertainty, but he had never particularly resented these occasions or even thought these particular white people incorrect for being fearful or at least skeptical. Even *he* was skeptical of black people at times. And white people didn't seem exactly equipped for survival in the actual world. If he were white he'd be afraid of black people too, he thought. He knew he'd be afraid to walk down Flatbush Avenue, or pass a dark cluster of boys on the street at night. And in a way he was glad they were afraid; it made him safer in *his* world, higher up on his own personal totem pole.

A bus groaned by close to the curb, spit dust and soot into his face. Too late, Aaron tried to shield his eyes with his hand. He held his breath. Rudy Giuliani smiled warmly from the placarded rear end of the bus. Below the photo-

70

graph, bold-faced times-style letters hung together in some beguiling caveat. "What the fuck." Aaron cursed lightly to himself. He spit in the direction of the bus, and wiped his face with his hand.

Taxi's honked their horns at each other and were flagged down by somber suited men and shag-haired women with short skirts and plain, expensive bags. The turbaned men in the driver's seats bent resentfully to their wills and hurried them off to their destinations. Aaron moved closer to 72nd Street. The sun reflected off the shining buildings and polished storefronts. As he neared the subway station his stomach began to swirl again with the thought of Sha. Sha had said that they *had* something, but what he had meant exactly, Aaron could not be sure. He hoped without knowing what to hope for, but knowing enough, at least, to never let Sha see it in his eyes.

The turnstiles at 72nd Street clicked incessantly, and when Aaron shoved through he was just one click of thousands, one tiny bubble in the violent crashing stream which swept perpetually through the City, cascading over every brick and stone, careening around sharp corners of buildings, splitting lamposts and fire hydrants and parking meters. This ceaseless stream corroded the City as it went, wearing down and softening its jagged edges, blunting its cold right angles into warm curves and subtle slopes, leaving sediment and debris washed up onto its side streets and into its gutters. But the City stood still, with its peaks and its valleys, like the mountain that it was, the violent stream that ran down and around and through it somehow building it up again, always, even as it tore it down, constructing newer, sharper angles atop the old and blunted ones, erecting prouder peaks, seemlier spires. And Aaron did his part, and was swept effortlessly beneath the City through the tunnel of the 2 Train Brooklyn bound.

When he swung open the heavy front door of the house, the still in the hallway surprised him. He had expected a warmer welcome.   He had expected the sun to be streaming into the house through the windows in the front, but the hall was dark and still, and though it was seventy-five degrees inside, seemed cold. It was after noon, and he hoped Sha would be there soon. He walked into the kitchen and turned on the television, opened one of the cabinets and pulled down a bright cereal box. When he tipped the box, a tiny plastic figurine clinked against the side of the bowl. Anise never bothered with the treasures at the bottoms of cereal boxes; she never had; but Aaron was always surprised, nonetheless, to find one falling despondently into his bowl.

He watched the one O'clock installment of daytime tragedy eagerly and with enthusiasm. Blonde bimbos defined the parameters of their acute love triangles.

The two O'clock he watched with anticipation and suspicion. Sexy moms battled their daughters over the lengths of their skirts.

By three O'clock he was hardly paying attention at all. Out of control teens staked their claims to debauchery, knowing there was no tomorrow.

Four O'clock brought fear and uncertainty. A black man in a blue suit petted and empathized with the abused. Sha would have to come soon; Anise would be on her way.

At five O'clock he was outraged, terrified. He paced the kitchen floor as if it were a cage, looking through the metal bars on the windows, wondering why Sha had not come. *Why would he say he was coming, if he wasn't? Why?*

At five-thirty Anise came and he ignored her. He vanished into his room and stomped back and forth, his fists clenched, cursing himself, cursing Sha. He flew his foot into the base of the dresser and change and CDs and cologne bottles toppled off, clanking noisily around and behind it.

At six he heard the front door open and close, and his mother's heels coming down on the hardwood floor. When she called him later for dinner, he yelled up the stairs that he had already eaten and was not hungry. "Get up here, boy," she yelled back. "You think I cooked this food for my own health?"

At dinner his mother grilled him about the interview and Anise looked at him suspiciously as she picked over her peas and rice. Aaron picked over his too, and answered his mother's questions, choking down bites of chicken and not looking either of them in their eyes.

In his room that night he sat silent and alone, with the television off, brooding and licking his wounds, still half expecting, hoping Sha would come knocking at the door.

But Sha never came, and Aaron twisted and turned and kicked in the sheets until they were wrapped tightly around him like someone bound and gagged. Finally, he was very still and quiet and drifted into a brief, exhausting sleep just as the tiny window began to glow softly at the corner of the room.

SEVEN

120 Schermerhorn, Brooklyn's grim pinnacle of justice, sits solemnly atop a mountain of misfortune just at the foot of the Brooklyn Bridge. The structure itself, a behemoth of granite and Bessemer steel assembled initially by hopeful Irish workers in sullen clothes and caps, now quietly dominates the entire block and houses a hundred years of anxiety and exasperation and fury. On Tuesday and Thursday mornings, just before nine, a line begins to form at its gaping, pillared mouth. By ten o'clock, three sides of the great gray building—Smith, State, and Schermerhorn—are lined with shimmery disgruntled Brooklynites, there to plead their cases, or accept the pleas offered them by a machine greased with the certainty of their guilt.

Familiar and fragmented, concepts formed tenuously in the minds of the men and women waiting, were shaped into sound over curling tongues, buzzed and broke against Sha's ear as he inched slowly toward the jaws of justice.

"—The girl with the little handicapped boy? Yeah she just had another one and it had to stay in the hospital a long time, too. And then, you know what? They wouldn't even give it to her; they gave it to her sister instead. They get a lot of money now too, girl, cause they keep all them foster kids."

"—That's that shit, son. Jakes drive around in taxicabs now. Follow niggas to the spot. Bag they ass right there."

"—I can't wait til Mommie get out of lock. We gon have a nice party for her too, cake and everything. The whole nine."

"—You see all these cops out here now? That's cause last time a fight broke right in front of this muthafucker. Shit on lock now."

"—I busted the other girl's head open too, but it didn't come out on the rap sheet. I guess they wasn't worried about her, they was thinkin about the one who had to get the stitches. When the ambulance came, and they came to me, I said 'I don't need shit. Take care of *that* bitch.'"

"—Hell. By the time we see the judge, they have a warrant out on *our* ass."

This whirled around him like a funnel cloud, until suddenly the whirling stopped and half-made threats and resolutions were suspended in the air above, then clanged metallically down to the pavement. The sound that stopped all the others, that brought all the explaining and excusing and demanding to a tremulous halt was the clear determined banging of a bell. Across the street, clinging to a rusted street sign with one hand, a tiny little man banged the thing relentlessly up and down. He was very old and very black and very bald except for a few filthy gray dreadlocks, and in his jaundiced eyes swam the clear conviction of insanity. "Raaaaascaallls!" he began to yell at the top of his wee lungs. "Raaaaascaaaals!" The bell he continued to beat up and down, and the sound of it, and the sound of his small rasping voice, stopped them all in their tracks.

For one endless moment, the crowd rimming the edge of the building was smitten with the old man's crazed rebuke, a message made the more urgent and castigating by

76

his utter dereliction. He looked as if he had been through every depth of hell, had danced and caroused and been possessed in the most intimate and perverse manner. His audience clicked their tongues, and kicked their feet against the pavement and drummed their fingers on their folded arms; they looked briefly at each other, shame and uncertainty in their eyes, and then began their quick and uneasy dismissals:

"Fuck that nigga talkin bout?"

"Crazy mufucka!"

"Oh, he *know* he got a touch. Now, what you was sayin?"

Sha said nothing, just stared quietly at the man for a moment, took a long, ferocious pull of his cigarette, then turned and stared solemnly ahead as before. The boy whose jaw he had smashed his fist against, he now thought, had hardly been worth it–hardly worth the dust and the sun and the line around the block and the curious and accusing eyes staring out of the cars and trucks and buses rolling down Smith Street. He had stood on the very spot, on that very square of cracked cement, twice before in three years, thinking exactly what he was thinking now–it just was not worth it. It had never been worth it–the fights at Coney Island, the nickel bags in Bushwick. None of it had ever been worth a damn. But here he was, this, the third time in three years and none of it ever worth anything. Before Schermerhorn it had been the juvenile court building at Adams Street a block away and that had not been worth it either.

He had never been in actual jail. But he knew the holding cell of the precinct–the foul smell of aged urine and the one icy cuff on the wrist. He knew the brassy ring of the second cuff sliding against the stainless steel pole in the wall, the dry spit on the fiber-glass window–a decade's worth of tiny encrusted curses hurled venomously from the mouths of the despised. He knew also the cold, fleshy contempt in the eyes and in the hands of the police, their undisguised, unapologetic aversion to the life he struggled so hard under, and their utter irritation that he continued to survive it at all.

The crowd's murmuring had grown louder now and more self-conscious over the wailing and bell-ringing from across the street. But finally the weary messenger, tired of his task, or perhaps simply having said his piece, brought his gruesome hymn to an end, and removed himself quietly from the premises. The line began to rustle and curl and snake more swiftly through the arched entranceway of the building. Huge metal detectors scanned each of their bones one by one; key chains and pagers and coins chimed together and dropped dutifully into plastic containers. The brooding police looked apathetically into side pockets of purses and backpacks and ushered their owners in to judgment. Sha passed through the officers' thick gaze and sent his own sneer flying in their faces. Gilded elevator doors opened and closed and sections of the crowd were lifted up into the heart of the beast. Sha watched the passengers examine themselves in the polished brass inside. He did not look at his own reflection; he knew what he looked like.

When the doors opened on the fourth floor he stepped out. The halls hummed with retellings of all the hustles and twists of fate that had brought each of them there, and with half-hearted speculations on the ones that could carry them safely out. Attorneys spoke to their clients in a costly and incomprehensible shuck and jive. Sha looked down at the yellow desk appearance ticket he had retrieved from his pocket and moved slowly toward the designated door.

Courtroom CC-19 was long and rectangular and wide. Rays of sun burned too brightly through tall windows down on the twenty rows of benches over the long length of the hall. The judge's bench looked down on the room from its high pedestal at the prow. Low murmurs rose up to the high ceilings from the people on the benches and from those still shuffling in through the doors. Papers rustled in the hands of uniformed men who hovered near the judge's bench. Sha walked toward them down the aisle, dropped his yellow paper routinely into the wire basket on the table just before them. He wanted it to be over. It was as bad as jail, he thought. The police with their badges and their guns. The convicts and ex-convicts and convicts-to-be, each with badges of their own–badges of contempt and disgust and self-loathing–and with guns probably too but for the machines to detect them, any and all likely to detonate at the slightest disturbance, stacked tightly atop each other on the benches, looking suspiciously at each other out of the corners of their eyes. But at the same time they were jovial, purposeful, though Sha could not see this, and some of them so connected to each other, so thrown together in the same simmering crock of shit and malfeasance, that they formed complex and tragic relationships with each other that very day.

It was right here at Schermerhorn, perhaps only yards away, maybe on the next floor or down the corridor (he could not remember) where he had met Joel. It was August; he had just turned eighteen. He could only remember that the courtroom had been a tiny one, and that the woman bailiff had looked at him strangely when he entered it and smiled. He had instinctively looked around for a seat in the rear but there was none. He had resigned himself finally with dread to the front, when he heard an emphatic shuffle and thump and knew what it was–the reluctant clearing of some bundle of belongings from the crowded wooden bench onto the floor. Sha turned toward the sound and saw a slim emblazoned young captive signaling to him with an upward nod and detached motion of index finger toward a now vacant segment of bench. Sha acknowledged him with a brief nod of his own, and moved quickly onto the seat.

"Cool," Sha said obscurely to himself as he eased into the space on the bench.

"All right," the boy answered back.

Sha had not thought anything at all of him. He had

noticed his clothes, bold and baggy and bright, with emphatic Ts and Ps and Hs stamped strategically and exultantly over them, and the big diamond studs he wore before Sha had seen them worn that way, two in one ear, one in the other. Puerto Rican he looked to Sha–the curl and the cut of his shiny black hair, short at the sides, long on top, tawny skin, long lashes. He was not handsome, not in that café-con-leche fashion so rare and essential to the City. He was thin, and his face was thin, lightly pocked and speckled with the remnants of an acnied childhood. But he was put together, and his clothes, and the way he stared noncommittally and stoically ahead at all times created around him a certain air of calm.

Court-appointed attorneys called their clients into the hall and one by one the cases were called. A thin chatter came up from the back of the courtroom, despite the bailiff's earlier admonition that there be no talking eating reading or sleeping. The judge was a large dark woman with hair lighter than her face. Her eyes were reprimanding and hard, her voice soft and unintelligible from Sha's seat at the back of the room. As she glowered and examined and assessed, the small clock above her jerked its black hands across its face. The bench became less and less crowded and Sha became more restless, sighing and dropping the heels of his boots heavily against the floor. The boy next to him leaned forward and said in a voice almost a whisper, "You got the same bitch I got probably."

"What?"

"The lawyer. You probably got the same one as me," he said. "The white lady with the short hair." He pulled his flattened hand unceremoniously about his face.

"I don't know," Sha said. "I ain't seen her."

"Is your last name M thru S?"

"Salvador."

"Salvador?" He pronounced the name in Spanish and looked at him. "Yeah you got her. She got everybody M thru

S, unless you got your own attorney."

Sha shook his head.

"You got her then," he said, pressing his lips together. "And she's a bitch too."

Sha looked at him. "You know her?"

"*Do* I?" he said and rolled his eyes into his head. "I almost had to fight the bitch out there in the hall two weeks ago."

Sha smiled briefly.

"Fucking cunt."

Sha looked at him again, concerned, amused.

"I hate her," he said. "I fucking hate her."

"Why's that?"

He leaned closer to Sha. "Because she wanted me to cop to something I know nothing about. Assault. Now look at me. I have never assaulted anyone in my life except one time and believe me *that* bitch had it coming."

Sha glanced cautiously around him then, moving his eyes and nothing else.

"Anyway," Joel went on rhythmically, pronouncing his i-n-g's, "I told her 'no, I'm not copping to no assault when I haven't assaulted no one.' And do you know what she said? She said, 'Don't be an idiot.'" He looked at Sha. "Yes," he said. "And I said 'Okay, you must be new sweetheart, because no one calls Joel idiot.' And when I told her watch her mouth, she just looked at me dumb with her big fucking hair and told me come back in two weeks."

Sha shook his head. "So what did you do?"

"I didn't do anything. I just came back in two weeks like she said."

"No. What did you *do*? Maybe not assault. But I know you not sittin here for no reason."

Joel stopped, looked up and down at him a moment. "I was chilling in Williamsburgh," he started, slow, emphatic, pleased. "With this white dude. In one of those big lofts down there under the bridge. It was nice too, so I was relaxing, and I had my feet up on the table just like I was at home. And pretty soon, out of the blue, he asks me do I smoke dope. And I said 'Dope? What kind of dope?' So he got up and he came back with this little gold box. And he lifts the lid and it was full all the way to the top with powder. So I put my finger in it and I tasted it and I said 'Oh no, that's alright. You go ahead.' Cause I do a lot of things, but what was in that box is one kind of dope Joel does not do. So then he pulled out this little pipe, and I never seen nobody smoke it out of a pipe, but he put it right in the bowl and smoked it just like a rock. You ever heard of that? Me neither. But it must have been good, because two minutes later he was nodding and sleeping right there on the sofa. And what was I supposed to do? Sit there and wait for him to wake up? No. I clearly ran that nigga' pockets and bounced. But soon as I got outside the police was right there. So they said can they ask me a few questions. And I said 'Questions? Questions about what?' And them talking about I fit the description of a young latino male that just punched a old lady in the face. And I said 'Look at me. Do I look like the type of person who would punch a old lady? Are you kidding? My mother would kill me.' But I guess I did look like the type because they searched me then and after that it was all over. They found the wallet. And of course they wanted to know whose wallet is it, and while I'm at it what am I doing in the area. And what am I supposed to say? I just got this nigga and he's white and he's upstairs very much nodding out? I don't think so. And I don't have time to chit-chat because the owner of the wallet is going to wake up any minute and realize I have all his dough *and* his credit cards. And I don't want to tell them I'm coming from his house, but what *can* I tell them? That I'm just out for a nice stroll in lovely Williamsburg at three o'clock in the morning? I don't think so. So I'm trying to think of something and them just looking and who do you think comes running out of the building barefooted and with no shirt on? That's right. But the Jakes don't see him because their back is to him and he's across the street. He sees them though, and hauls his scary white ass back inside very quickly. So they arrest me for something I don't know nothing about, and I'm sitting here in court two weeks later for assault and the damn attorney is telling me plead guilty and take community service. Now, I have got nothing against community service," he said, and paused, "but Joel…"–and he pointed his finger toward his chest–"Joel isn't pleading guilty to nothing. Uh-uh. Because then, the next time something happens, this will be on my record, and they'll lock me up even quicker then…"

Back in courtroom CC-19 the sun continued to stream through the tall windows and Sha began to sweat. He patted the dampness at his brow with the palm of his hand. The back of the bench in front of him was scratched with engravings. The words there rhymed and declaimed, sprawled in loose cursive or uneven print, declared the ancient borough rivalry of the City succinctly without meter. *Brooklyn Zoo. The Queensbridge Reprezenta. Uptown Baby. Uptown.*

Sha lifted his eyes and let them pass briefly around the room. He hated New York. As much he could hate the only place on earth where his life made sense, the one place in the world that gave him meaning, framed him and the things he did, made them intelligible, provoking. But to Sha, New York was a task, something to be gotten through or around, a series of mishaps and misfortunes waiting to happen, to be avoided only with the most excruciating attention to detail, the most rigid concentration.

In New York anything could happen. You could be struck down by a taxicab or an ambulance or a bike messenger. Your subway car could crash into another at Times Square. The police could get you. A tunnel could collapse. Your neck could be snapped in a hit and run.

But what could he do? Retreat to the hinterland? Flee to Miami or Texas or California, where his Wallabees were mistaken for bobos. Where people thought his hair needed to be combed. Where he was incomprehensible because he was contextless. They could keep their pimp shit–their bootyshake and their gangster lean. And then there was Aaron. As much as he wanted to escape his life, and the keloid it had deposited in his chest, the reflection of himself in eyes for which he was custom made, was something he could not live without.

"Salvador?" A young attorney pulled his blue implicating eyes up off the stack of paper in his hands.

Sha glanced up, folding his face into the frown he knew the man would be looking for. Their eyes met briefly and the doors swung fast behind them as they disappeared into the hall.

EIGHT

The great borough of Brooklyn, like any civilization worth its salt, erected, early on, a great monument to war. It is a grand white arch in a wide round plaza, and it is there signaling greatness as buses and dollar vans sputter and men in the park bend in the shadows. Facing the arch, a white replica of all the grand triumphant arches of the world, a more unclever construction broods. A wrought-iron grill rises up its face–fifty feet high and paneled, with fifteen bronze figures looking down on the people coming in and out all day long through its wide revolving door. It had always struck Anise that so many of them were animals. White Fang and Moby Dick. Babe the Blue Ox.

CeCe lifted her eyes. "Why they put all them animals and stuff up there," she asked, her head tilted back.

"They're characters."

"But why they put them up there like that?"

"Because it's the library, CeCe." Anise liked CeCe most of the time.

"I hate animals," CeCe said, and pinched her nose between her thumb and forefinger. "They stink."

Anise frowned, pressed her lips together.

To the right of the sculpture, on the front of the building, was a huge engraving. Sharp letters etched in stone.

HERE ARE ENSHRINED
THE LONGING OF GREAT HEARTS
AND NOBLE THINGS THAT TOWER ABOVE THE TIDE
THE MAGIC WORD THAT WINGED WONDER STARTS
THE LEARNED WISDOM THAT HAS NEVER DIED

Anise had always had a curious relationship with words. Even before she could read them, she would sit with Aaron at the kitchen table, her dolls and stuffed animals cast to the side, admiring the way the y's and the j's dipped below the line, peering into the perfect hole of the o. She would assign meaning to the black marks on the pages of her brother's books, deciphering them incorrectly, until Aaron would huff and say, *That's not what it says, Niecey.*

What's that say? she would ask, placing her little finger cautiously upon a clump of letters. After he answered, she would wait several minutes before asking again. She did not want to irritate him. She would have the next clump all picked out, though, holding her little finger watching her brother's face. Aaron tired eventually of the asking and sat her down finally on the stoop with the tattered old deck of alphabet cards he had used and that his mother had never thrown away. Anise was delighted as the pretty marks on the page became sounds coming easy over her lips. Sound then became sentence. *Here is the house.*

She read everything then, in books and out of them, but it was still the sounds that words made, more ever than what they meant, that moved her. One frigid morning she sat on the living room floor of her aunt's apartment on Kosciusko transfixed before the television screen. She was barely four years old. She hadn't known who the woman was or what she was saying or why. But her words, and the way she said

86

them—*A rock. A river. A tree.*—with that grainy voice and those perfect pauses had charmed her like the saccharine song of a pied piper. She was smitten, and the damp stern eyes staring out of the soft brown face, demanding everything, conceding nothing, had dampened Anise's own eyes, and made her work her little lips into the shapes of the magic outlandish sounds issuing relentlessly forth from the wide-stretched mouth of the woman. Until Jesse punched the remote from behind her cloud of smoke and the words were gone.

To Anise, everything was words. The ones flaking and peeling from bills and flyers posted on buildings and stuck to the sides of mailboxes and on bodega windows. Words uttered in Spanish or Italian or Chinese by the tan and olive and saffron-stained travelers on the train. Words buzzing in the intercom over their heads: *3 Train to New Lots. Stand clear of the closing doors.* Other words hypnotized her, held hostage her hungry imagination, more at times than those in the books she read. More than her double-dutch chants or her grandmother's quick patois. They pulsed through and stirred her in ways other words did not, came dropping down arrogantly through the kick of a base drum, pounding out of car speakers and headphones, sailing through the air and into her mind's eye. The pictures these words painted as they danced gritty and precise over the tense tight larynxes or were spit treacherously from the pouty painted lips or hung ethereal, ominous in the air over the clean chrome microphones, were as vivid as any she had known: intricate peals of passion and aggression and alliteration.

Anise would sneak into Aaron's room, quietly remove one of the clear plastic cases she had come for. She would steal away to her room, flip through the colorful jacket, past the parental advisory, to the flat drop of platinum within. She would retrieve the portable disc player her brother believed he had lost from beneath the foot of her bed, place the disc carefully inside. Her finger rested lightly on the tiny triangle that meant play and with the slightest pressure, the slightest urge of her will, the words came running over the loops and the breaks, rising and falling and changing shape, tumbling into staccato, recycling themselves again and again.

Everything was words to Anise. Everything. Until the day she discovered her mother had never loved her. From then, in everything she looked for it, for the shape and design of that thing she did not know but knew she had never had.

Anise pulled her few books to her chest and spun through the revolving door in front of CeCe and behind her Aunt Jesse, under the animals' bronze stares. Jesse always walked ahead. Anise hated her. She lit her cigarettes on the stove and walked to the store in dirty house shoes. She had only been coerced into taking Anise to the library at all by Anise's false claim that her books were overdue and amassing huge late fees, which fees Jesse might conceivably be held responsible for under the circumstances. That CeCe join them was a last minute request, asked shyly once they were already in the street. CeCe had waited at the corner with her two dollars carfare as Anise said.

Jesse was her father's sister. Her father who had vanished in a flurry of indifference when she was born. Over time, Anise had acquired an indifference of her own to combat this man's, just as her brother had. But her brother's was enviable, Aaron having at least some memory of the man toward which to direct his feelings. Anise had never seen him, and had therefore only the vaguest assumptions about her father's despicableness to hold on to.

Jesse turned to Anise, not slowing her gait or the speed with which she chomped her pink cud of gum, pointed to a cluster of iron tables. "I'm a be down here, Neicey. Don't take all day, either."

Anise dropped her armful of books into the opening

in the long curving mahogany and walked on. CeCe followed. The main hall of the library opened up above them like a small magnificent sky. On the escalator CeCe whispered, "Why she always act like that? I hate her."

"Me too," Anise said.

The books she wanted were on the second floor. She read novels now, and went calmly through them alphabetically, discovering, discarding, exhausting the life's work of some poor genius in whatever days or weeks. Some time earlier she had found misplaced under the Bs in fiction, a massive paperback, with a castle caught in black and white suspension on the cover. Sycamore trees spread out in the foreground. Spires shot skyward from the structure's mansard roof. The note inside the cover said: *Plaza Hotel, Grand Army Plaza, Manhattan, 1907.* Knowing full well that Grand Army Plaza was not in Manhattan at all but right there in Brooklyn where she stood, she had toted the heavy volume spitefully out to the check-out desk along with the others she had tucked under her arm.

In the dollar van on the way home Anise opened the book and let her eyes flutter over the photographs and illustrations: images of old-fashioned white ladies with parasols and fine white children, men in flat black hats. Anise wondered what it would have been like to be one of those ladies, strolling down the ancient promenades in corset and hat and long white gloves.

There had been only one brown face in the volume, taken by accident, it seemed to Anise. The composition perfect: The family coming home from abroad. Their carriage not yet stowed away in the carriage house, its ornamented rear end protruding slightly, auspiciously into the photo from the left. The man and his wife locked in an elegant pose, their exquisite travelling clothes and their fair-haired young son somehow unruffled by the journey. Behind them rose an intricate marble entranceway stopped on either side by square pillars topped, each, by the armless bust of a woman.

At the very right field, a uniformed black girl stared with one eye, the other half of her head and body cut off by the discriminating eye of the photographer. Anise touched the girl's skirt, feeling vaguely sorry for her. Her possibilities seemed so obvious and so few.

Anise knew what it felt like to be trapped, cut in half by circumstance. She felt betrayed by her mother's lack of vision, crippled by her mother's blackness, bored and annoyed by the station she found herself in, tied to that long lane of exhaust and overflowing trash cans between Newkirk and Kosckiusko. She was born into a world where the brown people were believed fools and which probably was right. But she had always felt the circumstances to be temporary, at least. She had never felt there were things she could not do. She knew there was injustice in the world, knew there were people somewhere who wanted to stop her. But their ability to do so she doubted very seriously. She believed she could outsmart them, whoever they were.

Anise had finished the book in two days. She learned about urbanism and metropolitan architecture and how Richard Morris Hunt changed the culture of New York with his apartment houses. The *culture* of New York. This was strange to Anise. She had never thought of New York in these terms. It was where she lived. It was not a culture. It was a constant. The tribes of Central Africa were a culture. The people on the covers of National Geographic magazines were a culture. New York was New York. It was nothing else.

But it *became* something else. She read about the first graded streets and the pious old families with impeccable manners and Dutch names: the Van Rensselaers and the Schermerhorns and the Stuyvesants. The Gilded Age and the transformation of the city. The first subways. The first blacks. The first trickle of Jazz into the City. She read about the Harlem Renaissance. The mob. The Bessemer process and the vertical climb of the City. The Empire State building. The Chrysler. The millionaires. The billionaires. Their wives. Alva Vanderbilt. Leona Helmsley. She read about Brooklyn, the Bridge from City Hall to Cadman Plaza. The brownstones eked out of the endless supply of chocolate-hued sandstone from New Jersey. Erasmus Hall Academy and the metamorphosis of Flatbush Avenue. The replacement of the Jews with Jamaicans and Trinies and Bajans. She read pages and pages and pages, and soon, the soiled city around her began to shine with a new light: The glitter of history, the certain gleam of a future.

Anise had always thought there was something important about the City. Now she knew. New York had all the possibilities of the planet, all the drama and danger and intricacy and intimacy and estrangement of the entire world, tucked into three folds of rocky island, sprawled around the filthy mouth of a dollar green river, stacked a hundred stories high over its slick foundation. The City was alive. And for Anise, it was books that had breathed life into it.

They stepped off the escalator. High walls of books rose on either side of them as they went down the aisles. Some of the titles were familiar to Anise; she had already read and returned them, and they had been put back on the shelves.

"I don't like these kinda books, Anise," CeCe said after a moment. "Let's go downstairs."

Anise gave her dirtiest look.

"Why you always get these boring ones?" CeCe tipped a volume out from the shelf and looked at it.

"Shut up, CeCe," Anise said.

CeCe sighed. "I have to go to the bathroom."

Anise glared at her. "That's why I don't never want to bring you nowhere."

"You asked *me* to come!"

"You probably don't even have to go."

"I do too."

They looked at each other, Anise squinting her disgust. "Well, just go then," she said finally. "Hurry up."

"You have to come with me."

"Well, I'm not. I don't have to go to the bathroom."

"But we're supposed to stay together. Something might happen."

"Nothing's gonna happen, CeCe. Just hurry up. I'll wait for you here."

"But my mother said to—"

Anise pinched her hard on the arm. CeCe cried out. "Be quiet before you get us in trouble! If you have to go, go. I'll wait right here."

CeCe held her arm, frowning.

"Go on," Anise said more gently then. "Then, when you come back, we'll go downstairs together. Okay?"

CeCe turned reluctantly, holding her arm, went slowly out of the maze of books down the long hall toward the ladies room. Anise kneeled and tipped the blue corner of a book out of the bottom shelf. Its matte cover was hard and pictureless. She read the title. Pushed back the cover and read the first lines. She always read the first lines, listened to those first words clap together in her mind. She pulled another book from the shelf. On the cover, four blurred figures in watercolor sat at a canopied café table. She turned back the cover, flipped to the first page. CeCe's face appeared above it.

"What are you doing?" she hissed over the book. "I thought you had to go to the bathroom."

"I do but—"

"But what?"

"But there's a boy over there."

"Over where?"

"By the bathroom."

"CeCe!"

"It's not my fault," she said. "He's just standing there by the bathroom and he's—"

"So what if he's standing there, CeCe. There's always boys standing everywhere."

"But he's... saying stuff."

Anise looked at her. "What do you mean, *saying* stuff?"

CeCe looked back at her with her nervous, twitching lip. "He's saying nasty stuff."

Anise closed the book. "Where is he?"

CeCe raised her arm weakly, pointing vaguely off behind her. Anise got to her feet, turned the corner past the shelves of books, looked out the entranceway down the hall. "I don't see anything," she said.

CeCe's lip quivered. Her eyes dampened.

"Oh don't start crying," she said, sharp and impatient. "Wait here. I'm going to look."

"No! I don't want to stay here by myself."

"Will you shut up, CeCe," Anise said. "You're gonna get us in trouble. Now stay here. I'm going to look." She started down the hall. "You better not be lying either," she said and went on.

She went quickly down the hall toward the ladies room. CeCe was lying. Or she had invented it all somehow and believed it. That would be more like her. Anise stopped at the restroom door. She looked around her. Nothing. CeCe lied. She had made it up, of course. She had known all along. She leaned over the railing then and looked down over the main hall. People moved back and forth, and she could see her Aunt Jesse sitting at one of the little iron tables drumming her fingers impatiently. She sighed to herself.

"Psss!"

Anise turned around.

"Psss! Come here."

She looked again and something caught her eye. A row of dark wooden phone booths clung to the wall. Something moved inside one. She came closer, looked inside. There was a boy there, sitting quiet in the shadow behind the half-open door, the phone pressed to his ear.

"Was that you?" Anise said to him through the door.

"Course it was me," he said and slammed the phone down. "Who do you think it was? I have to tell you something."

"What?" she said looking at him through the not-quite-open door.

He pulled the door back slightly. Anise could see him now and he stood, leaned toward her. He was light brown with light brown eyes and smaller even standing up than he had been sitting down. He looked hard at her. "You want to do something?"

"Do what?"

"You know," he said looking hard at her and touching the delicate tips of his fingers to the front of his pants."

Anise's face closed. "I'm gonna tell."

The boy flung the door open. "Tell then!" he yelled at her. "I don't care. They ain't gonna do nothin anyway."

"Yes they will. You'll get in trouble."

"No they won't, stupid. I'm retarded. They can't do anything to you when you're retarded."

"You don't look retarded."

"You don't know," he said. "There's people smarter than you that know, doctors and everything that can tell if a person's retarded. Just get away from me. You don't know nothin." He slammed shut the door again and sat down, picked up the phone and pressed it to his ear.

"What's wrong with you?" she said through the closed door.

"I told you I'm retarded."

Anise stepped back. She looked at the boy through the glass and wooden door a moment and turned to leave. She could see CeCe down the hall, peeking out from behind a bookshelf, holding herself to pee.

The door slid half-open behind her. "I thought you were pretty at first," the voice said. "But not now."

Anise came back to the door. She looked in at him there through the glass and the half-open door with the phone to his ear, staring ahead of him at the wall.

"Get away," he said. "If you ever come back here again, I'll take you in the bathroom and pull your pants down."

Anise pulled her lip up and turned and left.

"Did you see him?" CeCe said jumping and holding herself. "You saw him right? You saw him. What he say?"

"Come on CeCe," she said. "Let's go."

"He say something? Something nasty? You scared?"

"I ain't scared."

"But what he say to you, Neicey? What he say?"

Anise did not look at her. "Nothing," she said. "He's retarded."

NINE

"Sorry baby girl, not today. If I could, you know I would sweetheart." Sha shook his head sternly, blew a clean blast of smoke from his mouth.

"Not even a ten piece, daddy?" The woman sent her bony fingers nervously through her thin limp hair. She knew Sha had meant what he said. What she felt in her veins had made her ask again.

"Uh-uh," he said, shifting the tiny plastic bag in his mouth. "No movement on the credit, ma. I need some cash."

She looked at him, her mouth frowned, her eyebrows turned down.

Sha opened his eyes wider so she could see them. "What?" he said, shrugging and spreading his palms. Her mouth opened slightly, as if she would speak. Sha breathed and spun her around lightly by the arm. He smacked her on her back then, sent her stumbling down Church Avenue. She sent over her shoulder a last pitiful look of despair and pulled her dirty tank top up slightly in the front. "Come back with some cash, baby," he said, too soft to be heard.

Sparks adjusted his gold and diamond-chip fangs with both hands. "Give a bitch a break, why don't you," he said, lisping and spitting through his teeth.

"Get the hell out of here, man," he said. "I know *you* don't give a fuck."

"I *don't* give a fuck. But look at her." He shook his head. "Fuckin pitiful."

"Well help her out then, why don't you." He tugged at his cigarette and tossed it smoldering to the street.

Sparks shrugged. "She ain't ask *me*," he said. "These mufuckas know better. No dough, no show, with me."

"Yeah, well...you know me. Mr. fuckin nice guy."

Sparks laughed, pulled his jeans up slightly on his hips. "Why you been grippin so hard the last couple days, anyway, Sha? You ain't been out here hard like this in a long time."

"Bills to pay, baby. You know how it is."

"No doubt."

Sparks began to toy again with his teeth. Sha looked at him.

"That's a new one ain't it?" he said. "Where you pick that up?"

"Last night," Sparks said, golden. "We stuck these niggas at Grant's Tomb."

"Slow it down, cowboy. Slow it down."

"Oh really?" Sparks said, smiling.

"Yeah, really. I keep telling you about that shit."

"I hope you know, " he said, "I don't take advice from no nigga do more dirt than me."

"Nobody do more dirt than you."

A drab little man came quickly up the block. A ragged beard clung to his jaw. His mouth worked incessantly.

"What you need, old man?" Sparks said when the man reached them. He was taller than them both, but to Sha he looked small. They all looked small, no matter what size. The man pulled two little fingers out of the pocket of his small polyester shorts, and they swayed there slightly in front of him. Sparks stepped back off the curb, dropped down into the line of cars sitting heavy and motionless along Church Avenue. He glanced quickly around. His hands flew to his head, furrowed through his tangled hair. He leaned over slightly, and first one, then another tiny white bag fell onto the hood of one of the cars. He swept them up into his hand, stepped back up the curb, and dropped them into the man's hand. The man handed him a crumpled bill. "Aight, old man," he said, glancing around again. "Beat it. You makin me hot."

The drab little man did not say a word, turned and vanished down the block. Sparks bent over, peeked into the side mirror of one of the cars. He straightened and turned to Sha. "You see anything?"

Sha shook his head.

Sparks leaned down to the mirror again. "I got two more on me," he said. "The rest I got stashed." He motioned with his head toward a pile of garbage and cans near the street. "One of these mufuckas found my shit, cause I came back from the store one day and went to look for it and it was gone." He made a final quick adjustment at the mirror and straightened again to Sha. "Fuckin crackheads," he said.

"Crackheads, my ass," Sha said. "Them niggas you run with got your shit. You already know."

"Aw, come on."

"Sparks," he said, "I ain't tryin to tell you what to do. Or how to run your shit. But you know good as fuckin well Torious and that Haitian mutherfucker is dirty."

"Yeah, they dirty. But they ain't crazy."

"Okay, baby boy. Okay. You just hold it down. I'm only tellin you this cause you my people. Me and you been friends since way before Flatbush. Since before any of these niggas was thought of. So you just watch yourself. You heard?"

"I heard," he said. "I ain't new."

"Give me a square," Sha said then, and Sparks shook a cigarette up out of his pack. Sha lit it, reached into his mouth with the fingers of his free hand. "Take this," he said, shoving the tiny soaked bag into Sparks' hand. "You owe me one."

Sparks looked down at his hand, then back at Sha. "Where you goin?"

"I'm goin," he said. "I been out here twenty-four hours almost." Sha raised his hand to Sparks. They pulled together and their shoulders touched.

Sha turned and Sparks bent again to the mirror of the car. He wanted to hurry, to double-step himself down Flatbush to Newkirk Avenue and to Aaron, but he was too tired; exhaustion clung to his limbs, crouched on his shoulders as he walked, injecting his stride with a languor that was uncharacteristic. He normally *liked* to walk, to saunter quickly through the neighborhood, *his* neighborhood, with a purpose, as if there were some appointment he was running late to, but stopping to say hello and pound his fist all along the Avenue. As every avenue he had ever lived on in Brooklyn, Sha had instantly made Flatbush his own, did not delay in apprising its residents, young and old, of his limitless talents, of the many ways in which he was indispensable to them all. He knew he had very little to *do*, actually, to accomplish this; he had only to be—and this he was good enough at. If he was smooth and interested and gave them each a tiny, personalized performance of the drama that was his life, then that was enough. If they could see him and know him, and if he would allow himself to be caressed by them slightly, allow them to be intimate with him in some way, then that was enough. That was enough for them to take care of him, each in his own way, each with his own tiny contribution to Sha's existence. *Let me get a square, pa-pa*, he would say, or, *I know you gonna throw a few extra in there for me, ma*, or *Why don't you ride me down to Fulton Street real quick, son? You know I'll get you back.* But he never got any of them back really, never attempted even to repay any of the considerations given him, believing, of course, that he had

100

paid in advance, and with the most precious currency. And for most of them, this was enough. And those for whom it was not, who refused him his recompense, vanished instantly out of view. They no longer existed. But so serious a reprimand was rarely necessary—there were few so obtuse, so impenetrable as to not see the art in him, fewer still so unwise as to not find it worth *something*. And it wasn't a matter of resources; they didn't have to *have* much to give, but they had to be *willing* to give at least a little piece of whatever they had.

Now he was unanimated and listless, his presentation shamefully under par. By the time he reached the corner of Newkirk, having garnished only a loosey and a pull of chocolate along the way, he had almost decided to go home. He could smell himself, and feel the dirt under his nails and on his skin. He didn't want to see Aaron this way, but he knew if he went home first he would never come out again, would collapse on the tiny sofa he slept on and miss Aaron for the third day in a row. But it was not only that he missed Aaron, which he did, strangely; he knew that the damage done by his non-appearance the days before could only advantage him with the appropriate tending, the perfect second move. Aaron had to be crazy about him. He required this of them all. But with Aaron there was something else, so fresh and terrifying he could smell it: He loved Aaron—or *wanted* to. And he had never wanted to, had never been *able* to love any of them, ever. He had, in fact, at some point despised them all, resented them for their weakness and lack of control, terrorized them for daring to think for a moment even that they were worthy of the tiniest piece of him. But with Aaron there was the always-gnawing suspicion that he was not only worthy of him, but more rare and perfect than Sha could ever again hope to be. He was unassuming, unaware, all his hopes intact.

Sha pulled himself up the stoop, let his feet rest briefly on each step. At the top of the stairs he sighed and rapped his knuckles against the door, slapped the doorbell with his palm. He lowered his head, fixed his eyes upon the spot where Aaron's eyes would be when they looked out at him through the opening door. When the lock clicked and the door opened, there he was. There was something newly lean and daring in his stance. He looked ready, his white wife beater over the V of his waist and shoulders, his feet slightly apart.

"What's up?" Aaron said and looked at him.

"Sup, little man? How you?"

Aaron made a small, aerated sound, almost a laugh. "I been alright."

Sha raised his eyebrows carefully. He looked past Aaron into the hall. "Is it all right if I come in?"

Aaron hesitated for a second, stepped back, opened the door wide.

"You sure it's okay?" Sha said, but he had already come past Aaron into the house.

Aaron closed the door. He guided Sha into the kitchen. He would not take him to his room. He wanted the order and disinfection of his mother's kitchen. He wanted Sha to understand the coolness and cleanness. No sloppy hostility. No assumed intimacy. The kitchen.

He had settled it in his mind. He confessed reluctantly to himself the things he felt for Sha, the blizzard of infatuation and attraction and new kind of like laced with fear that seemed like something else. He admitted the glint of hope Sha had been to him at first. He had been fool enough to believe that the shell he had always supposed his life to be did not have to exist. That the shatterproof husk of hiding and hunting and raw longing unfulfilled was *not* a life. That perhaps there was a different kind of life for him now, peopled not by the phantom attachments of his youth, the fading best friends he had propped up like scarecrows along the emotional thoroughfares of his life, but by a real breathing heart-pounding sturdy Sha. But now he knew that whatever he felt for Sha, whatever hope and satisfaction and new-fangled like (like love) was not worth it. Nothing worth being that thing he had long decided he was not. And even if he could live with *himself* knowing, which he nearly could not, even more impossible to stomach was that bleak unbearable knowing by someone else. Even if that someone else were guilty too. Almost worse for that since then they could see him and know him the better.

"I been wantin to see you," Sha said, sitting down in one of the kitchen chairs.

Aaron stood above him at a safe distance. "Why's that?"

"I know I was supposed to come a couple days ago but I been—"

"A couple days ago?" Aaron stared blankly at him.

Sha leaned calmly back in the chair. He pulled a cigarette from somewhere. "Can I smoke in here?"

Aaron hesitated. He could not let that bright clean ridiculous kitchen of his mother's be infested by Sha's smoke, where not even a stray smell of grease was allowed to linger once the cooking was done. He could not allow it, had no authority in his mother's house, and he hated Sha now for asking, and believed he had only done it to humiliate him, and underscore again Aaron's utter inability to pose any threat.

Aaron made him a quick dirty look. "Come down-stairs," he said, and turned into the hall. Sha followed, and the staircase creaked beneath them.

In the basement Sha lit his cigarette and sat down on the bed.

Aaron closed the door behind them. The cigarette glowed against the dimness of the room. Aaron sat down at the foot of the bed, reached to turn on the television. He stared at it.

Sha sat with his cigarette. He brushed Aaron lightly across the back with the back of his hand. Aaron shook his head and said "Uh-uh," and moved slightly away.

"What?" Sha said and laughed. "What you goin through? I was just askin for a ashtray. What, you gettin romantic? Aw, that's a good one." He laughed again. "Give me a ashtray, son. Stop crackin jokes."

Aaron sprung up. "Look man, I ain't down with none of this shit. I'm not like you. I—"

"You sure in the hell ain't. You can say that again."

"I don't *want* to be like you."

"Don't worry. You could *never* be like me."

"*I* aint no homo."

"You a girl, son. Look how you actin."

"You don't even know me!"

"I know your type."

Aaron shook with rage and disbelief. "Why don't you leave?"

Sha did not move. He flicked the ash from his cigarette onto the floor. "I leave when *I* get ready," he said.

"I don't even want you here."

Sha stood up, dropped the cigarette on the floor. "You don't want me here?" he said, and came closer to Aaron. He stared at him. "You don't?"

Aaron stared past Sha, furious, encased in shame. Sha reached behind Aaron then and grabbed him.

"What you doin?" Aaron hissed at him, tearing his hand away.

Sha grabbed him again behind and they struggled, dropped in a blur to the floor. Aaron pulled and twisted and jabbed but Sha was quicker, stronger, and *sincere*, his body and mind fighting together for the same thing, while Aaron's went independent on opposite sides, his mind fighting for pride and self-respect and for what he was before anyone had seen him, his body struggling limp and half-hearted for what it did not know, against bliss, against that indefatigable hormonal might of a boy passing through his sixteenth year. He felt Sha stiff against him, and his own reluctant stiffness in

104

the instinctive hanging darkness. He hated Sha now for everything, for being strong and assured and correct, for that exactness and pride and inextricable hold on his maleness that should have crumbled a dozen times but didn't. For all those things in one that baffled and smote him and threw his entire system of evaluating and ranking himself into the finite pecking order of the world into utter ruin. He jabbed again once and felt the back of Sha's hand come down across his face. He breathed finally and surrendered and went up with Sha to the heights of peril.

TEN

While her mother scribbled and moved papers back and forth beneath the soaring clocktower of the Republic National Bank, and her Aunt Jesse stared with stagnant eyes at the glittering television screen from behind her iron cloud of smoke, Anise moved her little feet stiffly past the fruit stands and shoe stores and blue and white ice cream truck jingling and chiming down Flatbush. She had never walked more than two blocks in those flat black shoes reserved for Christmas and Easter and times like it, but today she had walked four miles, three of them unnecessary, with one yet to go, in the shoes grown smaller since Easter, so that she went stiff and mechanical like a black plastic doll with hair to match.

She had come down Utica from Kosciusko, then to Church and onto Flatbush Avenue, walking an almost complete rectangular revolution, adding three miles in the heat and too-small patent leather shoes to make five in all out of two, with one left to go. In her hair were two red ribbons her mother had attached the day before. She had combed Anise's hair back, humming, on her head, into four perfect plaits, each curving out and attached again at the bottom to make two black hearts of hair, glassy sheen-sprayed, one inside the other. Anise had not complained once, and at night went to sleep with the pillow rolled up tight beneath her neck and her arms folded across her chest like a miniature shrunken grandma sleeping stiff and arthritic and unmoving. When she awoke she sat straight up in the bed without turning her head or mussing her black plaited hearts. She had put on a crisp blue-jean skirt and t-shirt and her sneakers and put the patent leather shoes in her book bag with her books, and when she heard the horn of her Uncle Jack's black El Dorado at eight-thirty she went out without saying goodbye to her mother.

In the pink-tiled bathroom of her Aunt Jesse's apartment on Kosciusko she had taken off her sneakers and put on the too-small patent leather shoes and rolled her long tube-socks down into fat white collars around her ankles. She escaped her aunt's notice easily enough, and when she said she was going out to play, Jesse only huffed irately from behind her cloud of smoke and turned up the volume with the remote.

Outside on Kosciusko CeCe and Keisha Armstrong twisted their arms at opposite ends of two frayed jump ropes until Keisha caught Anise in her peripheral and let the ropes fly off and turned and pointed down at Anise's feet and screamed: "Ughhhhh!"

Anise walked on quickly not looking across the street at them while CeCe shouted after her: "Where you going Neicey? Where you goooo-in?"

That was four miles ago, before she had sat down on the curb halfway down Utica, taken off the shoes and torn off the socks and thrown them into the street still rolled down to the ankles. Now she moved her feet slow and stiff but steady in the flat black shoes that pinched with every step, having walked four miles in an hour and a half along the perimeter of that unnecessary rectangle which was the only way she knew for sure to go. At certain few points along the way, where there were no trees, or where the earth swelled up under the cement, asserting itself against that thick crust of manmadeness by which the natural topography of the borough had been long obliterated, she had been able to see that four-faced clock at the top of its domed tower beneath which she knew her mother was scribbling and shuffling unawares. When she would see it she would smile to herself, but nervously, and in spite of the pinch of the shoes, because she knew her mother would never suspect or think or care to.

Now on Flatbush, she could not see the clock, but its big and little hands still whipped around its four faces at once and the blue and white ice cream truck jingled and chimed past, marking off time with its slow elliptical revolutions around the neighborhood. She passed the dollar stores and the laundromats and on through the wafting smells of Jamaican beef patties and cook-up and Dominican beans and rice. Rottweilers and pit bulls plowed past ahead of adolescent boys at the ends of taut leashes. Giggling knots of Muslim girls floated by under their berkas, through the wisping smoke of incense stands, their Air Jordans moving quick beneath their skirts. By innumerable stiff and tiny steps Anise moved closer to that undefined something she had created and shaped in her mind until it assumed, almost, some sense of parameter, a faint set of borders in profile against the stark emotional tangle of her life. On one side of it was the boy, smaller than she was almost, the color of honey, with those eyes both clear and fragile, and aloof at the same time, as if they could not be expected to see on their own as a matter of course, but could only be coerced, massaged into sight by careful degrees. On the other side she saw herself, older in her own mind, or perhaps not older but mature, sophisticated, fluid in her movements, standing there on her own side of that pale undefined construct with her lips parted and her pants pulled down.

At Empire she stopped, looked both ways into the traffic. The light changed and she crossed the street slow and stiff and steady in that excruciating claymation lock-step with which she had ambulated fearlessly now through four sections of Brooklyn and which felt at last like walking a long unraveling bed of nails. She was close now, the only thing separating her from what she believed she would find trembling in that old-fashioned phone booth of the unclever book-shaped building facing the triumphant arch in the plaza was the barren quarter-mile of Flatbush Avenue where the furniture stores and knish-stands and Chinese carryouts came to an abrupt halt and the Park opened up wide on one side and the gardens on the other. For the first time since she had crossed that first street on Kosciusko with Keisha's and CeCe's voices climbing behind her, she was afraid. She saw herself small and vulnerable and alone on that barren green quarter-mile of Flatbush without the camouflage of shouting children and bustling distracted adults and wheezing dogs and dollar vans to protect her. She stepped up the curb crossing Empire and was alone now on that thin sidewalk that sloped up ribbon-like toward the plaza with only the cottonwoods and maples whispering on both sides of her and the traffic whipping down that stretch of Avenue without stores or intersections or bus stops to slow it. For a moment she thought she would turn back, but she had walked so far in the pinching shoes and bright summer sun with that even brighter vision of the trembling honey-colored boy encased in the antique phone booth there to prod her on that she could not turn back, would not turn back now from the vague unstipulated watercolor of her mind with the boy on the one side and herself on the other with her pants down.

So she walked on, stiff and doll-like and anxious and faster now with the shoes going clack clack clack along that long upsweep of sidewalk between the swatches of green. She was afraid, but the plaza grew nearer now and nearer, the sidewalk shortening up the hill before her and flowing out long and straight and narrow behind. As she came up, two Jewish ladies came down from the plaza in dark dresses to the ground, pushed past her with their purring strollersful of infants, looking from Anise to the long strip of sidewalk behind her and back again but saying nothing, and Anise walking fast clack clack clacking and not looking back.

Finally she was there, sliding along the side of the building on those last few yards of walk before the plaza, the soaring clocktower of the Republic National Bank peeking through the trees at times grim and forewarning. She entered the building, spinning through the revolving doors and on into the hall. She clapped her shoes onto the escalator step and rode up calm and metallic with her feet throbbing and shoe-stabbed but so happy to be there finally so close and moving closer up that contrapted stairwell where she would not even have to move her feet except one last time to step off it and there she would be with the boy looking at her now through the glass, or rather, being coerced, cajoled into looking with those clear aloof eyes by something he could not miss or mistake now because she had tried so hard.

She went mechanically up and up, stepped off the escalator and to the left, her feet stiff and smarting through those last few steps before she would see the boy who would perhaps see her and who would certainly at least pull her pants down like he said whether he saw her or not. She went down the corridor above the great main hall of the building not looking down over the railing at all but focused on that old row of elongated wooden cubes with phones in them and hopefully too with at least one trembling honey-colored boy, situated so convenient there to the bathroom where surely he would take her like he said. She drew up clacking to the first and looked in, and to the next and the next but he was not there, so that she searched the bathroom, looking under the stalls, and paced the hall outside and then the hallways and criss-crossing columns of books that gridded the building from hall to hall, from one end of that hulking unclever edifice to the other, through the untold volumes of human logic and learning and paginated keenness that offered no clue to her whatever clack clack clacking in pain until she was spit out lifeless through that wide revolving door battered and exhausted and sat down on the stone steps under the engraving to think of the long walk home through the forest of over-

111

flowing trash cans and dog shit and exhaust in the ugly too-tight shoes under the grim gaze of the clock until she was lost in the horror of it and cried and cried and cried and cried and cried.

NIGHT

ONE

There is nothing more dangerous than daylight. People know this. They hide behind dark glasses and duck under awnings to avoid it. They walk on the shady side of the street to keep it off their backs. People in Brooklyn, though—many of them—are oblivious to this fact and drink in the summer sun with wild abandon. Some of them (the young ones) bare themselves to it recklessly, fly in the face of caution, pushing young chests out to the sun, imperiling delicate new shoulders and loose-swinging limbs. Morning glory legs shoot through tiny strips of denim and stroll undaunted through the sun, wobbling on the unauthorized inches of new shoes. They don't know, or they don't care (the young ones) about the danger the day brings. They crave it feverishly, knowing it is their happy destiny to be stripped of all that they are.

Aaron had always anticipated the glare and adventure of summer. But this summer something kept him indoors. June tore by with brilliant tenacity, stopping now and then only to claw at the windows of the slatternly little house on Newkirk. Aaron stayed inside, locked into his dim envelope of doubt and confusion with Sha during the days, venturing out to work at the theater only in the evenings once the damage had been done. It was these secluded mornings and afternoons, tucked into the shadowy uncertainty of his room in the basement, that would blaze forever for him more than any of his days in the sun.

Outside the world continued—buses groaned, the sun burned in the sky—but inside, at the bottom of that creaking staircase, in the false twilight of their cube of confusion and doubt the two of them thrashed on oblivious as if there were no world but that one—boxy, dark, surreal. Aaron crouched inside himself, preparing for that day not far off when he would kick away with Sha for good and not look back, not even turn to say goodbye or I'm sorry or anything else but just go on easy and deliberate into the world and erase from all memory the brief shameful episode of his life. His birthday would be the end of it, and in some sadistic way he looked forward to it, could not wait to see Sha's face when he realized—the Sha who thought he knew so much, who was always right with the upper hand. He had wanted it to be sooner, but the original date set had come and gone three days now and, *anyway*, he thought, July 17th would be one month exactly and he would be seventeen on top of it and too old after that to ever justify or forget. So his birthday it would be, and until then he would stay with Sha (during the days at least) and make him pay as much as he could in advance for the shame and discrepancy that would be there on that meticulous record he knew was being kept somewhere of his life long after he had chosen to forget. He tried what he could to chip away at Sha and tear down that thing he did not even believe was a façade, but which angered him even more for being real. He was furious, offended at Sha's ease and insentience, at his lack of shame and remorse and apparent knowledge even of what he was, and he needed so badly to make Sha feel and understand the disgrace of it, to bring him down from that imaginary high ground above the floods of guilt and dis-ease that choked Aaron still.

But Sha was a genius of manipulation and self-control and all the things Aaron was only now experiencing his first acid-sweet taste of, and he had faced so many adversaries more cunning since his childhood that he was hardly touched by anything Aaron could think of to say. He had heard it all before and worse. And he did not believe Aaron anyway, when he seemed unimpressed. He was the brightest thing the boy had seen, he was sure, and whatever wall of false disregard Aaron was able to erect between lovemaking was not only false but disingenuous too. Still, something in the boy's coolness shook him. Not because he did not know that it was manufactured, but because its manufacture was flawless. And though he had long mastered his emotions and crafted around himself an exquisite shield against attack, there was still on the jagged surface of his heart that tiny pinpoint of vulnerability from which emanated all the shame and self-doubt Aaron believed did not exist. It was there, though, profound and gnawing and hidden behind a lifetime of rote empty adages with which he had learned to separate himself from that cursed line of humanity which to him and to Aaron and to the world were abominations.

"You can't keep comin over here every day, son," Aaron would say to him. "Niggas gon start thinking something."

"What do I care what these mufuckas think?"

"I care. I don't want everybody knowin about this shit."

"If anybody knows anything, it ain't because of me. Trust me."

"What you mean it ain't cause of you? You think I had a whole bunch of niggas comin by here every day before you came along?"

"No. You was sittin here by yourself with your little sister."

"At least I wasn't out here fuckin every homo moving."

"Don't worry about who I fuck with. Watch *your* fuckin step."

"Watch yours. What you think gon happen when your people find out? Your boys you be with on the block?"

117

"I don't give a fuck."

"Oh, you that tough?"

"I know how to handle myself. I ain't your average."

Sha came every day. And every day Aaron opened the door for him reluctantly and quickly and between lovemaking they fought. But the time between lovemaking was hardly any and time between fights less; yet, somehow, in the crags between abuse and caress were hidden those frail bright moments when they would simply forget to argue, forget their mortal enmity and speak calmly and clearly to each other and unfold. Aaron talked about his mother whom he hated, and Sha about his who had hated him. He told Aaron about Mike and the Infiniti and the Algonquin Inn. And, glossed together, into a neat ecumenical account, as if they had all been a single featureless and nonspecific face instead of the rising wall of faces and body parts discernible one from another only by the minute gradations in his memory of the things they had given him, he told Aaron about all the others—the hustlers or athletes or thugs, older or younger, with more experience or less, the fakes, straight boys, professionals, one night stands, week-long obsessions—all the hopeful contenders he had never loved, had less than cared about even, *or so he said*, until Aaron came along. He never said anything about Joel.

But Aaron would not allow himself to believe anything Sha said. He did not believe Sha would stay with him. Even if he could find a way to stay with Sha.

"You don't care about me," he would say. "You just think I'm young and dumb and don't know no better."

But in the dim cubistic world they moved in he could not know better, could not be sure of any thing except one, which he knew instinctively without needing to see that domed soaring clocktower or its four exact repugnant faces broadcasting the hour north south east west, or hear even one time from within that soundproof airtight enclosure the roaring jingle and chimes radiating out of the blue and white ice

118

cream truck circling for so many contiguous summers since before he was even born that he would not have known to listen for it anyway. In that world—muted, six-sided, with its two stark-naked inhabitants, where nothing ever could be seen or understood, where Sha's body against him was like a lean piece of heaven so hellish and unthinkable precisely because it had been thought and dreamed about so intensely, so often, since before he was even thirteen or twelve or eleven, where nothing could be recognized or known—he knew one thing and one thing only: that he would have to get away from Sha, and that it must be soon.

But he could not get away from him now. And instead of even trying, he fixed the unarbitrary date two weeks out on that timely continuum and continued to fight and make love alternately with him. Or sometimes simultaneously. And when Sha would fall off to sleep he would pull back the crisp bright sheets his mother had laundered and not looked at and stare at him each time in more shock than the last. He could not have imagined, even those brief weeks before, that that body so dreamed-about, that prototypal arrangement of limbs and pelvis and chest, which he sometimes believed he had conjured out of his own mind it was so exactly what he had prayed over, imagined since thirteen, twelve, eleven, would be so ultimately destructive to him and to every lie he had ever thought explained him. He could not have known how impossible it would be to bear the fact-heavy gaze of his co-conspirator. He could not stand for Sha to look at him, and he could only tell himself that it would all be over soon.

Outside the sun blazed, and though he never once saw it during this time, he imagined it going up and down like a yo-yo over that grim soaring clocktower under which he knew his mother was not even scribbling or shuffling but staring straight ahead at the walls of her tiny flourescent cubicle with the same vacant idiot's eyes she stared at him with. He was sure they called her stupid at work. She was

119

pigeon-toed and skinny and mean, and her witlessness man-
ifested itself not in any one thing she ever did or said or in
any one of her million sets of ridiculous voodooey beliefs
inherited from her predecessors, but in her innate ability to
speak endlessly on and on. She droned shrilly and constant-
ly and apparently without the slightest need ever to think
about what she was saying, as if talking were to her like
breathing or heart-pumping. He could not understand why
she had ever had children in the first place, except maybe to
boss them around and nag endlessly at them and ask them a
million rude and loaded questions from before they could
even understand what she was saying. She had to know
everything, and not, as he and probably Anise too had realized long ago, out of some deep maternal caring or concern,
but out of sheer business and the need to meddle. She wanted every detail of every detail of their lives, and Aaron's
response and defense to this was to tell her absolutely nothing, to answer only *yes* or *no* or *I don't think so* when it was
absolutely necessary to avoid the sting of his mother's hand
across his face.

His worst and most recurring nightmare now was that
his mother would come home from work early one day and
descend those dark creaking stairs and find him and Sha
together in bed. He dreamed this at least once nightly and
sometimes oftener and each time he would wake up shaking
and drowning in a pool of sweat. He knew this event could
not happen. His mother had never in her life come home
early from anyplace, and in the last six or seven years had
only come down that dark staircase for any reason once and
that was to slap him across the face after he had let her call
his name (her voice rising more shrill and outraged each
time) for ten minutes straight without answering. So he knew
it could not happen, but he could see her eyes, glowing and
contemptuous as they would be if she were ever to know any
of it, and the thought of it made his stomach sick. Not
because he was afraid of loosing his mother's love. Like his

sister, he did not believe he had had it. Nor did he seek her approval. He did not want it. What he feared was something in those minute idiot's eyes, something sharp and intelligent and inexplicable he had learned to watch for over time and which transcended her usual dullness and inability to understand any of what was happening around her. He had known it always, that brief unmistakable flicker just beyond the opaque eyes, faint but certainly there, which indicated some knowledge of something, but articulated nothing of her own outlook or opinion as to what exactly the thing was. So he had always known it, but the moment he had learned to dread it was its own. He was perhaps nine, and had bent over to pick up one of the anatomic blonde dolls his sister had already begun to discard. He was bent already, and his arm beginning that slow deliberate outstretch when he felt his mother's eyes. He looked over his shoulder and there she was, standing in the doorway with her eyes not wide or shocked or reprimanding even but just for once seeing behind the gray glaze, seeing him locked in that curious stooping pose which not spoke but screamed something about him that even he had not at that time had occasion to understand. She was seeing something, and she was saying something to herself about it behind the eyes. He had straightened immediately and his arm recoiled and he turned without looking at her and walked away out of the room.

He had been guarded, secretive before, but since that instant had become diabolically so, and the fury engendered by that bleak knowing look in her eyes that did not yet threaten or reprimand but that said *I know, I know, I know something about you that you probably do not even know yourself* became the blueprint for the rest of his life. He would never allow himself to become that awful thing he believed he had seen in his mother's eyes, not just because it was terrible in itself, but because he would never allow her to be right.

Now, with Sha, in their little square universe, where he could not even stand to look at Sha until he was asleep

121

and could not stand for Sha to look at him at all for the same reason he could not stand his mother to, he could only wait and bide his time until the end, when he would see Sha's face when he realized he was wrong. But as the big and little hands continued around the faces of the clock, with the sun yo-yoing up and down behind it, he found himself more and more anxious and afraid. He realized how difficult, how nearly impossible it would be to live without Sha now that he had lived with him, and it was not just that faint depression that would be there in the bed next to him once Sha was gone. He knew there was something between them now beside the physical, a creeping addiction to Sha's posture and diction, an ability to anticipate what he would say before he said it. All of this he felt happening around him, that essential something moving not only between them now but out of them, filling up that cubic space of universe until he could almost hear his ears pop. But still he waited, waited to see Sha's face when he realized he was wrong.

Except that he was beginning to know, to understand now that Sha had not been wrong, and that his mother had not been wrong, and in the ever-expanding futility of it, of the lies and evasion which no longer even sufficed, a darkness began to descend upon him slow and still until he could no longer see his life at all. And it was only then, in the darkness of total eclipse that it came to him, almost as a joke, a small outburst of air through the nose: He would kill himself, and be free of it all, and prove them wrong wrong wrong wrong wrong.

TWO

Ahmed Radwan-Dana's tiny store on Broadway was preferred among the cigarette smokers of its bustling corner of Bed-Stuy ten to one. The store was not the nicest nor even the most conveniently located to those hacking residents of the little swatch of Brooklyn, but the young Mr Radwan-Dana was shrewd or reckless enough to sell the precious mint-green boxes of carcinogens which normally cost seven-fifty for five dollars to his regular customers. It was this ground-breaking policy, and not the nickel candies or cans of ravioli or dog food, that drew the laboriously inhaling and exhaling customers around distant corners from Kosciusko or Hall or Linden past two or three other bigger or more well-situated establishments to his. None of this truck in mint green boxes was legal, of course, but two of Radwan-Dana's brothers shared a taxi-medallion and each time the cab went out and came back in through the Holland Tunnel it carried in its trunk an air-fresh case of the velvety green boxes from New Jersey.

Anise's Aunt Jesse would never have walked the extra block and a half to the store on Broadway, even to save two dollars. There was a perfectly good bodega three feet from the door of her apartment building and she went there every day with her seven-fifty tucked under the strap of her bra. One day, getting off the J Train from a rare trip out of that equilateral tangle of streets and square brick buildings and elevated train tracks between Putnam and Broadway and Kosciusko and Stuyvesant she stumbled into the little store unwittingly and put her seven-fifty on the counter in front of Ahmed and said: "One hundreds."

"No one-hundreds," Ahmed answered, running his eyes over her, and sliding a pack of Newports onto the counter next to the money. "But I give you these for five dollars if you come regular."

"Regular?" she said. "I live on Kosciusko."

Ahmed shrugged and lifted a five-dollar bill off the counter. "Your choice."

Jesse took the cigarettes and change and looked at them stupidly for a moment. She looked up finally through her long bangs of human hair. "Can I send my neice?"

Since then every day Anise trudged the long block and a half down Kosciusko to Broadway through the heat and the filth past the smoking peanut stand and identical barking rottweilers with her Aunt Jesse's five dollars folded into her jeans pocket. She would lay the crumpled bill on the counter along with the illegible four-word note her aunt had sent without even signing and Mr. Radwan-Dana would lean over to her from the high counter with the cigarettes and say: "You smoke too much my little friend. Now, put these in your pocket so we don't have trouble."

Today the walk seemed longer than ever. The disc of June sun that had dominated the skies had given way to an even more fiery July one that moved boulder-like and incomprehensible through the city. She could feel it on her shoulders now, crouched and infernal. She walked on. She drew from her pocket the creased five dollars and the creased note and read it: ONE PACK OF NEWPORTS. She looked at it a moment and let it go, and it floated down over the curb into the gutter. She walked on, beneath the curling toes of the ancient Clarks and Air Jordans dangling overhead from the telephone lines. She wanted to keep walking, past the elevated train tracks and chunks of brick, out of the forest of trash cans and screaming sun and iron clouds of smoke to someplace she could breathe. Where there were no mint-green boxes of Newports or evil aunts or shuffling mothers to interfere with her life. And where she knew there would be someone who would look at her and see what she was. See the thing that her mother and her aunt and her brother and Keisha Armstrong and the little honey-colored boy and everyone had failed to see all this time: that she was pretty and kind and capable of being loved.

She turned the corner onto Broadway. The smell of roasting peanuts and burnt sugar and exhaust flew up from the street with the cries of colicky babies. She entered the store, and placed the folded five dollars on the counter.

"You again?" Ahmed boomed from behind the counter. "What do I keep telling you about these things?"

Anise took the cigarettes and went out. On Broadway the traffic moved on the street and the trains roared overhead. She looked both ways down the block, through the pillars of light and shadow coming down from the hulking canopy of metal into the street. Then, less with her eyes than with her stomach she saw it, and knew before being able to identify any feature except perhaps the honey-colored skin, and the stance, and with even the most uncertainty regarding those because of the moving shadows of the trains. So she was not sure as she felt herself move, hardly even on her own legs, toward him, toward the little honey-colored figure half-hanging, half-leaning, absurdly small against the green expanse of tracks. She came closer. She could not see his face, but she could see his tiny back and the back of his neck and the soft waves of hair on his head. With one little honey-colored hand he held on to the green girder of the tracks.

She approached and she knew it was him, would have known it was him, she believed, had she seen only the tip of

125

his little finger or the top of his head. A dog barked loud somewhere behind her and he turned and looked, with clear honey-colored face and eyes, not past but through her as easily as he would have looked through a pane of glass. Anise's stomach dropped out of her, and she knew he had not seen her. He had fixed his eyes on her exact physical coordinates, on precisely the point where she stood, but he had not seen her, and Anise knew it at once.

She looked at him standing there, small and strange and beautiful just before her, not seeing her, still hanging on to the huge upslanting girder with one hand. "What are you doing?" she said finally.

He was looking at the space where she was, where she would have been had she not been glass, with the clear fragile eyes, which perhaps out of all she was, could recognize the cuff of her pants or her eyebrow or the square bulge of cigarettes in her pocket.

"Watchin the trains," the boy said. "What does it look like?"

Anise thrust down her little brows. "The trains are up there," she said, motioning with her head. A train rushed overhead, dragging it's long shadow over them and on into the street.

"Where you live," he said. "Where's your mother?"

"My mother doesn't live over here," she said. "My aunt does."

"Oh. Why's that, I wonder?"

"Why's what?"

"Why don't your mother take care of you?"

Anise shifted. "She has to work."

She stared at him, watched as he turned, still clinging to the girder, looked out down the diagonal blocks into the street. She came up beside him, watched silently for a moment as he stared out over the street. "Where do you live?" she said finally, uncertainly.

He turned and looked at her with what seemed like

126

surprise, as if he were only now seeing her for the first time, yet still, Anise knew, not seeing her at all. He motioned vaguely with his hand. "I live on the top floor."

Anise followed the line of his hand with her eyes. A set of identical brick buildings rose and hovered in the distance.

The boy dropped his hand. "We used to live on the fourth floor, but it got burnt up in the fire." He stopped and stared at her. "My brother did too."

Anise moved her head. "Your brother got burned up?"

"Yep. That's why my mother can't take care of me. She has to stay in the bed."

"Why does she have to stay in bed? Did she get burned, too?"

"No," he said quietly. "She's not burnt. She just stays in the bed, that's all."

"Who takes care of you, then?"

"Grandma Sadie. She takes care of me." And he made a low grunting sound in his throat.

Anise looked at him. She said nothing, just stood with him there on the corner watching the traffic and the rushing train-shadows move back and forth over the street.

"You like birds?" he said suddenly, turning on her again the clear eyes, eyes at once animated and dead as plastic.

Anise shrugged. "I don't know."

"Well, you want to see one?"

"Okay."

He led her then and she followed just behind, crossing Broadway beneath the green towering tracks. They went toward the buildings over the cracked cement, across gutters running with incandescent liquid filth. He did not speak to her or look at her until he stopped abruptly before a tattered chain-link fence, turned down the eyes intently.

"See it?"

Anise came up beside him and followed the eyes down. A flat black stain stared up at them, hardly discernible except for the gaping beak and crooked wing. "Eww," she said, pulling up her nose. "It's dead."

"I know it's dead," said the boy then looking at her.

She was disgusted, but she could not take her eyes from the flat mangled bird and could not stop thinking that she was exactly like it, fossilized in filth, mouth gaping but no sound coming out.

The boy turned his eyes briefly on the bird again and turned and looked out over the street. "Want to go to the playground now?" he said without looking at her.

"What playground?"

"Between the buildings," he said, and moved his arm slightly.

Anise looked at the identical square buildings. She touched the bulge of cigarettes in her front pocket and glanced back over her shoulder toward Broadway.

"Come on," the boy said, and moved away ahead of her.

The playground was one sagging monkey-bars and two unidentifiable fiberglass animals, faded from the sun, quivering on springs in the rough cement. Anise sat atop one of the animals, which perhaps at one time had been a dolphin. The boy swung relentlessly from the scalding monkey-bars, his little legs kicking beneath him.

"Once," the boy said from the monkey bars, "when I went to Jesse Owens, I fell off the monkey-bars and cracked my head, and I had to go to the hospital and get stitches."

"Jesse Owens has a monkey-bars?" she said, looking at him.

"They used to. After I cracked my head they took it out."

"Oh." She rocked for a second. "What school do you go to now?"

"I go to Ricin," he said and looked down wearily at

her. "*You* never heard of it. It's a school for kids who don't know how to act."

Anise thought for a moment. "You seem like you're acting alright now."

"Sometimes I don't," he said, and let go of the monkey-bars.

Anise shrugged. "When I saw you before you were worse."

He turned fully on her then those wide clear eyes, which would only have made sense in the face of a stuffed animal, and the vivid bewilderment and unrecognition in them screamed so loudly at her that she held on tight to the jagged little porpoise to not fall off its back. He did not even recognize her. She dismounted on her own then, throwing her little leg over the ruined fiberglass. "I have to go."

The boy said nothing, but kept the eyes on her, followed quietly at a distance as she went. At Broadway she looked at the light, looked both ways and crossed. She didn't look back, but behind her she heard him, his little voice rising over the traffic: "Come back tomorrow!" he said. "Come back tomorrow or I'll pull your pants doooooown!"

THREE

As time spun intractably away from Aaron, for Sha it stood still. The days passed not continuously minute by minute, but in a series of three-dimensional freeze frames, without movement or breath, a summer frozen in blocks of glass. By the fourth of July, desperate for air, unaccustomed to resistance, to not being fallen madly and immediately in love with, and unable fully to comprehend the situation, Sha decided to take matters into his own hands. He had gone on long enough with the boy petting and entertaining because he had cared. He had cared about the boy and that had been the big mistake. He had made him believe he possessed more power than he actually had, and at that exact moment the boy had seized it, taken hold around the neck of something that had been only a fiction, but was there now, real, as plain as day.

Now, advancing up Church Avenue beneath the streetlights and gunsmoke he felt as if he were standing still, could see himself dark and immobile, another blocked instant in the mounting pile. He had not invited Aaron out of affection, but cunningly, because he knew Aaron could not say no. He knew that Aaron was alone, by himself and not wanting to be, with no friends, no boys, no crew, nobody

131

because he was meek and quiet and afraid. And Sha had been quiet with him too, locked down there in that cubic cellar speaking in low tones to the boy between fights things he had never said to any of them. But now he would let his voice boom, out of the boy's lair, out here in the world that he dominated, the world of people and places and things and not just talk, the dry dumb talk of a boy grasping power for the first time. Now Sha would take control, re-take it if it had ever been lost in the first place and force Aaron to regard him as the world did.

He knew Aaron did not want to come. He understood the limits of his own power. He did not want to go anywhere with Sha. In Aaron's little world beneath his mother's feet where they could only be compared to each other Aaron could win, grasp that recently non-fictionalized power boldy around the neck and win without seeming even to try. But in the other world, a world of movement, unlike those blocks of glass, where people were looking, where Sha was on top, little Aaron shrank to a flea. The power he had in the dark was of no consequence in the light because it was secret, because the fragile distinctions made in dismal corners of rooms by and between men who sleep with men fall to pieces before the rest of the world. The world knows the truth as well as the men do and the world has no interest, no interest at all in caressing or manipulating that truth because it is as fundamental to the world's well-being as the lie is to the men: A fag is a fag.

Somehow, the lie, which was that some of them were fags, homos, queers—and that some of them were not, had gotten away from Sha. He had always relied upon it. He had based his life and his character on it. Made a career of it. Now suddenly the lie had turned on him, *been* turned on him by a boy who was not one-tenth the man he was. But he had told the boy too much, had voiced too often and too loudly his distinctness from the them, his disdain for them, until Aaron had understood, actually heard and understood that *need* in

132

Sha's voice to be distinguished from them, and to be distinguished from them *by him*, in *his* eyes. And Aaron had looked at him with those eyes and knew that Sha *was* distinct from them, and distinct from *him*, and when he looked back at himself he hated what he saw, more times ten than he had before. But rather than bow down to Sha at that moment, admit his inferiority on that scale of what is a man, he swooped in on that hint, that pin-point of vulnerability and sunk in his talons deep. He smeared together Sha with the rest of them, blurred his purportedly one-sided and dominating involvement with them into an incestuous entanglement of dicks and mouths and dirty assholes, of shrieking homosexuals of whom Sha was the Grande Dame, the whore of the gay parade, the worst of the worst. And that was the moment. That was the moment when Sha believed it, or admitted it, because somewhere in him he had believed it already, had believed the truth instead of the lie, knew that any distinction between any of them was only a charade.

But none of that mattered now. Whatever the truth was, he would build his own, rebuild the lie until it looked like the truth. Was hard like the truth. And out here under the gunsmoke and streetlights and dim blotted stars was where he would do it. He would not pass his days in blocks of glass frozen between those crisp sheets, the boy tearing at him with his talons. Even if he loved the boy. Because that didn't matter either. Now he would show the boy something, and he would do it effortlessly because now he didn't care. Love him or not, he would put him in his place, strike the life out of him with easy strokes, kindly. And he would not enter the boy's house again.

As he came up Church Avenue, swatting emphatically at some invisible airborne pestilence, pulling heavily on his cigarette, he became suddenly at ease. Now that he had decided his path, resolved something coolly and decisively, he felt a certain rush of goodwill. The cunning melted away and the affection came back and he knew he would be glad to see him. But he would never give an inch. And he would not enter the house.

He looked around him at the throngs of people in the streets, scanning for the boy, listening to the firecrackers and M-80s crackle in the dark. Strands of flourescent light fell out of the scratched fiberglass windows of jewelry stores and fruit stands. As he approached the train station, the crowd became thicker. Brown waves of faces, taut with youth, whipping around him, laughing and yelling to each other from opposite sides of the street. Then he saw him. Just his face brown against the orange tiles of the station. Not a face so different from the others there bobbing and shifting but somehow different altogether. Flared triangle nose. Lips pressed together. The boy was beautiful. He would give him that.

Then Aaron saw him. His brow furrowed faintly and he looked away, waited for Sha to come to him through the crowd.

"Don't act like you ain't see me," Sha said, as he approached. "You know you can pick me out of a crowd."

Aaron looked at him and laughed, and Sha laughed back. Because they were still crazy about each other, stunned by each other, despite the fear and trepidation. And there were still times when neither of them could hide it, when neither of them wanted to.

"Come on," Sha said and pressed Aaron's hand slightly beneath the surface of floating faces. He led him out of the crowd away from the station, toward Flatbush Avenue.

Aaron followed. He had *not* wanted to come. He understood vaguely this idea of power, though not in the stark terms to which Sha's clicking mind reduced all human inter-action. And though he was lonely, he was used to it, accus-tomed to observing dates and events with a pang from a dis-tance. But he had not reached either of these questions when he agreed to meet Sha at the station. He had dropped down below the surface of his former reality. He was enveloped in

134

darkness. Decisions had become too difficult. All the effort for one day was expended getting out of bed in the morning after his mother had left to open the door for Sha. After that he could only lie there, next to Sha or beneath him, folded into the sheets, lifeless. His only moments of light floated down to him now in fragments, a refracted glow from Sha's teeth or skin. He would hold him around the neck, at the shoulders weakly, looking up but avoiding the dark eyes, wondering how he would finally leave, resolute he could not stay. He still clawed at Sha when he could think of it, but mechanically. He had become too tired to fight. He could not get out of bed after Sha left him in the afternoon to shower and dress for work. He would call in sick. Exhausted. So when Sha told him to meet him at Church Avenue at ten 'o clock, Aaron did not want to go, but he had been too tired to say no.

Sha had perceived the silence, the languor, but he believed it a part of the boy's plan, a highly contrived silent treatment to further restrict his flow of air. Now he led and the boy followed. And to Aaron it was a relief, a welcome reprieve from paralysis, the brown faces churning, white teeth bare with exhilaration, the crackling fireworks and the smell of smoke. He was happy to be there in the world, to be with Sha, or as close to happy as he could now imagine, and he would not think about the rest of it, about leaving or his birthday or the bald little alternative that had come through his nose that first time three days ago. He would think only of right now, *be* only in this moment right here.

As they walked people nodded or spoke to Sha. Some of them, perceiving that they were together, spoke to Aaron too. Sha smiled and nodded back, smacked hands with some of them, kissed some of the girls on the cheeks. He lit a cigarette, held it above his head as they moved through the masses.

"Let's go to the park," Sha turned to Aaron behind him. "Maybe we can still see some of the fireworks."

They turned down Ocean toward the park.

"Sha!" A voice came through the dark. "Yo, Sha!"

Sha looked up, raised his hand over his head and waved. "Wait a minute," he said, nudging Aaron. They crossed the street, their lean silhouettes passing through the headlights inching along Ocean.

At first they could not see Sparks' face, only his long backside horizontal across the trunk of a car, the metallic halo of his red baseball cap glinting under the streetlight. He lay on his side, his elbows relentlessly churning as he groped and tickled and pinched beneath the scant draped clothing of the absurdly young girl who faced him. Squeals and grunts rose in time with the motion of his arms.

"Aw shit," Sha said with mock disgust as they approached. "Get a fuckin room! Come on." He grabbed Sparks' arm. "Nobody want to see that."

Sparks twisted his head around and his gold and diamond-chip fangs sparkled. Aaron saw the eyes and gilt smile and for a second he forgot to be nervous. In this moment of distraction the flushed little lady seized her opportunity and sprung up, strappy-sandled, from the trunk of the car. "That's *him*," she said indignantly, and touched her fingers to her crumpled hair. "He's so nasty!"

Sparks sat up. "*I'm* nasty?" He adjusted the v-neck of his sleeveless cotton sweater and a glint of gold peeked out around his neck. "Smell this," he said and shoved two long fingers under her nose.

The girl's nose wrinkled.

"Hm," Sparks grunted. "That's *you*, girl."

Her mouth shot open and she inhaled sharply. She smacked his hand away. "You nasty mutherfucker! I hate you." She turned, pushing a last hiss of air through her teeth, and scraped furiously away on her sandals in the dark.

"Page me later!" Sparks shouted after her.

Her middle finger flashed defiantly as she disappeared.

"Stinkin bitch," Sparks said happily to himself through his teeth.

Sha shook his head. "Are you retarded?"

"*That* bitch is retarded," he said, motioning into the dark.

"This my man, Aaron," Sha said, moving his head. "This Sparks."

Their arms arched and their palms cracked together.

"What up," said Aaron.

"Alright," said Sparks.

"Where your people at?" Sha said then, glancing around him.

"The only people I got is you."

Aaron's pupils dilated to take in Sparks. Sparks felt it and ignored him. "You got something to drink?" he said to Sha.

"Nah, son."

"Well, I know you got some trees."

"Nope." Sha said. "No trees."

"Aw, Jesus." Sparks threw his hand up, brought it down hard on his leg. "What is this, a goddamn ice cream social? It's the fuckin Fourth."

"Yeah." Sha smirked. "Time to spend some cash."

"I *been* spendin." Sparks voice rose hysterically. "You know I always spend mine. I ain't no cheap mutherfucker like you, Sha. I ain't—"

"Ah, shut the hell up. Come on."

Sparks lifted himself off the car, all long arms and legs, his tangled hair coming out from under his cap. "Let's go to the corner."

The corner bodega was tiny and bright. They filed down the aisle.

"They ain't got shit in this store," Sparks said into the refrigerator case.

"Heinneken," Sha said. "Guinness too."

"You know I drink the big boys."

137

"Not tonight." Sha slid the case open, took out three brown bottles, slid one into Sparks' hand.

They filed back toward the front down the tiny aisle. They put the bottles on the counter and the thick Dominican behind it moved his furry arm back and forth with small paper bags. "Four-fifty," he said, pushing the bottles toward them in the bags.

Sparks reached for his Guiness and hesitated for a moment, looked at Sha. Sha raised his eyebrows and looked back at him. He took the two remaining bottles off the counter and handed one to Aaron, looked at Sparks again.

"Ah damn, now why you playin, son." Sparks voice rose and cracked. "Why you—"

Sha tilted his head slightly. "Come on now, Sparks."

"What the fuck, man! You always pull this shit."

"Son, you know I gotta pay the lawyer. You gon take my money and let me go to jail?"

"Ah hell!" He leaned around Sha and looked at Aaron. "What about him?"

Aaron shifted on his feet, opened his mouth to speak.

"He ain't got no money," Sha said quickly. "Just pay, nigga. It ain't gon kill you."

"Ah Jesus, goddam!" Sparks huffed and fumbled in his pocket, slapped four dollar bills and two quarters onto the counter where it was swept up into the fat hairy fist of the Dominican.

In the street voices and car horns, the smells of smoky flesh leapt up at them from all around. The little black briquettes of the neighborhood had ashed over, settled into the tiny grills or oil barrels cut in half sitting on the sidewalks, but the smoking continued in the absence of open flame.

They stood on the sidewalk, tipping their bottles up from their mouths, watching the people pass by. Aaron looked around him. Sparks scowled.

"Let's find your people, Sparks," Sha said. "I want to smoke."

Sparks mumbled something and they departed grace-fully, like a flock of glistening starlings. Their stride was clean. Their quick feet hit the pavement, hips and heads moved slightly and exactly. The bright tiny shorts of children flew by as they spilled the bottled beer down their throats. Sparks pulled instinctively ahead, letting his lazy eyes scan the darkness and the cones of light. Sha looked at Aaron. "You alright?" he said.

Aaron shrugged vaguely, tipped his bottle up and drained it.

Sha looked at him. "You drunk?"

Aaron laughed and tossed the bottle to the ground. "I ain't drunk."

"Drunk off one beer," Sha said. "Fuckin shame."

Sparks turned around then and shouted at them. "Look!" he said, and flung his arm out. He stepped into the street, crossing diagonally toward the other side. Aaron and Sha followed, cutting between the cars and gypsy cabs purring irreverently behind their headlights.

Jay Toriace and the Haitian Claude leaned against the red brick wall of a ruined courtyard across the street, a long, glowing Dutch Master full of counterfeit Blue Hawaiian passing between them.

"You know what," Sparks said menacingly, stepping up onto the curb, "ya'll some funny-actin—"

"What?" Toriace said shrugging, his crooked teeth coming out of his mouth.

"You know what the fuck I'm talkin about."

"Go to hell, Sparks." Jay looked at him. "If you would buy some quality weed sometimes instead of that garbage you always bring around, niggas wouldn't be mad to smoke with you sometimes."

The Haitian smirked quietly and blew a cloud of smoke into Sparks' hair.

"Pass the weed, son."

Claude pulled at the weed again slowly and looked at

Toriace, passed it finally to Sparks.

"Will you tell this nigga he be smoking some bullshit, Sha," Jay Toriace said then to Sha, sweeping his eyes over Aaron.

Sha shook his head. He said, "This my man, Aaron." He watched Toriace.

Toriace raised his chin slightly, said nothing. He turned to Sparks. "Okay. Okay." he said. "Two pulls and pass. You ain't at home."

Sparks stared at him, tugged again at the brown blunt, passed it to Sha.

"Son," Jay Toriace said then shaking his head, "that ain't no damn oregano. That shit costs. From now on, you don't pay, you don't smoke."

Sha laughed out loud, choked and doubled as his lungs seized on the smoke. He straightened and looked at Toriace, smiling. "Ah," he said with a final cough, his voice a comic falsetto, "that's a good one." He raised the blunt to his lips and pulled again deeply. He passed it finally to Aaron, who took it uncertainly.

Aaron's eyes went around quickly at the staring faces of the boys. Then he smoked, his eyes low on the Dutch, his lungs pulling fiercely. He pushed the smoke through his nose and it rushed down over his shirt. He pulled again, still not raising his eyes, examining the glowing end of the blunt quietly. Jay Toriace sighed, a draft of air through the crooked teeth. Sha looked at him, his brows raised in warning. Toriace's mouth shut over the teeth.

Aaron took a final pull and extended his arm vaguely with the short brown blunt. Jay Toriace reached for it. "Yo, let me hit it again real quick, Torious," Sparks said, taking it from Aaron, whipping it to his mouth.

"Goddamit, nigga. That ain't no local shit."

"I know. I know," Sparks said, suppressing the smoke, his eyes closed to a squint. "'s good shit, son. Good shit."

140

Toriace took the blunt from him finally, his face tight and irascible.

"Yo, let's get the fuck out of here," Sparks said. "I gotta piss."

Toriace shook his head at their swaggering backs as they moved away down Ocean. The Haitian leaned toward him. "Fuck those nig-gas," he said in his accent. "They say that one is a fag anyway."

"A what?" He looked at Claude, the jagged teeth exposed in his open mouth. "Who?"

"That one," he said, moving his head. "Sha."

Jay Toriace looked down Ocean again, squinting and perplexed. "He don't *look* like—" he said and stopped. He held the tiny piece of blunt between his thumb and forefinger and smoked. The smoke wound up from his hand. "I knew there was somethin about that mutherfucker I ain't like."

***

Three rivers of piss poured over the yellow bricks of the big building off Ocean. They had visited two further identical bodegas and consumed six additional brown bottles of beer among them since the first, winding through the neighborhood circuitously.

"Shit." Sparks lay his hand on the wall above him. "I swear I almost pissed on myself."

"Me, too." Aaron twisted his head around. "Somebody's comin."

They adjusted themselves quickly and skirted around the corner. Aaron stumbled on the pavement and fell to one knee. "Damn, son," Sparks said, taking his arm. "You alright?"

Aaron looked up and laughed. "Shit," he said, "I think so."

"Look at you," Sha said taking his other arm. "Tore down off three beers." They pulled him up.

"I ain't. I tripped."

"Tripped on what?"

"On that..." He looked behind him. "...whatever that was."

Aaron's head swam. He felt free, his troubles floated-off on a stream of brown beer, his worries wafted on Dutch Master smoke. He wondered why he hadn't thought of it earlier, of drinking and drugging his tumult into oblivion.

"Let me find out you a lightweight, son," Sparks said.

Aaron belched into his fist. "I ain't no lightweight." He paused for a moment. "I think I'm high off the weed."

Sha said, "I doubt it. I don't know what them niggas *thought* they had, but it wasn't nothing special."

"Sure'n the hell wasn't." Sparks adjusted the fangs. "Dumb asses. Think they smokin hydro just cause they go way the hell uptown to get it."

"I told you about them niggas a long time ago."

"You ain't gotta tell me nothin," he said shaking his head. "I already know. Now on, it's strictly business."

"It won't even be that for me. Soon as I make enough cash to do what I gotta do, I'm done."

Sparks frowned.

"That's my word, Sparks. If I make it through this one, I'm done. I'm getting too old for this shit." He put his palms together, rested his chin spuriously on his fingertips. "God, please just let me get through this last piece of bull-shit," he said, casting up his black eyes, "and I promise I will get the hell out of Dodge and be done with this shit."

Sparks looked at Aaron, rolled his eyes.

"And please forgive these ignorant-ass mutherfuckers right here, God, cause they know not what they do. Blind to thy light and to thy truth, God. Amen." He made the sign of the cross, incorrectly.

"Asshole," Sparks said. He took a cigarette from his pack and lit it. Smoke poured from his nostrils. "You ain't goin nowhere, nigga."

142

"Okay. See what happens."

They neared the corner and the square bodega that squatted there. Sha said: "I want a beer."

"Yeah," Sparks said. "You buyin this time."

"That's what you think."

Sparks hissed through the gold and diamond chips.

Sha took the short from between Sparks' fingers and pulled on it fiercely. He snapped his arm and it sailed into the street. A thin string of smoke hovered as he vanished into the bodega.

Sparks shook the last two cigarettes out of the pack and crushed the box in his fist. It fell among the other trash and debris on the sidewalk. "You smoke?" he said, offering one to Aaron.

Aaron shook his head drunkly. "I'm cool," he said, and waved it away.

Sparks smiled at him. "Just trees, huh?" He slid one of the cigarettes behind his ear, lit the other.

Aaron nodded.

Sparks moved the cigarette between his fingers. "So how long you been knowin my man?"

Aaron hesitated. "Not that long," he said.

"He live on your block?"

"Around the corner."

Sparks pressed his tongue against the backs of his teeth. "Me and Sha is family. We used to live in the Johnson Houses when we was kids." Smoke curled up from the cigarette and he put it to his lips and pulled. "He's selfish," he said. "That's because of his family. And how his mom did him. But there ain't nothing I wouldn't do for him. He knows it. That's the only problem."

Aaron looked at the ground. He wanted to claim Sha too, to express something clear and absolute but he could not.

Sparks watched him. "I wasn't sure about you at first," he said. "But you alright." He pulled again at the cigarette. "If you cool with Sha, you cool with me."

Sha came out of the bodega. "All they had was cans," he said. "Let's walk."

They began to move slowly, the heavy night air parting around them as they went. Sha threw his arm over Aaron's shoulder and the cut gold on his wrist glinted against his skin. "You asleep? You ready to go home?"

Aaron shook his head. "I'm cool."

Sparks ran his eyes briefly along the length of Sha's arm. "Son, why you don't get that link melted down into a ring? Trade it for some studs or somethin."

Sha looked at him. "What I look like?"

"Bitches love that shit," he said. He tapped his cigarette with his thumb. "You slippin, son. How many females knockin on your door?"

Sha looked at him, calm and ironic. "How many you think?"

Sparks turned his eyes ahead and slowed his gait. "Shit," he said through his teeth. "Sha, look."

Down the block, in tight blue and black, two hulking police officers lumbered toward them. "Damn," Sha said. He let his arm fall from Aaron's shoulder. "Chill, Sparks," he said. "Just be cool. They don't even see us."

"Why *don't* they see us?" Sparks hissed. "We see *them*. Let's go."

"Don't." Sha said. "If we run they gon fuck with us."

"They gon fuck with us no matter what, son. That's Delgado. You know he hates me."

"No. We got to—"

"What did we do?" Aaron looked at them. "We ain't—"

"Don't worry, baby boy," Sha said and touched him. "Everything's cool. We gonna just stop right here." They all stopped. "Now we gon turn around real nice. Come on. Ain't nothing happening." They turned slowly, moving in the

144

direction from which they had come.

"Come on," Sparks said. "You know we can skirt on these fat bastards."

"No. Keep walkin. All we got to do is walk." He turned to Aaron. "I know you tipsy baby boy. It's cool. We just goin around the corner."

The rubber heels of their boots thudded against the pavement. Their feet pulled instinctively to the left. They neared the corner. "They ain't even payin attention," Sha said.

They turned. Out of the corners of their eyes they could see the blue shirts and glinting badges. The officers looked up out of their broad pink faces. Aaron's stomach jerked and fell.

"Wait a minute guys," they heard over their shoulders. But they were already running. Their feet pounded, tearing up the block and into the street, around cars and fire hydrants, beneath the spreading canopy of trees to the other side. Grim rows of brownstones rose on either side of them. The dull clamor of the police was behind them: handcuffs jingled; guns thudded in their holsters; the hum of polyester was in their ears.

Sha pumped his arms. His eyes flew back and forth. His lungs clenched again and again. "This way," he shouted as they flew around the corner at the end of the block.

Aaron came wide around the turn and catapulted into the street. His legs threw him forward still. His mind was frantic, his body all adrenaline and sinew, snatched out of drunkenness and languor into taut sobriety.

"No! This way!" Sha shouted at him, drawing him back to the curb. "Right here!"

A pinched gangway separated the rising apartments on the corner from the row of brownstones extending the block. Aaron jumped and slid and slipped through the opening after Sha.

Sparks emerged first, crashing through the yard on

145

the other side of the gangway. Sha flew after him. Aaron came then, tripped over a gutter, fell to his knees. There was a hollow crunch of aluminum. He whipped his head around. The fleshy faces of the police floated at the dark entrance of the gangway.

"Come on!" He heard Sha's voice. He sprung to his feet, the incomprehensible click and gargle of the police radio behind him. He vaulted over a low chain-link fence. Sparks and Sha were already on the other side. Twenty identical fences separated twenty thin quadrate plots before them. Aaron hovered for a moment at the next little fence, looked over his shoulder, sprung over to the other side. They were behind him, but they were coming, and he could feel himself rushing on a flood, before the drone of polyester and radio garble.

They tore through the next yard and the next, knocking over lawn chairs and tomato plants and Weber grills, leaping over fences and landing on the other sides on the tips of their toes, graceful strong and synchronized, like three masters caught in the climax of a ghastly midnight ballet. Aaron could feel the officers behind him; he kept his eyes on Sha, jumping when he jumped, dodging when he dodged, straining to see anything in the dark plots of land illuminated only by the glowing rear windows of the buildings rising up around them on every side.

Sha kept his eyes on Sparks. He knew he trusted him. He knew Aaron was behind him and afraid. Then he heard Sparks just ahead in the dark—a terrible, rankled sound of fear coming from deeper down than the throat, the low sound of dispair. His stomach sank.

"Shit!" Sparks said and slapped his palm against the wall.

It took Sha's eyes some short second to see the brick wall that stood before them, and not a millisecond to comprehend its significance. The wall separated the overgrown rectangle of flax and crabgrass they stood in from the vain

146

delicate garden on the other side. "Goddammit," Sha said, whipping his head around. Aaron was coming over the shrubs in the next yard and he could hear the police crashing behind. Three stories of brownstones blocked their paths on the right. The twenty quadrangle plots dropped away to the left, fifteen feet down, into the long identical plots of the houses opposite.

"Shit," Aaron said, reaching the wall. "Shit! What do we do? They're..." He glanced over his shoulder. The blue shirts of the officers loomed closer, bobbing and bending as they heaved over one jingling chain-link fence after another.

"Hold it!" one of them yelled, and they could see his hand move toward the holstered black handle at his waist.

Aaron shivered. His eyes locked on the gun.

"Come on." Sha growled at them. He dashed away to the far end of the yard. Aaron and Sparks were after him, arms pumping, legs kicking out behind. The fence at the back of the yard rang out as Sha hit it, a cold dead sound like a cymbal. He leaned over and peered down into the plot below. "Come on," he said, and lifted one leg and then the other over the fence.

Aaron and Sparks made the fence and threw their heads over it.

"We can't," Sparks shouted. "It's too far!"

"Come on!" He screamed at them, balancing on the ledge, clinging to the fence. "We got to!"

Aaron straddled the fence and shifted himself to the other side. His feet hung over the six inches of ledge. His eyes sunk into the murky tract below. He thought maybe he was dreaming.

"Hey!" screamed Delgado from the next yard.

None of them turned their heads to see, but the same iron-clad image of the pasty-faced cop cocking his boxy .45 flashed in all their minds at once. In what seemed a single move, they all leapt from where they stood and flew down into the shadows. Sparks had thrown himself from the other side of the fence and turned in the air so that he landed backwards and tumbled onto his back. Aaron's knees buckled beneath him and his palms clapped the bricks of the patio fanning out around them. Sha was up over the fence and into the next yard, yelling at them to come on before they had even realized they were on the ground.

They stayed close to the wall, in the shadows. Again the fences flew under them. The moonless sky above blackened the shadows that wound around them. Aaron looked around him. Curious silhouettes glowed in all the windows.

"There ain't no way out of this shit." He said out loud. He looked ahead at Sparks and at Sha. They were still moving. "There's no way out."

Sha gasped something inaudible, tossing his head back but pressing on. His lungs ached. They were all tiring now, and out of the corners of their eyes believed they could see Delgado lowering himself down onto the patio from the ledge above. Sha ducked under a vined clothesline. Quick flashes of white came through the leaves. Twigs crackled. Aaron vaulted the fence with Sparks and ducked under the vines. Foliage whipped over their heads. They emerged at the end of the enclosure, flanking the rear lots of the buildings on Church Avenue. The dull clang of metal drifted down from a fire escape at the backside of one of the buildings. "Come on," Sha hissed from the landing. They clamored up the escape, gasping, peering down into the geometrical patches below. They could hear the clicking garble and the movement of feet. Aaron looked up through the rungs of the fire escape. Sha had already vanished onto the roof. Sparks was pulling himself over the ledge. As Aaron neared the top, he glanced again over his shoulder. A streak of baby blue was in the lot below. He threw himself up with the last of his strength, over the last rungs and onto the roof. Sha was on one knee, yanking at the handle of an aluminum hatch. Sparks bent over him, bouncing nervously on the balls of his feet.

Sha cursed and sprung up. He flew onto the roof of the next building. Again he was on one knee. He yanked again. Paint cracked and the little door flew open. Wood splintered around its mouth. They looked at each other and went down it, the little ladder ringing under the rubber soles of their boots.

Sparks pulled the trap door shut over him and followed them down the threadbare staircase of the four-family walk-up, through the clouds of curry goat and ginger tea coming out around the frames of the doors, out into the curtain of darkness.

FOUR

He doesn't want to. He doesn't even want to. I don't know why I came here with him if he wasn't because it smells like pee. I think that is a puddle of it on the landing. He is not even looking at me. He is looking at the rat. His eyes look like an animal's. Maybe if I pull them down for him he will look at me the way he looks at the rat. Maybe if I pull them down he will... But he is not looking at me. All he can think about is the rat. He is poking it with a stick. He always knows where the dead animals are. He is the color of honey. I don't know what he is saying but if I nod my head it will be enough because it is only about the rat. I wonder if he is really retarded. Maybe because he cracked his head. But if he doesn't do it fast I will have to go because Jesse will be mad if I don't bring the cigarettes. He is saying something else about the rat. If I nod he will be satisfied. He is poking it again with the stick. It smells like pee. I am going to stand up now so he will know I am going. He is still poking it with the stick. He sees me standing now but he is not saying anything. His eyes look like plastic. If he does not do it now I am going to go down these stinking stairs and out of here and never come back. Why does he keep saying he is going to do it if he's not? Why does he look at me like I am

151

a piece of glass? I am going down the stairs now because he is not going to do it. He probably thinks I am too ugly and black. He is the color of honey. I am going down. He stands up on the landing. He is still holding the stick. He is looking down at me from the landing but I know he doesn't see me. He is like an alligator or a crocodile. He just sees something moving. He does not care what it is. He is saying something but I can't hear. What, I say. What? What did you say? He is not talking about the rat. He is saying, Come back here. Come back. But I am not going back. I am going down the stairs. I can hear his feet on the stairs. Then I feel it in my back. Ow, I say. Ouch. I feel it in my back and I turn around. He is looking at me now. He is not holding the stick. The stick is on the stairs behind me. I touch my back where the stick hit. I am cursing at him now saying I hate you and I know I am crying because he looks like he is under water. I am going down the stairs again, running now. I hear his feet on the stairs. I hear him behind me and he catches my shirt. I swing at him with my fists but he has my shirt from the back. Now he is saying something. He is saying something in my ear. He is not talking about the rat. I stop swinging my fists so I can hear. He is saying it. He is saying he will make me do it. He will make me pull them down. He is telling me to do it now. I want to look at him but I can't because he is holding my shirt. I want to look at his eyes. He is saying it again, saying pull them down right now. I tell him let go of my shirt so I can. He says I better not run and I say I'm not, just let go of my shirt so I can do it. He lets go and I turn around and look at him. His eyes are like plastic. He looks at me like the toy camel on my mother's shelf does. He does not see me. But he is telling me to pull down my pants so I do. I pull them down but he doesn't even look. He is not looking down there at all. I wonder if he will pull his down now. I wonder if he will… But he is not even looking. He is looking up the stairs. He goes up the stairs and picks up the stick and comes back. I don't know why he wants the stick. He is not looking at me. He is not looking at anything. His eyes look like plastic. He is holding the stick. It smells like pee. He is the color of honey. He is holding the stick and he tries to put it down there between my legs but I jump because I know he used the stick on the rat. No, I say, no. Not with the stick. You used it on the rat. His eyes look like plastic. They look at the stick. I will use the other end, he is saying, and turns it around. But when he touches me with it I still jump because it hurts and I don't think he knows which end he used on the rat. He is probably using the same end on me. It smells like pee. He is poking me the way he poked the rat. But he is not looking at me. He is not looking at me the way he looked at the rat. His eyes look like plastic. It smells like pee. There, he says. Now you can go. So I pull my pants up and button them and go down the stairs. I look up at him and he is on the landing again looking at the rat. He is poking it with the stick. I know he is using the same end on the rat that he used on me. Next time I will not let him use the stick. I will make him take me behind Jesse's building. It doesn't smell so much like pee. Next time maybe he will look at me. Next time. Next time. Next time.

FIVE

He wants me to feel some kind of way but I don't. God forgive me, I don't. He keeps lookin at me with those sunken eyes and dark circles underneath expectin me to feel sorry for him but I can't. It smells like piss in here. It looks clean and white and I can hear the white shoes squeak in the hall but it smells like piss. He looks at me with those sunken eyes and dark circles and wants me to care. He's movin his fingers at his ears and sayin somethin. Uh-huh, I say, but I don't know what he's talking about. I ain't listening. I'm looking at his eyes. And his face. He looks dead already. He keeps movin his fingers at his ears, rollin em and sayin somethin. He wants me to feel something...Uh-huh. Uh-huh. It smells like piss in here. He's movin his fingers again. He puts his hand out and it looks like a skeleton. He says, Here. I open my hand under his and the three studs drop into it. I look at the sunken eyes again and, I don't need them, he says. I don't need them no more. He wants me to feel some kind of way but I don't. God forgive me. It smells like piss in here. I am looking down at my hand with the three studs sparklin in it like some fuckin constellation and I don't want to look at his face. He looks dead already. He never was beautiful, but God, he didn't look like that. Those sunken eyes were fearless. Used to be. He was *the only one of them that wasn't afraid. He wasn't never afraid of me not even once. He never was afraid of nothin cause he always expected the worst and predicted the worst and you just can't scare somebody like that who has already got his mind around the very worst thing that could happen. God, it smells like piss. Maybe he pissed on hisself. He looks dead already. God forgive me. I just want to get out of here, away from those sunken eyes. He used to look at me with them eyes past thick lashes. Used to. Through the mist and sleet. Freezin nights. Fearless. Comin around the corner at 42nd street, six, seven, eight times in one night. Eyes dilated from the drugs. Breath comin out in clouds under the Port Authority lights. And he would give me all the money. Every cent. He always wanted me to have it all. But he wasn't never scared. He wasn't no punk. He just wanted it like that. I figured that out later. He looks dead already. He's sayin something. He's tryin to say something but not with his mouth. His mouth ain't movin. He's saying it with his eyes. Dark circles but I can't look. I look down at my hand and there the studs are, winkin. Some kind of constellation. God, it smells like piss. I can't stand it. I got to go, I say. I got to… God forgive me. See you next time, I say, but I know it's a lie. He looks dead already. See you next time but it's a lie. It's a lie because…He looks dead already. See you next time, next time, next time.*

SIX

He is laughing at me. He is looking at me and his eyes are black and he is laughing. He is not doing it with his mouth. He is doing it with his eyes. He will not come to the house. Has not seen me in five days and can laugh. I forget how he looks almost. What he does to me. And can laugh. He is not doing it with his mouth. He is doing it with his eyes. His teeth are moving white and straight now. Saying something. I can't, he is saying, I can't today, baby boy. He is laughing at me. He is not doing it with his mouth. He is doing it with his eyes. Thinks I am stupid but I'm not. Come out here to tell him and he laughs. In the dark with his teeth white and straight and can laugh. Where his friends can see and are watching. Thinks I am young and dumb. He is not doing it with his mouth. He is doing it with his eyes. He will not come inside the house. As far as the stoop and stops. Will not come in and thinks I am stupid. Tells me to come out here and then laughs. Out here where his friends are and it stinks with piss cause they put their drugs in the garbage can and piss on the graveyard fence. Can not stop selling them for five minutes enough to go inside. He is laughing at me. He is not doing it with his mouth. He is doing it with his eyes. What will he do when I'm dead? What will his eyes do then?

Should have gotten away. Ran when I could. Now he has me by the throat. And can laugh. In front of everyone and can laugh. Thinks I am young and dumb. What will he think when I'm dead? He is not doing it with his mouth. He is doing it with his eyes. He is looking at me and his eyes are black and he is laughing. What will he do when...Next time he sees me I will be...Next time he...Next time.

SEVEN

Jonathan Fenimore Sparks' view of the world placed the Johnson Houses of East New York at the center of the universe. He was born in the outer vestibule of building 32-08 when the paramedics refused to get out of the ambulance and enter the gate and deliver him. That was a long time ago, before anyone had ever heard of Giuliani, before the streets were secured by the quiet removal one by one of brown and beige perpetrators out of all the indigenous swaths of the City. Still the seven identical buildings, shaped like crosses, rising out of the rubble and severed streets were part of him, crucial as lung or limb.

His mother had arrived to the Johnson Houses in a little airplane, her few scant Caribbean dresses folded into a wicker suitcase, her long hair up in a bun. His father had come there on the two train from the Bronx when the old neighborhoods were cut in half and the Cross-Bronx Expressway dropped down on top of them. For little Jonathan Sparks the Johnson Houses were an institution, the seven of them standing there, staunch guardians over the broken glass. Everything that had ever happened in his life had happened on one side or the other of a thin timeline, out of which the Johnson Houses towered, defining and dividing

159

his life into stark epochs. For Sparks, there were only two times. Two great eras of human civilization: The Johnson Houses and everything after them.

But the old sensory perceptions had failed him, crumbled under the weight of time. He could not remember the curling linoleum and bloody noses and vacant lots. The rats and fleas and pissy mattress. Forgot the barred windows and scalding radiators and exhausted cars immobile above the gray landscape in precious balance on blocks of cement. He remembered his life there clean, bright, happy, colored by valiant graffiti strokes, inhabited by sprawling personalities, larger than life. Before he left the Johnson Houses and everything went wrong he was happy. Before his father left. Before his mother died and her body went back to Vauxhall in something that could hardly be considered a coffin. Before his grandmother came finally from The Parish of Christ Church with her switches and coo-coo to take care of him.

All the million things about the Johnson Houses, as he now remembered them, were golden. Sha Salvador was among them. Like everything of the era, he remembered Sha strong, heroic, out of time, frozen in hyperbolic terms. Sha. Twelve when he was ten. Who smoked and played c-lo, and taught him to. Who always seemed to know what to say and to whom, and what to do, and even then with lightning hands. Fearless. Who could pick and win a fight with any fourteen-year-old in all seven buildings, and once he did, became their president and hero, won them all over and was gone. That Sha, who had only been at the Johnson Houses for a moment, secured his place in the myth of it, and now, for Sparks, was all that was left.

Sparks pulled his arm across his forehead. Sweat gathered at his temples and on his brow, ran into the shirt that clung to his skin. He glanced at the battered trashcan where he kept his stash, looked out over the block. He could see the traffic jerking and slowing at Flatbush, cars and

160

trucks and dollar vans in articulate procession under the glowing lights. Pedestrians moved too, in and out of the darkness, past the crumbling church and ancient graveyard, crossing Church Avenue and going out of view. Something caught his eye. The language of one of the bodies moving came to him through the din. He knew it was Sha. Slow, solemn, without the singing gestures. But it was Sha, unmistakably. He whistled. The head lifted slightly, turned, made a vague motion.

Sparks turned and looked at Jay Toriace and the Haitian standing yards off. "Watch my shit," he said. "I'll be right back."

Sparks went down the block quickly, his boots thudding on the cement.

"What the fuck," he said as he approached. "Where you been?"

Sha looked at him. "Where you think I been? Tryin to get this money."

"For the lawyer, right?"

"Yeah, for the lawyer."

Sparks' eyes flew over him. "You don't look so good."

"Don't feel so good."

Sha turned to walk and Sparks walked with him. "Sha, if you need money why are you stayin off the block," he said. "It don't make sense."

"It does make sense. You know why, too. The block is hot. What you think gon happen when Delgado or one of these Jakes run up? I'm goin to jail, that's what. That make sense to you?"

"So, what? You going to jail anyway if you can't get the money for the lawyer, right? You might as well take your chances now. You got to do somethin."

"More than one way to skin a cat."

"Like what?"

"You don't worry about that. You worry about *you* out here. The only reason they ain't got you yet is cause they

161

don't want to. They waitin for you to turn eighteen."

"Man…"

"Son," Sha said. "I gotta go."

Sparks touched his arm. "Here," he said. He held a bundle of folded bills in his fist.

Sha looked at him and looked at the money. He paused, took the money and was gone.

Sparks went back down the block and turned on Church Avenue. The spire of the church moved over him like the hand of a clock. The leaning headstones in the graveyard peeked out through the wrought iron fence.

"What happened, Sparks?" Jay Toriace said to him as he approached.

"What the hell you mean, what happened?"

"Wasn't that Sha?"

"Yeah. So what?"

Jay chuckled. "What, he scared to come on the block, now?"

Sparks looked at him, his eyes dark with disgust. "Scared?" he said. "What the fuck he got to be scared of?"

"I don't know. Look scared to me."

"Shut the fuck up, Torious," he said. "I don't want to hear it."

"I'm just sayin."

"*I'm* just sayin. Don't say shit else to me."

"Yo what is wrong with you son? You fuckin that nigga?"

"Watch your fuckin mouth. Don't say nothing you might regret."

"Okay. Okay." Jay Toriace said. "I know how you get down but, seriously, what about your boy? You know what niggas been sayin."

"Sha is a fuckin thoroughbred. You know as good as I do. You wouldn't be sayin no shit like that if he was here."

He laughed. "Yeah right. Tell me you ain't let that nigga suck you off sometimes."

162

Sparks felt something in his stomach turn over. "You startin to piss me off."

"Piss you off? I don't give a fuck about pissin you off, nigga. I'm tryin to let you *know* something."

"I don't want to know nothin. You got somethin to say, say it to him. Don't tell me shit."

"You is hardheaded, son."

Sparks turned his back to them. He leaned over the gate and lifted the lid of the garbage can. Jay's voice came over his shoulder.

"That nigga Sha is a faggot," he said.

Sparks winced. Whatever it was turned in his stomach again. He did not want to know. He reached into the garbage can and retrieved the brown paper bag full of tiny plastic ones.

"You hear me, nigga?" Jay said. "Your man is a fuckin homo. You ain't know that nigga was suckin dicks? Gettin fucked and shit?"

The paper bag crumpled in his hand. Of course he had known. Of course, somewhere, just below the sleek surface of consciousness he had always known. Even when he had not wanted to. And what had terrified him was that Sha seemed always on the verge of saying everything, disclosing the undisclosable truth.

Jay licked his lips. "Or maybe you like that shit, now," he said and threw his head back and laughed. "That it?" He flashed his eyes at the Haitian. "You hear this shit, black? This nigga suckin now too."

Sparks was frozen in his stance, the garbage can lid balancing in one hand, the brown paper bag clutched in the other. He clenched his teeth. He could feel the smugness of Jay's eyes, the vicious curl of his lips. As he turned, he shifted the beaten aluminum in his hand. The paper bag toppled to the ground. He stared at Jay's eyes, smug and triumphant as he imagined, at his foul, offending mouth, still half-open with satisfaction. He smiled, letting Jay see the glint of gold, and brought his arm around. The lid of the garbage can sailed through the air and into the smirking mouth of his transgressor. Blood shot from Jay's mouth, sprayed across the Haitian's face and chest, fell onto the sidewalk, huge drops of black rain. Jay doubled, his hands flew to his mouth, his knees buckled. Sparks snarled and drew his arm back and up. The Haitian's eyes had seen the flash of silver with the spray of blood across his face. He jumped then instinctively and flew from the path of Sparks' weapon hand as it came down across the back of Jay's head. There was more blood and the dull crumple of metal on flesh and bone. He brought it down again hard, a second time, and a third. The Haitian threw himself onto Sparks then, and they fell to the ground. He wound his arm around Sparks' neck, batted his head with his clenched other fist. Next to them Jay Toriace twisted in pain. Huge white eyes, curious and blood-thirsty, gathered around them in the dark. Sparks jerked his head back hard, smashing the Haitian's face. Blood poured over the back of his neck. He jerked again and the crunch of cartilage was in his ear, then the Haitian's howl, and the gurgle of blood in his throat. Sparks leapt to his feet, pulling himself up into his most menacing stance. He looked at them both, bloody and wormlike, clutching their faces and curled into sixes. He steadied himself, then drew his foot back, brought it forward swiftly into Jay's head. There was a thud and a gasp and he pulled himself back, shook himself, spit over them both. For a second he stood there, his chest heaving, his shoulders moving up and down. He turned, took several slow steps, and tore down the block, the blood baking and coagulating, the flecks on his boots turning from red to brown to black.

EIGHT

Gray ribbons of smoke rose up through the dusk of his room, curled back down like the tails of collapsing kites falling through a lifeless sky. His lungs ached, and the smoke seemed everywhere, rising and falling, weaving itself into the very fabric of the room. He coughed, and as he opened his mouth, black jets of smoke poured into him, rushing through all of his orifices at once, pumping him full of filth and emptiness, lifting him naked off his bed and dropping him down again violently.

Aaron opened his eyes. The television screamed in his ear, threw its gray light against his skin. He was wet with perspiration and his heart pounded, beating out its garbled message to all his oblivious extremities. He glanced at the clock. Its flat face blinked the unhappy news: Twelve-oh-two. He rolled onto his side, away from the glow of the clock, out of the damp circle of sweat he had been lying in. It was over, and Sha had missed it.

That day his sister had read to him from a book on astrology, stressing the numerological significance of multiple seventeens. A golden birthday, she had said, was always special. Aaron had begged to differ. His mother had given him two dress shirts and a six-pack of ankle socks. What Sha had given him sat in his stomach still, souring and turning over, becoming stiffer and more bitter every minute. What he had gotten from Sha, in the end, was what he had expected all along: empty promises and a flurry of dashed and ridiculous expectations. How could he have been so stupid? When he had known all along?

He lay motionless, hardly wanting to breathe, listening to the nonsensical hum of televised voices. A thin tear crept to the corner of his eye, but he blinked it away. He rolled onto his back. He wished there was something he could do, some way to pierce the straightjacket of shame that cut and bound. He had intended to leave Sha today, tell him once and for all it was through. But things had taken a turn. Something had changed. Sha had found him out. He had not come inside the house in two weeks. And when he came to the door he would look at him through cloaked eyes and not come past the stoop. But the further away Sha drew, the nearer Aaron wanted him, the handsomer he became, until he had decided to turn back from his plan, or almost had, decided at least that he would win Sha back, regain control, and from that more comfortable place decide. But Sha had not given him the chance, had made the decision for him, leaving him impotent, aching, out of control, an ice-blue despair coursing through his veins without him. It was his birthday. He hadn't even come to say hello.

He sat up in his bed and put his feet on the floor. He wished he was dead. He stood up, pulled straight his twisted clothes. He ambled toward the dresser, let his fingers graze the folded scrap of paper cradling the seven easy digits, the three bold letters. He couldn't call him. He wouldn't. He shook his head. He would rather die.

He turned and walked past the foot of the bed, reached the wall and turned back. He couldn't stay there, trapped in that little cube of room, the one he had come to think of as *theirs*, with the specter of Sha batting back and forth in it, and the sounds and smells of him fading from it, slipping through his fingers like sand. He looked up at the dark window in the corner of the room. The rest of his life would be as black as that paned square of glass. He sighed and stomped his feet into a pair of honey blonde boots on the floor. He had to go. He would go out the front door and he would not come back. He would kill himself. That would be the end of it.

He crept up the creaking stairs. The kitchen was dark, and he could see the silver flicker of his mother's television shooting eerily from her cracked bedroom door. He opened the front door quietly as he could, slowly, and slipped out, pulled the door shut behind him. Outside, the heat descended upon him, pulling moisture from his pores, depositing it on his skin in a thin film. He walked along Newkirk, casting his eyes up to the hopeless sky. There was not a star or a moon, or the passing light of a plane overhead, only the gray glow of the City casting itself up into the clouds. His heels dragged with every step and as he turned onto Flatbush he brushed against something passing. He did not know what it was. His eyes saw nothing but the faded simulacrums of Sha dredged up from that shining place in him that grew dimmer and dimmer now every minute. He did not know where he was going, but the thud and scrape of his heels was constant and, whatever he moved toward, the motion cooled the madness that boiled in him. Flatbush rambled by with its headlights and shop windows and distant rattling voices, unnoticed, unrecognizable. He wondered what he had done to deserve it, what, to have brought God's wrath down on him with such awful fury and precision. He cursed God and himself, cursed Sha, clenched his fists involuntarily. For the millionth time he wished he had never met him, and for the millionth time took it back a second later, rebuked the vileness of what he had said. But wouldn't it have been better? To have gone on with his pale, eventless life, to have felt nothing at all, than to feel this: the faint reminiscent flavor of a life he had tast-

167

ed but would never have? *Why, God, why?* He heard himself growl out loud, caught himself, shot his blind eyes out for a moment into the darkness. He walked on, retreated back into his own privately-lit world of regret and despair.

The clouds shifted cruelly above him, and around him the artificial world creaked and moaned. Trucks groaned and belched their filth. The park passed by on the left, the library on the right. The pinnacled clocktower rose into view and in a moment was upon him, staring down with two of its hell-red faces at once. He walked still oblivious, or entranced, turned mechanically down Fulton, past the grilled and gated window fronts behind which crouched the gleaming plunder of the lost civilization he discovered himself in—the precious metals of an age of angst, emblems of pre-disaster well-fare. Calfskin coats and gator boots posed in their cells in silence, locked fastidiously away with the baseball caps and basketball shoes, armies of branded boots set to march.

He turned down Adams Street; the gray court buildings loomed in front and back of him. Cars and taxicabs swept by toward the Bridge, and he followed their glowing taillights, the wayward mayfly, clinging to his duped instinct. Dark green letters hovered above him as the hulking Watchtower compound rose on his right: READ GOD'S WORD THE HOLY BIBLE DAILY. He trudged on. He only knew he was going over the Bridge once he was on it. With the hot river of mist oozing beneath him. And the white and red torrents of light sending up their spray of exhaust on either side of him. And the dark towers of glass rising all around him, before and behind, shining like syringes, shooting white lines of designer dust into the black bulging biosphere of the City. He stopped for a moment at the top, thought of throwing himself down into the traffic on either side of the slatted walkway, climbing over on one of the beams, plunging down into the bubbling water below. But on and on he walked, through the haze and confusion,

168

and the heat, alone lonely delirious, his head hanging lower and lower, his eyes seeing less and less. A van screeched beside him, blew its shrill horn indignantly. Aaron flinched, but pressed on, his mechanical feet still dropping heavily, moving him through the City by imperceptible degrees. The pavements threw up their dismal waves of heat and funk, and a faint roll of thunder sounded far off, faded against the slabs of steel towering above him like tombstones, casting black shadows, announcing the death of desire. He would never allow himself to want anything again. He would never be so stupid.

His feet chafed and burned now in his boots, but he kept on. He would not go back. He would die first. Broadway opened up around him, empty and wide. Headlights shined in his face. Occasional eyes rested on him, looked back at him as he passed beneath the million stark streetlamps along the way. He wondered where Sha was, who he was with. If he had thought about him. He blamed himself for everything now. For his pride and stupidity. He wished he could explain, wished he could tell Sha everything and make him understand. But he knew that even if he could talk to Sha, he would never be able to say the things he wanted to say. The impossibility of his life loomed clearer. He could not go on. He could not turn back.

A clap of thunder boomed above him and he raised his eyes again to the sky. He felt the rain on his forehead. He looked up at the street sign. Twenty-eighth and Broadway. He couldn't go home, but the street was speckled and steaming now with drops of rain. His feet screamed and throbbed. He was exhausted. He would have to do something soon. But how? What?

He turned down twenty-eighth street. The thunder cracked again and the sky opened up, sent its impenetrable wall of rain tumbling down into the city. Suddenly water was everywhere, crashing and spraying and flying through

169

the air. Aaron kept walking, thankful almost for the distortion the rain caused, and for the perceived break in the astonishing, dead-of-night heat. In reality, the rain was hot as the pavement it dashed against, adding only a density that choked and hung. Aaron's shirt clung to him. He looked down at his feet—all the crispness and blondness washed away by a simple summer shower. A green awning jutted out to his right and he ducked under it, watched the rain come down around him. He could hear, vaguely, the muffled pounding of music, and smell the faint odor of cigarette smoke mixing with the rain and oil on the street.

A door swung open next to him and he started, watched in alarm a figure emerge amidst the blast of smoke and music. She was tall and thin, her long hair thrown over her bare shoulders, her strapless gown hanging over her small, firm breasts, its hem brushing lightly against her ankles. At her shoulder a huge silk flower was set, the same color cream as her gown, and at the end of her long arm a cigarette burned in a holder, sending a spiral of smoke upward toward the turbulent sky. She did not notice Aaron at first, or seemed not to, and he watched her out of the corner of his eye. There was something strange about her. Something peculiar in the profile and the stance.

She raised the cigarette to her lips and pulled. "Do you take it I would astonish," she said suddenly, her eyes fixed in front of her on the pouring rain.

Aaron shifted his weight uncomfortably on his feet. He said nothing, uncertain whether she spoke to him or to herself, unsure of what she had said.

She turned and looked at him then, lowered and lifted her eyes curtly. "Does the daylight astonish, honey?"

Aaron's face burned. The woman stared at him. He wanted to dash away into the rain and never look back, to disappear without a trace from the woman, the words, the eyes. But he could not. For some reason he could not. There was something in her, in her voice, her manner, that

170

repulsed him, but there was something else, something silky in her words that begged him to listen. He squinted and looked at her.

Her hard face softened then and she laughed, tossed her long hair expectantly. "Oh, don't look so serious," she said, and touched the long cigarette holder to her lips. "I can't stand it. I am not one of those women who can stand things. I wish for the children's sakes I was stronger, but, oh…" She took a deep breath and looked out again into the rain. She looked back at him after a moment. "And you?" she said. "What about you, sugar? Can you stand things? Can you take a lot?"

"What?"

She shook her head knowingly, took a long pull of her cigarette, and blew it into the air.

Aaron watched her profile against the gray dripping rain. Brown bangs curled over broad forehead. Large fingers, splayed on her raised hand, curled around the silver cigarette holder.

She turned to him again. "Are you waiting for someone?"

Aaron shook his head. He noticed a tooth missing from the side of her mouth.

"Well, of course you are. I mean we're all waiting for someone now, aren't we? But why are you *here*?" She smiled strangely. "Alone?"

Aaron put his hands in his pockets, looked out into the street, made a small movement like a shrug.

"You don't say much, do you," she said, laughing to herself. She pulled at her cigarette again. "I never seen you before," she said after a moment. "Do you come here often?"

"Here?" He looked blankly at her.

"Yes, *here*," she said ironically, and raised both her hands. "Here, sweetie. The Clubhouse."

Aaron glanced back uncertainly at the black door

171

behind them.

She leaned closer to him then, smiled through the dark and narrowed her eyes greedily. "My God," she said with delight, touched his chin lightly with her long index finger. "You're just a baby. A precious little baby."

Aaron pulled his face away. He knew he hated her now. He knew why. But he knew also, at that moment, that he needed her, needed to be seen by her in that way in which only one as pitiful and repulsive as she could see him. He knew if he stayed he would be admired. And envied.

She stepped back slightly and extended her long arm. Jewels sparkled on her fingers. "I'm Magdalena," she said grandly. "The children call me Maggie. But you can call me anything you want, sugar."

He did not take her hand. He would not touch her.

She smiled cruelly, let her hand fall. "And your name is…"

"Aaron," he said, but regretted it immediately.

"And…Aaron," she said, tugging lewdly at her gown, "exactly how *young* are you?"

"Six-" he said and paused. "Seventeen."

"Well which one is it, honey? Sixteen? Or Seventeen?"

"Seventeen." He looked at her.

"Just turned?" she said, raising her eyebrows inquisitively.

Aaron looked at the sidewalk. The rain had diminished. "Today. Eh, yesterday."

"Today?" she said, and turned her head slightly. "Do you actually mean to tell me that today is your birthday?"

"Yesterday."

"Oh, yesterday, today. It's just a technicality, sugar. I know a scandal when I smell one." She grazed her long fingernails lightly across his shoulder. "Do you want to talk about it, sweetie," she asked breathlessly, batting her thin

172

lashes.

Again Aaron shrank from her touch. "What?" he said with blank disgust. "Talk about what?"

Magdalena stood up straight then and clasped her hands, inhaled thoughtfully and said: "I think we need you to have a drink." She turned in her cream pumps. "Come inside and we'll get you a little something to take your mind off everything." She pulled the door and it swung open, slammed shut behind her with a clap.

Aaron looked around him. His heart raced and shrank. The world had become a black slamming door. He looked around again quickly and vanished like a thief into the smoke and despair.

The cream outline of her gown glowed dimly and he followed it down the dark hallway behind the door, past the windowed cashier who shouted something from behind the glass. Magdalena swung her arms and hips. "He's with me, sweetie," she said inaudibly and kept moving. They stepped through a long curtain at the end of the hall. A man on a barstool sat at the entrance, looked with authority at Aaron. She wagged her finger in the man's face. "Uh-uh,"she said. "I got him." She motioned him on and swept around a pole to the bar. "Let's get this young man a drink," she said to the bartender. "Oh, something light. One Fifty-One or something." She gave a flourish with her hand. "I'll be right back. I have a little matter to attend to." She turned and walked away, leaving him there alone.

The grisly bartender smirked and slid a tumblerful of jet-black liquid across the bar. Aaron looked around him. A dim stage rose at the back of the room, and small groups huddled around it with their backs to him. There was move-ment on the stage, and in front of it, but Aaron could not tell what it was. To his right, across the bar, was a dark doorway from which flowed every few moments a procession of three or four dainty young men, all of whom looked at him more or less longingly out of the corners of their eyes. They were terrible, he thought. All of them.

There was a commotion in the crowd and a flurry of lightly clapping hands. Something cold and terrifying took hold of him as he watched Magdalena climb onto the stage, cock her big head slightly to the right and wait graciously for the meager applause to subside. Aaron snatched the glass off the bar and swallowed from its rim a mouthful of the awful contents. He gagged and glanced at the bartender. The bartender looked back at him. He seemed to be laughing to himself. Aaron swallowed again. It was terrible, but he knew he would need it.

"Okay, sugars," he heard Magdalena say hoarsely from the stage, "I have one important announcement to make before we move on to the next category. And maybe if you're all good little children Maggie'll do a nice little number for you when I'm done." There was a patter of hands. "Now," she said, and pulled herself up in her dress. "If we've told you children once, we've told you a million times, there will be no double entries from the houses in any category. This is a mini, sugars, not a maxi. That means," she said and raised her finger in the air, "that if you walk Face for Chanel, you are the only Chanel walking Face for the evening. If you're walking Realness for Guttione, you're the only Guttione in that category. Now it seems simple, doesn't it? But week after week, night after night, it's the same thing over and over. Last week five LaBeija's walked After Five Cocktail. Five!" she said and shook her head. "And then want to stand around in their evening gowns at the end of the night and wonder why there's no trophies over the mantle, honey. Don't spend all week crafting up these gowns and things just to get disqualified, sugars. Just to watch yourselves prance around on stage all night. We take what we do here seriously. Please do the same. Whew!" she said and drew the back of her hand wearily across her forehead. "Now that we got that out of the way," she said, and turned and looked into the shadows offstage. She nodded serenely

174

and the music was struck up. "Shit," she said into the microphone and swung her long hair over her shoulders. "These girls tryin to start a muthufuckin civil war up in this piece. Sister against sister and things." There was laughter from the crowd. The music grew louder. She sang:

All night long
Gonna give it to you, give it to you,
give it to you, give it to you...

Magdalena stepped down off the stage and was swallowed up by the crowd. Aaron swallowed the last bitter corner of his drink and set the glass on the bar. He hated it. This limbo he had stumbled into. But he would not leave. Not yet. He would stay. Stay and hate it some more.

Aaron shoved his hands in his pockets. "Where's the bathroom," he said to the bartender without looking at him. The bartender raised his chin to the dark doorway. Aaron looked around him and stepped cautiously around the bar. He ducked through the door, traveled down the steep staircase behind it. Two tiny queens eyeballed him through the dark as they passed on the stairs. The driving remix that had banged and taunted upstairs grew dimmer, faded into a familiar boom and kick knocking confidently through the lower level.

Downstairs was dark, and the figures that hunched over cigarettes or bobbed their heads at the room's periphery were darker, and faceless, yet somehow indisposable, undissmissable to that obvious and bottomless place to which he had long dismissed them all. He looked around. Three low doorways, dark and unmarked, loomed at the corners of the room. Which was the one? He hesitated, tried to discern some distinction between the doors. He felt, though he could not see their faces to be sure, that they were all staring at him, all seeing him much more clearly, through the maze of shadows and light, than he would ever see them.

They were scrutinizing his solitude. Picking apart his dismay.

He stared at the door closest to him, walked bravely up to it and put his hand on the knob. He tried to turn the knob, but it held. He pulled, pushed. It did not give. *Shit*, he thought. They were certainly all looking at him now, all clucking to themselves at his expense. *Now what*, he thought. What would he do now? Try every other door like an idiot while these faggots looked on and laughed? The bartender had probably lied out of spite, just to see him make a fool of himself. None of the doors was the bathroom. He was sure of that now.

"You lookin for the bathroom?"

Aaron looked up.

The person talking leaned over to him from a tall stool at one of the tables. Aaron looked at the boy's mouth. His teeth were small and straight and framed by pinkish lips. His stool was in shadows, but when he leaned over to speak his face passed through a needle of light that pierced the darkness from above. "The bathroom?" he repeated. Aaron nodded.

"Right there," he said and motioned across the table to the far end of the room.

He looked up almost into the boy's eyes, nodded again quickly and moved toward the door. He pulled the handle and as the door came open he braved a glance at the young man. He stood at the stall inside the tiny bathroom, letting the first flood of alcohol drain out of him. Maybe, he thought, everything he needed to forget about Sha was right out there in that room. He thought of the pink lips, the little square teeth. Maybe it was experience he needed. Maybe that would be the thing. Maybe then Sha would want him and respect him. Maybe then he could reclaim himself. And maybe, after, he would not want Sha anymore. Maybe he would want something else.

He adjusted himself and stepped back from the stall,

176

glanced at himself in the mirror. The first, faint signs of intoxication played around his eyes. He came out of the bathroom, stood for a second, letting his eyes adjust again to the darkness. He looked sideways at the boy at the table. The boy looked back at him, and the room took silent note. He stood for a moment, then moved again toward the dismal, folded staircase.

As he passed the table where the boy slouched cool and provocative on his stool, he shot a last steady glance at him, tipped his head slightly and uncertainly. The boy reached out in the dark and touched Aaron's arm with the backs of his fingers. Aaron's heart pounded. Fear. Doubt. Exhilaration. He pulled away and ducked clumsily through the doorway, his shoulder sliding against the wall as he fumbled up the stairs. At the top of the staircase he turned and glanced down behind him, stepped out into the bar. The music clanged ridiculously, and the elfin inhabitants of the place struck grave and curious poses. Aaron hovered near the bar, casting quick glances at the crowded area near the stage. There was something happening there, a curious concentration of noise and movement he could not see through the shadows and the crowd. A voice squawked shrill and relentless, incomprehensible over the music:

"*Work. Lady. Couture. Lady. Couture. Work. Work. Winning. Vogue. Work. Vogue. Take it. To the floor. Take it...*"

Aaron cut his eyes in disgust. Whatever it was, he did not like it, could not abide it, and as much as he was dying to unlock certain of the silvery secrets of the place, he would not stand for it. He was leaving; he would not come back. He moved toward the door, but as he did, out of the corner of his eye caught the bartender motioning him toward the bar. Aaron turned to look at him, and at the end of the man's hairy forearm, a single fat finger extended behind a short sweating glass. He tapped his finger in the air at Aaron, then again in the direction of the crowd. Aaron

177

glanced at the stage, then back to the drink on the bar. His head swam already, but he wanted to feel it more, feel everything else less. He stepped over to the bar and pulled the drink toward him, lifted it to his lips and gulped. His face folded and he dropped the glass on the bar. Now he could go. He moved away from the bar, toward the man on the stool and the heavy curtain at the entrance. He felt something across the back of his neck.

"I'm mad at you," Magdalena said, pulling her hand away. Her voice was deeper now than before. "You haven't been near me all night. And I wore this old dress," she said, gathering a portion of it in her hands, "only because I thought you liked it. I was planning on eating..." She smiled nervously. "Well, nevermind." She poked at her scalp with one of her curved nails. "You weren't leaving were you?" She said then in a different tone. She looked closely at him.

Aaron looked past her.

"Well, you can't leave yet," she cried. "The night hasn't even got going good, sugar. And I have so much to tell you, I'm sure. Well, you don't know it yet, sweetie, but you've caused quite a commotion around here. You've became a regular old superstar, girl. And you haven't even been here a hour."

Aaron dropped his brow sharply in disgust and moved away from her.

"Oh, don't take it the wrong way, sweetie," she said, touching his arm. "It's just that you've got everyone raving about you. Five or six young men, and I mean some of them strapping young things and quite attractive, have already asked after you."

For a moment the disdain in his eyes fell away and for the first time that night he looked directly at her.

"Oh yes," she said, her eyes lighting up. "*Yes.* And, well, I got rid of most of them for you already, because you wouldn't be interested, of course. I can tell by the way you look at *me*," she said and paused, touching her nail again thoughtfully to her scalp, "what you're interested in and what you're not. But there's one or two...But come," she said after a second, touching his arm again, guiding him. "Let's sit down and have a little drink and talk. Just for a minute."

Without awaiting any response she steered him carefully around the bar to a tiny table in the dark corner of the place. They sat down. Magdalena motioned something to the bartender and he emerged from behind the bar with two identical martini glasses in which swished identical amounts of a pale liquid, and two drowned cherries, identical in every way but one.

"Finally," she said in exasperation, crossing her thin legs, "a chance to relax. I've been on my feet for hours. But I shouldn't complain."

Aaron stared at his glass. He picked it up and took a drink. The cherry swished into his mouth and he bit down on it and a piece of his tooth broke off on the pit.

"Ouch," he said. "Goddamn." And spit out his tooth and looked at it.

"Well I hope you've enjoyed yourself, at least," she said then, not seeming to notice, stroking the rim of her glass with the tip of her finger. "Did you see that last thing? Ugh," she gasped.

Aaron said nothing. Felt his jagged tooth in the side of his mouth with his tongue.

"Oh, but you probably couldn't see anything, poor thing. They make these things so dark, now. I keep telling these children, 'it's not going to work hiding behind these dim lights, girls.' And the longer I do this, the darker these things become. It won't be long before these girls are in here stumbling around in the dark with no lights on at all and nobody seeing nothing. But I always say: nothing, storm or flood, must get in the way of our need for light, and ever more and brighter light." She cackled horribly. "The light is the truth and the truth is the light. These bitches can't take it, honey."

Aaron fired his barest look of pity and loathing, took a long drink from his glass.

"But I know you are not sitting here right now to hear me go on about all these boring topics," she said lovingly, leaning toward him over her glass. "I know you are sitting here for one reason and for one reason only."

Aaron looked down again at his glass.

"Oh it's nothing to be ashamed of," she said quickly. "A fine young man like yourself should have what he wants. Of course. Of *course*! But that's the big question, isn't it? Nobody ever knows what they want. And if they actually ever get what they think they want, God help them then because that's when the real drama begins, isn't it sweetie?" She had pulled a cigarette, this time without its holder, from some invisible place a moment earlier and now she lit it, held it between her lips and exhaled. "Don't worry, precious," she said sadly then, "I'm going to tell you every little thing you want to know. But first," she said, and smiled faintly, "first I'd like you to do me one little favor."

Aaron looked coldly up at her.

"Oh it's nothing like that, sweetie," she said, fluttering her hand. "Nothing like that at all. I may be old, but I still have my mind, after all. No, no, it's not that. I only want," she said and paused, "to hear you speak. I only want to know something about you, something precious from your own little mouth. Something about your life, perhaps, and I'm sure it is a very exciting life, indeed. Oh, yes, I'm *sure* about that. And I know it seems silly to you, but if you would just humor me a little. Sometimes, all the pleasure an old woman has is in watching the young ones. Watching their lives unfold right before their eyes. Everything. The joy. The pain. When you get to be my age," she said, and pulled again at her cigarette, "you look into the future and all you see is a long, dark highway filled with endless tollbooths and no exits. But you, well, you're just so…so of the moment. So perfect for the time. I just can't help but want to know you. So let's just talk for a minute. Like regular people."

If it had not been for the alcohol, which seemed to rush all at once to his brain, and for the undeniable desire he felt to gain something tangible and throbbing from the unfortunate wrong turn he now felt himself to have taken into the place, he would have gotten up right then and left without saying a word. But he did not get up, of course. Did not move a finger or a fingernail, only stared again intently at his glass, and pushed whatever remained on the surface of his one true self deep into the furthermost crags. He would never give her what she wanted, never allow her what he was sure she desired: to *see* him. A sleek facsimile was as much as she could hope for, a picture of aloofness and the happy days of youth.

Magdalena sipped her drink, looked tentatively at him over the rim of her glass. "I still can't imagine," she said suddenly, "what on earth you were doing out there all alone at such a hour. And not knowing even. Not knowing where you were, I mean. That is true isn't it? You did not know?"

Aaron nodded, his eyes on the glass.

"But where were you coming from?" she said in amusement. "Where were you going?"

"I wasn't going anywhere. I got caught in the rain."

"The rain," she said. "Of course. But what a happy little twist of fate. Because you are…I mean…you do *like* boys don't you?"

He released a long exasperated breath and looked around him over the bar.

"Well, of course you do. I mean, well, of course. But you've really got to ask. There's just so many…variations. So many ways of thinking about everything. And don't think it's just because of your age that I ask. That's not

181

it at all. God knows I've seen eleven and twelve-year-olds who knew exactly where they were going, and what they want, and how they want it. No, it's not the age. I mean, in this day and time if you're seventeen and haven't been *somewhere* or seen *something*, well, you're practically a late bloomer. Years ago, it wasn't like that, of course, but now, well... But you. You just have this look about you that makes me think you don't know one little thing even. But you have," she said and paused again briefly, "have actually *been* with someone?"

Aaron felt his throat close, his chest swell with pride, horror. The question, unanswerable because no sufficient answer could be made to communicate to someone like *her* the significance, and raw, glowing perfection of someone like *Sha*, hung bulging and dark as a weather balloon. In some strange way, though, he wanted to tell her, wanted to paint that precious picture for her of his inconceivable Sha and watch the fire of envy and self-loathing light up behind her eyes. If the brilliance of Sha could be conveyed, he thought, in even the obscurest of terms, he too would be illuminated and any hint of kinship between her or any of them and him would be erased beyond all doubt forever.

Maggie smiled in amusement. "Why're you going through it, honey? These are the easy questions. Especially this. I mean, there are really only two possible answers."

Aaron smiled for some reason—a faint, nervous, intoxicated flash of teeth.

"Well," she said impatiently. "Have you?"

Aaron inspected his glass again briefly and nodded, flashed his eyes at her uncertainly.

Maggie smiled and nodded her approval. "Sweetie," she said softly then, "you don't got to be afraid of me. You have everything and your whole life ahead of you. There's nothing I could do to stop you, now. Why would I try? I'm just a tired old queen with a long train ride ahead of her and nothing to look forward to but a warm enema from time to time. No," she said and shook her head, "I'm nothing to worry about. I just like to hear a good story sometimes, that's all. And I just *know* you got one, sweetie. So, come," she said, "tell me everything. I want to hear everything. What was it like, your first time? Was it everything you ever dreamed of. Was it the way you imagined it?"

Aaron moved his head again uncertainly, acknowledging but not answering.

"It never is, I guess." She stroked the rim of her glass. "But you'll never forget it. Never. Even if it is your uncle or stepfather or some disgusting old bird of prey like that. Still, it's never the same. Never so desperate and wonderful. Or painful. But you won't be able to appreciate that until later, of course." She looked at him through the spiral of smoke that curled up from her cigarette. "Was it painful for you, dear?"

"Huh?"

She angled her long thumbnail skillfully under a long strand of hair then and lifted it over her shoulder. "How old were you, sweetie?"

He tapped his glass. "Sixteen."

"Mmm," she moaned in ecstasy. "Sweet, sweet sixteen. Just last year."

Aaron pressed his lips together and looked at her briefly. "Last month."

Magdalena laughed loudly and then caught herself with an apologetic widening of eyes. Aaron laughed, too, in spite of himself, and reached for his glass.

"You see," she said and smiled sweetly, baring the black hole of her missing tooth, "it's not so bad, just to talk, now is it? Talking about things always makes us feel better. That is a known fact. And I can tell by looking at you that something's on your mind. Oh, I know you'll say it's nothing, because what else would you say at your age, but when you've been around as long as I have, sweetie, well, things just start to get clearer and clearer after a while." She sipped her drink and looked out over the smoky room. "So who was he? The lucky devil. And how did you meet? I want to know everything."

"You wouldn't believe it if I told you," he said coyly, a twinkle of intoxication in his eye.

"Oh, but I would!" she cried hysterically. "I promise I would! I would believe absolutely anything, honey. *Anything*!"

Aaron laughed again. "He lives on my block," he said. "In Brooklyn."

"Brooklyn. Of Course. Lovely."

"He's twenty-one," he said proudly, and watched her face.

"Twenty-one. Well, well." Maggie took a last long hit of her cigarette and crushed it into the tin ashtray on the table.

"But he's not like—"

"Not like any of *these* queens. I know, sugar. I know. That's why you've got yourself all in a tizzy over him."

"Well, I ain't—"

"I know you're not, sweetheart. That's why you were standing outside the Clubhouse in the middle of the night in the pouring rain." She paused. "On your birthday. Oh, I'm sure he's something else, honey. Something else, completely. And I think it's marvelous, just marvelous! But, what I really want to know, dear, is who..." she said, and paused again, "just who is zooming who?"

"What?"

"Oh, you know what I mean, sweetie. It's unavoidable, now. I already have an idea, of course. I mean, you know what they say—'butch in the streets' and so forth. Don't be shy now, tell Maggie everything."

"What are you talkin about?"

"Oh, don't be so *boring*." She rolled her eyes. "Do I really have to spell it out for you? You *know* what I mean."

184

Aaron stared at her, drunk, angry, confused. "Look," he said. "I don't know what the hell you're talkin about." He pushed his chair back. "I gotta go."

"Oh, don't go yet," she gasped, and reached across the table to him. "Not yet. We were just starting to know each other. And you haven't even let me tell you the most important thing yet. Just five more minutes, sweetie, I promise. I didn't mean to make you mad. I just...Oh, I just forget what it is to be so young and so...*tender*, sometimes. Don't be mad. Please. Just five more minutes."

Aaron scowled and said nothing, but stayed where he sat, a foot from the table, his fists clenched, eyes all but invisible behind their curtain of regret.

"My word," said Magdalena breathlessly. "I didn't know you were so sensitive. Really. I was only trying to ask a obvious question. What I was trying to say, dear, is whether you are a *giver* or a receiver."

Aaron stared at her, blank and astonished.

"Oh really!" she cried in disbelief. "Now, really, you can't be serious." She leaned closer to him. " Sweetie," she said then, attempting to whisper, "What I'm asking is whether you are a top or a bottom. You know, passive or aggressive?" She stared feverishly at him. "Are you a fuck-er," she enunciated painstakingly, "or a fuck-ee? What do you do, child?"

Aaron's head swam. His face burned. His tongue batted blindly around in his mouth.

Maggie watched his face. Her lips flattened into a vicious grin. "You don't have to say anything, sweetie," she said. "I already know."

Aaron glared at her. "You don't even know me," he said furiously. "You don't know shit."

"Don't I?" she said, raising the painted line of her eyebrow.

Aaron sprung up from the table and the chair he had been sitting on toppled loudly over onto the floor. "Man, I ain't got time for this shit," he said, and shoved the toppled chair with his foot.

Maggie sprung up then too, grabbed him by the wrist, sunk her ready nails into his skin. "Don't get mad at *me*," she hissed.

"Don't fuckin touch me." He yanked his arm away.

"Oh, don't be so silly," she said and grabbed him again so hard he felt tears in his eyes. "Getting mad about nothing."

Aaron was suddenly terrified. He tried again to pull away, but her grip on his wrist tightened.

"I am going to tell you something very important, right now, my dear," she said. "So listen closely."

Aaron turned his head away and she took his chin between the thumb and forefinger of her free hand, turned it back to her. "Are you listening?" she said.

Aaron stared at her, at the damp mounds of makeup gathering in the crevices of her face. His eyes twitched with fear and desperation and hatred.

"Do not," she said slowly, "ever be ashamed of what you are. One day—soon I hope, for your sake—you will discover or decide who and what you really are. When you do, be proud of it, my dear, whatever it is. And don't let a little thing like who's on top and who's on the bottom get in your way."

"It ain't even like that," he said, shaking his head despondently.

"Like what, sweetie?"

"The way you think."

"Well," she said, loosening her grip slightly, "how is it then?"

"Not how you think."

Maggie sighed. "You've said that already."

"We just," he said uncertainly, his eyes darting. "We don't get down like that."

"Would it be possible," she said softly then, still

holding fast to his wrist, "for us to communicate in English? You people just can not seem to talk about anything. Now, what are you saying, dear? You are not telling me that you and your, er, friend are not involved in a *physical* relationship."

"Well, we don't do that."

"So you don't *fuck*," she said, pushing the word through her teeth. "Well," she said, a hint of amusement coming into her deepening voice, "what *do* you do, dear?"

He did not look at her. He pulled his arm to test her grip. "We just mess around."

"Mess around," she repeated slowly and ironically. "Well, I'm not sure I know what you mean."

"I mean," he said angrily, "we don't fuck each other or no faggot shit like that."

"Oh, you're not one of those!" she cried. "One of those disgusting things that just *jacks* off–" She expelled the words repugnantly. "-and never says anything or does anything. It sounds sexual to you, doesn't it? I assure you, sugar, it is not. Not at all. Oh, but I don't believe it anyway. I don't believe a word. I mean it wouldn't be totally out of the question, of course. There is that certain category of trade that falls into that category, I know, but, well...Except that you're not exactly *trade*, now are you? I mean, to the unskilled eye perhaps but to me..." She shook her head. "No. No, if you had been actual trade, honey, I would have seen that immediately and been very strongly attracted to you." She squeezed his wrist. "But that wasn't the case at all. When I saw you, sweetie, all I wanted was to hold you. Like a mother would. That's why I don't believe a word of what you're saying. I know the type you're referring to. I know more than you think. And from personal experience, too, honey-trust. Yes, I know the type, but you're not it, sweetie, and I know there's more to the story than what you're letting on."

Aaron was no longer listening. Only waiting.

"Oh, I know you want to get away," she said. "And if it wasn't for the fear, and the idea you have that behind this flawless exterior there's a big old physical man tucked away who just might overpower you here in front of all these people—if it wasn't for that you'd have tried to get away by now, wouldn't you? Well, lucky for you I am such a nice person and not one to cause a scene. I'm going to let you go now, so you can run along and enjoy the rest of what you believe is your life. But you have to tell me now, once and for all, and in plain English, not that non-language you people speak all the time. I want you to say the actual words, now sweetie, as difficult as I know that must be for you. And don't you dare start with all these vagueries and things, 'mess around' and all that nonsense. Strict verbiage is what we're shooting for, so stick to the action words, honey. And not too many of them. I don't want you explaining, I just want you to say it. And I want to look at your face, too, while you say it. Because I'll know if you're lying. Now, tell me, sweetie, and remember what I said—think carefully about the words you'll use. Tell me what you do, sugar. Tell me now."

He hated her. He hated her, and in his mind's eye scoured the room for something sharp to stab her with, something heavy to hit her with, to stun her at least for the second it would take for him to fly down that dark hallway past the doorman and be gone forever. But he was afraid, afraid of what might happen if he failed and found himself flailing helplessly at the end of Magdalena's powerful arm or being devoured by the angry horde that would certainly descend if provoked. The only thing to do was what she wanted, to say something and hope she would let him go quietly and with only as much shame and humiliation as he had already been made to bear.

Magdalena lifted her black brows and tightened her grip on his wrist.

Aaron clenched his teeth. "We just," he said slowly through the pain, sweat running over his temple. "Grind."

Magdalena stared at him. "Grind," she said flatly. "*Grind?* As in *bump* and grind? As in dry hump? As in–Oh please, child. Please! What are you saying? That you are head over heels for this child and all in a tizzy and things, yet all you do is hump around like five-year-olds? Is that what I am supposed to believe?"

Aaron said nothing, but stared at the wall, his shoulders shrugging involuntarily, his head heavy as a brick.

"Is that what I am supposed to believe?" she shrieked again, yelling now, enraged. "Well, I'm telling you right now, sugar, I don't. I don't believe a word! And if you think for one minute that that disgusting little game you are referring to is in any way a acceptable form of intimacy between two human beings, you are wrong, my dear! Dead wrong!"

"Well that's what we do," he said furiously, exhausted, pulling toward the door.

"But it's not even sex! It's...It's ridiculous. It's kiddie sex, Lord. It's frauderism! Trepedism, girl! I don't believe it!"

"Look," he said, "I gotta go."

"Go?" She glared at him. "After you stand here and tell me that bold-faced lie, you think you can just waltz out of here without a care? I don't think so, sweetie. You deserve a good telling-off for that one, and I'm the one to give it to you."

As she raved, Aaron pulled more forcefully toward the door. He was leaving now. He didn't care how.

"First of all," said Magdalena, clutching him tighter, "remember this. All of life is a stage, honey. Everybody plays a role. Don't think you can get out of it through this stupid rouge you're putting on. I see what you're doing and it's disgusting. And irresponsible. Do you hear me? Be a man, child. For Christ's sake."

Eyes were on them now, and Aaron yanked his arm. "Get off me," he growled.

"No," she said, a vicious smile coming across her cracked red lips.

"Let go of me," he shouted, and pulled again violently, tearing his arm from her. He turned quickly and stomped away, past the brooding doorman who seemed softly chuckling to himself as he stared. But Maggie was right behind him, her heels clacking ominously against the unpolished floor.

"You're such a liar," she said behind him in disgust. "How can you live with yourself knowing?"

He was in the hallway now, and the darkness of it seemed to close all around him. He could hear his own breath, and the click of Maggie's heels against the muted clamor of the club. The door was just before him and around its sill glowed the gray light of a stirring City. He would be through that door in a moment, he thought, out into whatever was left of the night, and away from this place forever. But as he reached out for it, his palms open and ready to fly that black painted door off its hinges, Maggie reached out too and caught his shirt in her calloused hand.

"What's his name," she said, holding fast to his shirt.

But Aaron had had enough. He clenched his fist and all of his muscles tensed at once. He would break her face and be done with her. But as he drew back, Maggie grabbed him with her other hand, pulled him close so their bodies came together.

"Don't ever," she said gravely, leaning closer, bringing her lips to his, "ever make the mistake of fighting a queen, honey." There was a slight tremor around her mouth and when she opened it to him, a razor blade glinted against her tongue. She stared at him for a moment, then worked her mouth again and it was gone. "Now tell me his name," she said, pouting. "Before I hurt you."

Aaron's throat closed and he thought he would vomit. Tears blurred his eyes. "What do you want from me," he whispered in defeat. "Why can't you leave me alone?"

190

"Because you haven't told me his name."

"What?"

"His name, sweetie. His name."

"Why," he said to her and to God. "Why?" But her breath and her hair and her eyes were merciless and he knew there was no hope. His lips parted and he drew a bitter breath. "His name is Sha."

Maggie's eyes narrowed. "Sha?" she said slowly and emphatically. "Did you say *Sha*?" She looked at him staring at the floor, his eyes damp and bloodshot, his body tense and slumping and small. She threw her head back and a gurgle broke in her throat. She stopped and looked at him again, at the top of his head, stroked the pattern of his short black hair with her hand. "Oh, my dear," she said, laughing again, "it's not Sha." She raised her brows quizzically. "Is it?"

He looked up at her then, drunk and bewildered and half-blind with nausea and chagrin.

"Oh my God, it is," she said, and snorted in delight. "It is him, isn't it?"

"You don't know him," he muttered.

"*Know* him?" she said. "Everybody *knows* him. He's been with half the girls in here. Of course I know him, sweetie. I know him very well." She cackled again and let him go, cupped both hands around her mouth.

"You're full of shit," he said, and turned and flung the door open into the creeping green glow of night's end.

"No. No. No." She said, stepping into the doorway. "Never that. It's clean as a whistle, honey–trust." She ran her tongue over her teeth. "Which is more than I can say for your *boy*friend."

Aaron had stepped out into the street, and at a safe distance turned. "You don't know me," he screamed. "And you don't know him. He would never let you know him."

"For the right price, sugar, he'd let anybody know him."

"He would spit on you if he saw you."

"I should spit on him."

"You're a fuckin liar," he said. "And a faggot."

"Sha is a faggot. I am a queen."

"Bullshit." Aaron turned to walk away.

"You think I don't know him, but I do," she said over his shoulder. "It's Sha—black, nappy-headed Sha with the nice piece." She watched him stand still. "It's him, isn't it? Our little Sha?" Aaron turned slowly and stared at her, his eyes shaking and wet. Maggie laughed and stepped down onto the sidewalk. "No wonder you're not getting any sex, sweetie. You're both waiting for the same thing and bumping pocketbooks in the meantime. She likes to get *fucked*, girl."

Aaron could not speak. His head ached and swam. People had begun to trickle out of the Clubhouse and stared at him as they passed. He wanted to turn and run but he could not. He just stared and swayed slightly where he stood. Maggie looked at him and laughed again softly to herself. "But why're you gagging so?" she said. "Did you really think you could come in here all clear-eyed and clean-limbed and looking down your nose at everybody thinking you were so different? I know what you were thinking. You're thinking: 'I'm young, I'm strong and nothing can touch me.' But let me tell you something, sweetie. Every month as it wanes brings you nearer something dreadful. Time is jealous of you, don't you know? But I'm not. I wouldn't trade places with you for the world. Especially now that I know it's Sha. How did you ever get mixed up with her? You'll regret it, I promise you. Maybe for the rest of your life."

Aaron could not look at her. His eyes refused to focus. He felt suddenly naked and tricked and ugly, as if the only thing that had ever meant anything to him was being dashed to pieces right before his eyes. Maggie reached into her tiny, cream-colored purse and removed a cigarette and lit it. She came closer. "I know how you feel about him," she said softly. "I know you think he's so wonderful and so rare and with so many qualities so often. I've seen it a million times. That elevating excitement of the soul. But it's a sham, honey. Don't fall for it. If you're smart you'll never see him again. Someone like that can ruin your life and make you wish you'd never been born. Whew," she said and raised her hand to the sky. "Thank God I never messed with her, honey. And it's not because I couldn't have."

Aaron glared at her.

"She is bad news, honey. Isn't it obvious? I know you think he *belongs* to you, or whatever, but believe me he belongs to whoever's convenient at the time. Has he asked you for money?" She watched his face. "Well, of course he has. But that's not even the worst of it. I mean, she's been with so *many* people, done so many things. You really couldn't begin to imagine. I'd be afraid to kiss him, let alone anything else. Then there's that little Puerto Rican child she's been running around with since forever. Joey or Joel or whatever the child's name is. Disgusting little crack whore who used to walk the balls. Last I heard she was selling her body for coins. But that's his main squeeze, I guess. They've been together for years. All the rest were just sex, I suppose. Low sex. Or money. But I haven't seen Miss Joel in so long. Who knows, maybe she's dead. She was half-dead then. Oh, look at your face. You don't want to be hearing any of this, I know, but it's for your own good, sweetheart, believe me. As much as I would like to see you fall into the clutches of someone like Sha—just to teach you a lesson—I can't for my own reasons. She'll just use you and drag you through the mud like she did all the rest. Get away from her as fast as you can and don't look back. If you don't, it will be just a matter of time before someone somewhere is having this same conversation over you."

Aaron had heard the words from far off. His surroundings were a mystery to him, and he could not remember, precisely, how he had come to be where he was. He was dimly aware of something being slipped into his hand and when he opened it to look, a small scrap of paper teetered in his palm. He closed his fist and looked up. The boy was looking at him, pink-lipped. A faint hopeful smile and a nod.

"You see," said Magdalena thoughtfully, "there are other fish in the sea, sugar. And some of them not half as bad-smelling as Sha."

Aaron gave her a last silent look of contempt, turned and dashed through the dark, past the trudging patrons of the place, and did not look back.

Magdalena raised her arm langorously to wave. "Goonight Lu. Goonight May. Goonight Aaron, sweetie. Goonight. Ta ta. Goonight. Goonight. Good night, ladies, good night, sweet ladies, good night, good night."

NINE

Jersey City, New Jersey, like a shrunken hind leg of the City, loomed and bobbed closer through the scratched black glass. A night like the one that now spread over the city and sprawled out to blacken the windows of the PATH train plunging forward through the fouled fields of New Jersey none of them had ever seen the likes of. The hundred and twelve degrees that had cracked thermometers and ground air conditioner motors to dust during the day had now, at midnight, dropped off to a stifling ninety-two, hovered there impetuously awaiting the break of day. People in Brooklyn, of course, sought relief on their stoops or moved lawn chairs out onto the grassy squares of apartment buildings when air conditioners broke down, lay there hoping beyond hope for a cool breeze that would not come. For Aaron there was no relief, thrashing and sweating beneath the white hot body of a boy whose last name he did not know and whose first he could not pronounce. For Sha at least, rumbling down the Newark Line, there was the metallic black shaft cool against his thigh, and for the moment that was enough.

For him, it had been a great deception: the day

beginning, that false fresh coolness and calm, and for a moment he believed that everything, everything, *every thing* would be all right. But it was only a moment, dissipating fast, fleeing before the early smoke of his cigarette. Then the phone rang cold, sonorous, full of alarm, and he only looked at it and knew it had been a lie. The fifteen hundred dollars he thought would be the answer to everything were creased beneath the sofa, bound in fifteen rubber bands to avoid confusion. He could forget what he had done to get it, and whatever was in that sharp dark ringing cutting through the morning and his cigarette smoke, he could forget that too. He did not want to know.

He rolled onto his back and stared at the ceiling. He pulled at the cigarette, rolled forward again on the flattened yellow sofa cushion and let a long column of ash fall through the mouth of an empty green bottle on the floor. The phone rang again and he sighed, deep and smoky, reached behind him and picked it up.

"Sha." Sparks' voice came tense and fatigued over the phone. "What the fuck, son. Where you been?"

He did not want to hear it, the insistence, the child-like almost-terror in the voice of a boy who, like himself, had long pretended to be a man.

"You there?" The voice came again.

"Yeah. I'm here."

"Well, say somethin. What the hell is wrong with you? I been callin, comin by the house. Shit is goin down. You don't even know."

"I don't *want* to know."

"I ain't playin, Sha. We gotta talk. I'm comin over."

"Not now, man. Maybe tomorrow."

"Tomorrow? Son! Torious and—"

Click. He already knew. Somehow.

But he wasn't afraid. They were boys, kids, none of them with a heart between them or even blood in their veins. He had watched them for months. Sized them up and eval-

196

uated, assessed. Watched their mouths twitch and seize when they wanted to say something but were stopped from even thinking it with a sideways glance from his indifferent eyes. He didn't *give* a fuck. And he had let them know right from the start, let them see that they would respect him. And they had. Which was why they hated him now. He didn't know what they knew, exactly, what amount they had gathered or how, but that high thin almost-terror in the voice of his most fearless disciple had said it all. But he didn't care. They could hate him if they wanted. He would allow them that. He had made fools of them, after all, and for this he was willing to atone. They could talk amongst themselves. But if even one of them said one raw word to him, or so much as even looked at him funny, he would slit their throats and not think twice about it. He only felt sorry for Sparks.

Then the phone rang again. More dark and alarmed even than before. He picked it up and pressed it to his ear. "Look, Sparks—"

"Hello?"

The first creep of shadow he had felt right away, before Aaron had said anything else. What words followed were razor-sharp and had come through the receiver with such rote speed and celerity that Sha knew he had mulled over and arranged them, turned them over so that they were hardly even his own. But that first dark hello, full of doom and resignation, the sound of someone who could no longer care about anything, was all his, and Sha understood it instantly.

"What's up, baby boy?"

"Don't call me that."

"What?"

"You heard me. You're a liar. And a faggot."

"Whoa. Whoa. Whoa. Wait a minute…"

He had tried to explain, tried to make Aaron understand that it was all bullshit. Twisted and taken out of context. Manipulated by that sick raggedy bitch whom he had never even allowed within ten feet of him, whom he had never spoken a word to in his life except to say *get the fuck away from me* on the one occasion she had been drunk or delirious enough to approach him. And that had been years ago. Of course people knew him. Or acted like they did. Of course they wanted to claim him, or tear him down, or both, because they had never seen anything like him. He knew it as well as they did, and this was what infuriated them, that he owned it, that he claimed the difference between him and themselves and without the slightest remorse or mincing of words. They had to hate him, because they hated themselves next to him.

But Aaron would not hear any of it. Would not open his mouth except to say: *Whatever. Liar. Faggot.* And Sha was furious, clenched his teeth and paced the room, the telephone pressed to his ear, his voice rising uncontrollably, his words becoming loose and jumbled and full of fear.

"She's lyin," he screamed. "Can't you see that?"

"Whatever."

"You're fuckin naive, son. Don't you know all these faggots is the same?"

"You should know. You been with enough of them."

"Don't be stupid, Aaron. Lettin some dried up fuckin drag queen pump your head full of bullshit."

"Why would she lie?"

"The same reason they all would. They're fuckin jealous. They can't stand to see two niggas like us—"

"Like *us*?"

"You know what the fuck I mean."

"I thought I did. But you ain't what I thought you was."

"What the hell is that supposed to mean?"

And Aaron told him what it was supposed to mean, in the plainest of terms, and hung up the phone.

Sha had put the phone down, unable to swallow or

think, and a moment later the bell rang.

"I ain't here," he choked out to his sister, and a moment later she shuffled in on her yellow house shoes and set a small brown shopping bag on the floor beside him.

"It was Sparks," she said. "He said to give you this."

He opened the bag and reached into it. Inside, sheathed in a threadbare pillowcase, heavy as a brick, was the black nine millimeter and a note on a piece of paper: SHA. WATCH YOUR BACK.

But the Nine was for her.

Now, closer, Aaron's voice pounded through his head, that little voice weighted down with words heavier than they should have been, so that the voice itself sounded deeper, almost a man's. But he blamed *her*. He would get her. *Fuckin monster*.

The train lurched and shifted at the station. Sha nudged the steel at his waist and his fingers trembled with fury and anticipation. But not fear. He would kill that stinking bitch dead and no one would ever know the difference. There was nothing to be afraid of.

But there was. There was something, he knew, infinitely more terrifying than the easy slug he would plant in Maggie's stomach, or the empty threats of Jay Toriace or the idiot Haitian. There was the darkness, more black and unbreathable than the night around him, of which that first dark hello of Aaron's, that first creep of shadow was but the tip. It poured down on him now, descending into him by narrow pathways he thought had been long blocked off and constricted.

The doors slid open and Sha stepped out onto the platform. Heat bounced off the filthy tiles of the station and rose up from the crusted cement. It would not take long, he knew, to find that broken-down double storefront, the curlers and clumps of hair, dirty vats of wax and relaxer. And it would take less time than that to do what he needed to do.

She worked out of one side, they said, and lived out of the other, but her oil and her stench and the dead scent of burning hair would be everywhere, he was sure.

He knew he could find it from memory. It was a burden left to him by his mother, that he should always know where he was going. None of them—his mother, his brother, his sister—had ever been lost. Not even once. And neither had he. They had all received, through some inexplicable chromosomal shift, their mother's eerie ability to find anything—street, landmark, or dingy double-storefront. Which was the insult of her leaving. Because she wasn't lost, after all, wandering or alone, even up to now. She could have found them, could have found *him*, her baby boy, could have looked up to the angle of the street sign, or down to the shapes of the shadows falling over the street. She could have found him by the way the buildings and the trees shaped the sky outside. Even in the dark, she could have found him by that. Even drunk or in the pouring rain.

Which was how he knew he could find *her* now, the filthy bitch, though he had only been there once, though he had only been sixteen and never even gotten out of the car. He had been infinitely more interested, at the time, in the gadgety interior of the biggest BMW he had ever seen, than in the puckered peeling paint of the odd little hair shop, or the rail thin abomination that emerged out of it, and peered at him with such license that his skin had crawled. He had hated her from the moment he saw her—from that first wry smile and contrived toss of hair. And he hated her now.

Outside the station, oil and exhaust, the raw smells of the Garden State, came up to him on the waves of heat bucking up from the pavements. Dollar vans and gypsy cabs prowled the streets and the tangle of wires that crisscrossed over them sent all the bad news and electricity the filthy little city could use to all its estranged vicinities. He could find her by those wires, the way they had narrowed against the eaves of the building. The street had dipped there and he could feel the incline of the earth. *It was this way.*

As he pulled toward her, closer and closer, the sting of what she had done, what she had said, rushed back at him. There had been moments, since he first resolved early in the day to consummate his hatred for her with a final muffled act of aggression, that he doubted himself, moments when he had decided to turn back, forget the whole thing. But he had only, at these moments, to remember Aaron's voice, and his eyes—eyes which would never again see him, except as she did (or said she did)—to know that he would have no trouble, no trouble at all blowing the life out of her with a single shot because that was what she had done to him.

He walked on slowly, turning right here, left there, through the dank disordered grid of streets, his eyes plucking out of the sordid landscape those obscure but discernible bits of matter that would point the way. He knew he was close. People passed him on the street but he did not look at them, would not have seen them if he had. He turned again to the right and hesitated. His stomach twitched. *This was the street.*

He crept along, past the piles of garbage and debris that lined the street. Sweat began to pour from him, down his neck and back, out of his armpits. The misshapen little buildings of the street, like ragged piles of brick, rose above him, their two or three stories pounding heat and looming dark against the sky. He looked at the ground. Bits of glass and kitty litter were scattered at his feet, forming tiny barren mountain ranges in places, which he stepped over gingerly, wanting not to mess his boots. He looked up again and swallowed. A dim light glowed in a window to his right. *This was it.*

It still looked the same. *The piece of shit.* The same crumbling steps and gray cement. Wood siding over the formerly brick front of the building, paint peeled and torn. Two doors. Two front windows: a light in one, and in the other, now dark, her name, in curved Spanish letters. As he came up the steps, his fingers fluttered instinctively over the bulge at his belt. He turned to the right, to the door of the one she lived in, knocked hard on the glass. There was a brief rustling inside, and a movement of shadow over the blind. Then he heard her voice, muted and indistinct beyond the doorsill, and the aluminum sound of the blinds against the glass. The door swung open and her shrill voice spilled fiercely out into the street.

"Goddammit, bitch," she shrieked blindly. Then her body stiffened. She looked at him. Her eyes widened and mouth fell open. Then Sha was in the apartment and Magdalena stumbling backward onto the floor. The door closed behind them and Sha reached back to lock it. He kept his eyes on her.

"What is *wrong* with you?" she said, getting up and smoothing the front of her pale satin nightgown. "And what are you doing here?"

"What do you think?" he said, staring, coming further inside.

"Well, I'm sure I don't know," she said, touching a long nervous finger to the brown stocking on her head. "But I'm right in the middle of something, sugar." She glanced at the door. "And I'm expecting company any minute. I thought you were them."

He moved toward her slowly. "I ain't them," he said, and his eyes flashed.

Magdalena rolled her eyes, sighed her phony exasperation. "Look sweetie," she said, fidgeting slightly and smoothing her slip again, "I don't know what all this is about, but this is really not a good time for me. I have a show tonight, sugar, and late already. And obviously," she said, spreading her thin arms, "I have a lot of work to do before then. So if you don't mind…"

Sha smiled and said nothing. He looked around the room. It was low and dark, its only light creeping forth from a small shaded lamp on the cluttered vanity near the wall. A

202

mirrored ribbon of smoke spiraled upward from a cigarette in the ashtray, and next to the vanity was a tiny mirrored table, upon which a small mound of white powder and several glass and metal instruments sat, reflecting themselves in its surface. Clothes were everywhere, racks and racks of them: vivid beaded monstrosities strewn about on hangers and falling over the backs of chairs, huge shadowy things coming out of drawers. It looked a mess, he thought. A fuckin mess. And so did she.

Magdalena breathed again restlessly. "Honey," she said. "It's not going to work, your coming here. If it's about your little friend I really don't understand what you want me to say." She looked at him a moment. "I think you should leave."

He laughed softly again and stared at her. "Is that what you think?"

"Well, yes, honey," she said. "I mean, I really don't see what you could possibly hope to accomplish..."

He dropped his hand slowly down below his belt, drew out the heavy piece, let it fall loosely at his side. He looked at her. "Let me worry about that."

Magdalena's eyes bulged white, flitted instantly from the shining barrel of the gun to Sha's blank face and back. Then a smile, unlikely, apprehensive, began to form around her eyes, bloomed delicately into a full decayed show of teeth. She laughed once, a single high-pitched bubble of sound. She looked at him again, and at the gun, laughed deeper and darker, throwing her head back and sliding her hand over the satin front panel of her gown. She stopped suddenly. "Sweetie," she said hoarsely, her eyes wide and smiling, "you don't really expect me to believe you're planning on using that thing, do you?" She pursed her lips skeptically and raised both hands to her head to adjust the nylon cap. "Oh, not that I don't think you're capable. I mean, I'm quite sure you can shoot straight, honey, so long as you don't have to shoot too far. But even then you'd need some kind of motivation. Some reason why. And as for me, well, obviously I haven't done anything so terrible, have I? What, spilled a little tea?" She smiled softly. "Surely, that's not it. I mean, you must know by now, what, with all your experience, that we all pay a price. A price for what we are. And let's face it, sweetie, you're something of a celebrity. I mean, there aren't many *of* you out there. So of course the girls will talk. You can't stop that. And people want to know." She looked insistently at him. "You don't want to hurt me," she said, gliding across the room away from him. "I've been more than fair." Magdalena paused at the crowded vanity, picked a small glass bottle out of the forest of tiny cylinders and took it in her hand. She glanced at him through the mirror. "Maybe you just want to talk," she said, and sprayed gently at her breasts. "You must have so much on your mind. I mean, with your life and all. Oh, let's don't be enemies," she said, seating herself at the vanity. "Maybe we could be friends to each other."

Sha pulled his lip up. "I'm gonna kill you, you dumb fuck."

Magdalena quietly clicked open a large makeup case that sat before her on the vanity. "Everybody needs a friend from time to time," she said, dabbing at a drab pool of liquid.

"I don't," he said behind her. "I especially don't need none like you."

"Like me?" She smiled and stared at him for a moment in the mirror. "Do you really think you're getting anywhere trying to separate yourself from everyone all the time? Everyone, after all, goes the same dark road, sweetie, and the road has a trick of being most dark, most treacherous, when it seems most bright. You're not so different." She smeared a band of makeup across her face. "You're not so different at all."

"Ain't I?" he said, patting the gun lightly against his leg.

"Why?" she said. "Because you're a boy? Because

204

you can walk around comfortably living in with everybody else? Because you've erased all the mistakes, all the flaws, all the giveaways to make *your* illusion perfect? We're exactly the same, you and I," she said, working the liquid over her mottled face. "Exactly."

"We ain't nothin alike, faggot. Look at yourself. You wearin a dress. You got tits, you fuckin freak."

"This," she said in disgust, running her hands over her gown, "is *not* a dress, honey."

He came closer to her, raised the barrel of the gun to the back of her head. "Do you know when I kill you nobody will even care? You're a fuckin monster," he said, and put his finger on the trigger. "You're better off dead."

Magdalena closed the lid of her makeup case and stared thoughtfully at herself in the mirror. She reached for the cigarette that still burned in the ashtray, raised it to her lips and pulled. "Somewhere," she said, expelling smoke from her lungs and crushing the butt into the ashtray, "somebody could be saying the same thing about you."

Sha dropped the gun again to his side. He stared at her in the mirror. "Why did you do this?" he said. "Why?"

"What I did," she said, "was nothing. Absolutely nothing." She drew a tiny, frayed eyebrow pencil from the clutter and, leaning forward into the mirror, began to drag it heavily back and forth over her eye. "I did what any woman my age would have done. I comforted him, the poor thing."

"You lied."

"Did I?" she said, pausing for a moment and raising her one incomplete eyebrow. "Don't tell me you never rode in a hot rod, honey. Or had a late date in the second balcony. You ought to know Maggie always has at least one ear to the ground."

"You did lie, you fuckin faggot."

"Could you please," she said, looking at him in the mirror, "restrain from using this type of language in my presence. That's such an ugly little word, don't you think? And really not applicable at all." She sat up straight in her seat. "Now as far as the lying goes, I did no such a thing. Well, you should have seen him, the poor child. Standing there all alone. And with that look in his eye—you know what I mean. That look someone gets when they've simply lost *all* hope." She considered Sha briefly in the mirror. "Well that was how he looked. Just so cold and alone. And when he told me it was you... Well, what are the chances? When he told me it was you I just wanted to reach out to him, to put his little head down against my breast and say 'I know. I know, sweetie. I know.' And him looking so heartbroken and destitute, and blaming himself. Well I just felt so *bad*. And I wanted to reassure him. And he was so confused, so very confused about everything. Well, I just tried to explain..." she said, gesturing upward with her hand, still holding the eyebrow pencil. "I just tried to explain that some people...Well, let's face it, sweetie, some people are simply not relationship material."

"And who the fuck are you," he screamed at her, "to say anything about me?"

Magdalena blinked into the mirror, one black eyebrow hanging ominously, swimming in pools of foundation.

"Huh!" he screamed louder, shaking the gun at her. "Who the fuck are you?"

"Careful, honey," she said, leaning over to the tiny table next to her. "You'll bust a gasket." Magdalena picked up one of the small silvery instruments from the table, scooped a tiny mound of white powder onto it from the table's mirrored surface and held it to her nose. She sniffed and it was gone. She turned slightly and motioned to him with the little apparatus. Sha just stared furiously, his teeth clenched, his fist tight around the pistol. Magdalena shrugged, leaning over, set her tool down again on the table. She leaned forward into the mirror then and began quietly to construct the absent eyebrow.

"Honey," she said after a moment. "I don't mean to

be cruel. I don't, really. But there are things we do in our lives that simply cannot be taken back. Things that must be tallied. Accounted for. There's no use trying to hide them away from the world, honey. No use in that at all. Because no matter how big or how small it is, or how perfectly you've taped it down or concealed it, there's always that moment when you just have to say, 'here it is honey. All of it. So take it or leave it.' And believe me, sugar, that moment would have come for you eventually with or without my help."

"Nobody asked for your fuckin help."

"Maybe not," she said. "But you needed it whether you know it or not." She examined her eyebrows for a moment in the mirror. "Boys like you always have the same problem: communication. None of you ever seem quite capable of it. You never say anything to each other. It's always just 'fuck-this', and 'fuck-that', 'son-this, son-that'. Why do you call each other that? It's so ridiculous. Sometimes I just want to shake you. And Aaron—my God, he's worse than you. You'd think he never learned the language. But that's neither here nor there, I suppose. The point is...well, the point is that maybe you can tell me things you can't tell each other. The point is I knew you'd never tell. And he has every right to know. I felt responsible. That's why I spoke."

"You did it out of spite."

"I did it because I was afraid for him. I was afraid of what you might do to him."

"*Do* to him?" He looked at her in the mirror then, and at himself, and their dim reflections seemed suddenly and gruesomely fused. "I loved him," he said, almost a whisper.

"*Loved* him?" she said and laughed. "Oh. Wouldn't it be pretty to think so? You should have loved yourself, honey."

"I loved him," he said again hoarsely. "He was the only one. The only one," he shouted. "And you fucked it

up, you fuckin faggot! And you did it on purpose. Because
you hate me. Because you can't be me. Cause you could
never have the life I have. All you got is fuckin dresses and
makeup and all the rest of this bullshit," he screamed, and
leaning over with the gun, sent all the little tubes and canis-
ters flying off the vanity and onto the floor. "You hate me,"
he said. "So you try to fuck up the only thing I ever gave a
fuck about. The only thing, and you try to take it from me,
right? Right?"

"No my little pearl," said Magdalena. "You must
gather your own sunshine. I have none to give you."

"I tried," he said, shaking. " I tried to give you a
chance."

"Oh, chance-shmance, honey," she said. "A chance
is not something you give. It's something you take. And
you've taken quite enough of them already in your little life,
darling. Don't you think? I mean, in the end, isn't that why
you're here at all right now?"

"I'm here because nothin else matters," he said. "I
don't care what happens now."

She laughed cruelly. "Oh. You don't have to make
leading lady conversation for me, honey." She twisted the
top off a tube of lipstick. "We've known each other too
long."

"You don't fuckin know me."

"Don't I?" Painstakingly, Magdalena began to apply
the heavy red lipstick to her lips. She pressed her lips
together, pursed them a final time to examine the color. "Do
you remember the first time we ever saw each other? Hmm?
Do you?" She looked at him a moment in the mirror, set her
eyes forward again on herself. "Well, I'll tell you, sweetie,
when I saw you that first time I knew right away. I said to
myself 'Now *she's* something. She's someone.' I looked
right at you and I said: 'Now there's somebody that could
really make a splash.' And you did, I suppose. In your own
way. Not how I had hoped, of course. But still it was some-

thing to watch." She ran a thin finger over her eyelid and stared at herself in the mirror. "When Clyde brought you by here that first day—You remember Clyde don't you? He's dead now, of course, but when he brought you here that day, well you should have seen him, so giddy and excited. And aglow. And surprised, too, now that I think about it, like a child who's found something precious at the bottom of a Cracker Jack box where he expects to find only a flimsy paper doll or a …scratch-and-sniff or something useless like that. He had told me about you, of course, because he always told me everything, but when I finally saw you for myself, well…then I understood. And the things he said he *did* with you, my God. Well, I must admit I was shocked. You were so young. And he was such a big man back then, and you so small. I remember when you first looked up at me out of that car window, how tiny you looked in the passenger seat. Now sometimes I think it was the tint or because it was getting darker outside because you never looked that way to me anymore. I suppose I used to feel sorry for you at first. Until I realized you were depraved. Baneful. Flagitious. An evil little bitch honey. And I admit I admired that at first in a way. You know, a woman who knows how to get what she wants. But, girl, you take it too far. Do you have any idea what you did to that man? How he cried like a baby? Or how many others there have been since who cried their hearts and their eyes out because of you? But do you care? No. You only care about yourself. And on to the next, and to the next. You can't just go around playing with people's emotions all the time and expect nothing bad to happen. You've spread yourself too thin, dear. Just take this as a life lesson."

He aimed the gun at her. "I'm gon teach you a lesson," he said. "Get down on your knees."

She turned from the mirror and feasted huge eyes upon him. "You're just being polite," she said. "I know you don't really want to—"

"Get down on your fuckin knees!" he screamed, shaking the gun at her.

Magdelena swung her legs around effortlessly and knelt before him. She looked up at him eagerly. "Sweetie."

"You should have never," he said gravely, "thought I would let you get away with it."

Maggie clasped her hands together, touched them to her chin. "Oh faithless and pervert generation..." she said breathlessly, "there is nothing covered that shall not be revealed; and hid that shall not be known."

Sha touched the cool barrel of the gun to her forehead.

"Bless them that cuss you. Do good to them that hate you. For he maketh his son to rise on the evil and on the good, and sendeth pain on—"

"Fuck you."

"I speak to them in fables: because they seeing see not; and obviously hearing they hear not..."

"Shut up!"

"What I tell you in darkness that speak ye in light: and what you hear in the ear—"

Sha raised his hand suddenly and brought the gun down on top of her head. There was the muted thud of metal and the shrill cry of Magdalena as she fell backward into the tiny table behind her. The table crashed to the ground, shattering its mirrored surface, sending rocks and powder and tiny metal instruments flying through the air before them. Maggie sat up and touched her hand to her head. A trickle of blood ran out of her hair and into the makeup on her forehead. She looked at her hand and the blood on her fingertips and smiled strangely. "What?" She said bitterly. "Do you think I never been pistol-whipped before?"

"I don't give a fuck."

Maggie laughed cunningly. "How original," she said, sliding slowly backward through the shattered glass. A flash of silver glinted among the shards and Maggie placed her hand over it.

Sha stood over her, staring down with ravenous eyes. He leaned over and with his free hand seized the front of her gown. The gun hung loosely in the other. "You should a never done this."

"You," she said, "should have done your homework, honey." And with a skillful flutter of nails took the glinting blade into her hand, flung it forth with such rapid force and exactness that even Sha's lightning reflex could not have matched or anticipated. She aimed for his throat, and had it not been for the flash of silver Sha glimpsed out of the corner of his eye and the quick instinctive jerk of chin, would have sliced clean through it. Still, she was too quick, he not quick enough, and when he jerked his chin back and to the side the blade opened his face and the cool crystals clinging to its surface turned to fire in his flesh. Sha howled and let go of her. His hand flew to the fire in his face. Magdalena stared, inching backward over the carpet of glass. Sha looked at his bloody palm and then at her. His eyes narrowed to tiny slits of pink. He came quickly toward her, his head light, the gun heavy in his hand. Maggie dropped the blade in the glass. She looked up at him and a defiant smiled passed briefly over her face. Sha raised the gun and brought it down swiftly again on her head. Maggie winced and fell back; her arms jerked and flailed, her feet kicked blindly at the glass. Again he raised the gun and again brought it down on her. And again. And again. And again.

Magdalena lay there, sprawled and silent, her hair matted with blood and makeup, her tiny hormone-shrunken penis peeking curiously out from beneath her tousled gown. A circle of blood fanned out slowly over the shattered glass, and in the distance the lights of the city flickered into darkness.

TEN

Sparkling at the edge of a vast black ocean is a Silver City. We know it is there, because it is always there, rising like a mammoth in our minds. Those who have seen it with their own eyes have been blinded, struck down by its light. Those who have not are smitten still, because they feel it and have seen its glow forever pulsing at the horizon. But at half past midnight, on the hottest day ever recorded, the City fell dark, and the glint and glow were gone.

For Aaron, slipping desperately from one darkness into another, it was a nightmare. But the monsters that howled after him in the dark were not monsters at all, but the sound of his own voice, at once shrill and gutteral, crying out into the spanking new silence of electricitylessness. After, the city would remember this night for its darkness, lock away in its collective consciousness all the dim towering visions as myth. But for Aaron, hardly aware even of the loss of light, it was the horrible sound of his voice and that last poison kiss to the collarbone that would stand as symbols of his sudden exile from innocence.

Aaron bit down hard on his lip, but the sound was still there, more pained and animal-like for his efforts, as he

213

strained against the bleak thrust and counterthrust which was his undoing. Aaron could still not be sure of the boy's name. The scrawl of the creased scrap of paper that had been thrust on him in front of the Clubhouse was useless, and whatever Aaron called him, the boy responded, so it was no matter. What mattered was that it was not Sha, which was why he was there in the first place, which was why he had agreed to any of it. Which was why he howled now desperate and forlorn. Because it had taken only one touch from the boy for Aaron to know his mistake, for him to know that he had never wanted any touch but Sha's. But at the same time, this realization thrust him forward, into the depths of despair, toward an end that was no end at all, but the grim beginning of an era of enlightenment as dark as the night.

Aaron had been determined, for reasons he had not yet begun to unravel, to deliver up to the boy—hardly more man than himself—what Sha had never asked him to. But even as he did, and the boy shifted inside him, there came to him the sudden and cruel realization that, defining as it may have seemed, the thing at its heart was a question of mechanics. The sheer pain of it he could stand, but that sound—horrible, effeminate, wimpering—that filled the room when the stereo went out was far too much for him to handle.

Aaron dug his nails into the boy's skin, but he only moved faster and more frenetically, lunging forward and pulling back with that urgent instinct, that raw painful desire that is the capstone of youth. But Aaron had had enough, and in a single quick movement pivoted his hips and threw himself out from under the boy.

"What's wrong," the boy said frantically. "What happened?"

"I...I gotta go."

So he went. And the boy flicked the switch stupidly again and again.

In the street darkness had descended. Only headlights gleamed, and flashlights around the necks of children awakened by the panic in their parents' voices or the heat of apartments where fans and air conditioners had whirred to a halt. No televisions buzzed or washing machines churned. No streetlights shined down their cones of light. The only sound above the din of bewildered voices was the horns of cars and the scream of a siren far off. But Aaron noticed nothing. It was dark. It had been for days.

He walked, ran, stumbled. Then reality rushed all at once, and he seized upon it and understood. *There was no light.* It was not just the traffic light before him, not just the streetlight above him; it was every shred, every flicker he had ever known that had failed him, left him in darkness, unrenderable. It sooted his skin and blinded his eyes and got everywhere, into his clothes and hair, clinging like a vine, robbing him of everything he had ever needed to survive. In his mind's eye he could no longer see himself. He had been something once, he knew—alone but erect, with clear lines and definition. Now he was something else—shapeless, enshadowed, and with nothing more to show for his gruesome metamorphosis than the bitterest sweetest memories of Sha and the lingering ache of a coupling meant to discredit, that in the end had only restored Sha as the original, as the beginning and the end in his mind. But he hated Sha. He hated him for making him love him. He hated him for dirtying him, for making him *this way.* And he hated him for still seeming perfect, so goddamn perfect, when there was every indication he was not. Aaron stumbled suddenly and fell to his knees. The pavement bit his skin. His stomach heaved and he vomited. Tears ran hot and silent. He was vaguely aware of a hand at his shoulder and quiet words being spoken. But he would not be comforted. He would *not* be consoled. He sprung up, desperate and confused. Glass shattered nearby. He had to go.

His feet began moving, *but where? Where?* Where could he go that was not contaminated, rife with the taint of his new-fangled shame? He wanted to die more than ever. He needed something he could no longer have. He ached to be clean.

Fiended for morality. Wanted no more of the filth and confusion of men. The shame and secrecy and rending self-hate. Had to find in the world some way of being or die. He would not live like this, could not, in disgrace, unable to raise his head, unable to bear what he was. He could no longer suffice the lie. Nor the lie him. It was not enough. Did not satisfy. He had to *be* something else, *would* be something else now or die. He would refuse his body, rebuke his despicableness and his desire, go on cold and hypnotic, detaching nerve from nerve, retraining his body and his mind until there was no trace of that secret pulse, that hard high compulsion toward his own kind, despised through the ages, from Sodom and Gomorrah until now. He had never touched a woman, never wanted to. But he would now. Somehow. He would find a way to be whole, entomb himself beneath wife, family, look upon the men as the world did. That was what he needed: blinding routine, the drone and cloak of family. He thought of his own: defected father, cruel idiot mother. Only his sister was redeemable out of that fell salvage yard from which sprung his crooked family tree. *His sister*. It struck him. He had to find her.

He ran quickly, clawing through the darkness, toward his aunt's apartment on Kosciosko. Anise was there, he knew, left for dead while his mother traveled out of town, where and why he did not know or care. He should have kept her with him, *his sister*, should have kept her close, to protect her, to protect *himself*. And he would now; he would not let her out of his sight, the only clean thing left. Would keep her out of the claws of the bumbling mother, the evil aunt, to sully and spoil. He would take charge of her now, no one else could be expected to, teach her right from wrong as they had not taught him. Maybe then he would be safe.

He looked around him in the dark. Hordes of people were in the streets, moving, churning, some with candles now or tiny radios buzzing and clicking. Faint reflective circles were being made by bicycle tires as they spun. He was close. He had to be close, because the boy lived in Bed-Stuy too, in that dark tiny cupboard that would haunt his heart and his mind and become the crux and focus of nightmares to come. He was close, but the streets confounded him at every turn. Each block seemed darker and more foreboding than the last. All was unrecognizable. At points he thought he would turn back or simply lie down where he was on the pavement, close his eyes and be swallowed up by the night. But he could not turn back, because turn back to what? To where? Where was he going? Where been? Nothing was certain now. Nothing clear. The darkness around him spun into color and he felt himself falling. His legs vanished beneath him. There was a sharp pain in his chin and darkness.

In the moment of his unconsciousness he dreamed, dreamed that it was all a dream. He had opened his eyes in bed, *his bed*, that first expectant day of summer. There was no impossible blinding light coming through the little window. No unbearable mask. No choking heat. No inviolable darkness. There was only shadow, obscuring and imprecise, and the cool white sheet across his waist. It had all been a dream: Sha, Maggie, the boy, the Clubhouse, that terrible tiny room—all a dream, dark and unshorn but gone now, leveled to dust by the involuntary act of opening his eyes. He could hear the jingle and chimes of the ice cream truck, the voices of children on the street. But the voices changed, deepened, and the music did too, grew coarser and louder until it roared, became violent like the snapping of piano wires, the wooden crushing of darling music boxes. A voice came:

"Is he dead?"

"He ain't dead. Probably had a heat stroke or something."

"In the middle of the night?"

He tasted blood. Then it was back and pounding. The grim facts of his life rose up again more dark and outrageous than before. He got to his feet, stumbled again and fell, picked himself up again and was running, going in the right direction now he was sure, though the streets gave no signal, toward his aunt's apartment on Kosciusko. Around him, voices rang out of throats cloaked in darkness. Feet pounded the ground. Then he knew he was on Broadway.

The tracks of the J train hulked above him, strange and silent. He ran still, though his head and his lungs ached, bathed in perspiration, unable to stop. Then he was on Kosciusko, beneath the sagging telephone wires, only that long block and a half of uneven cement and crumbling brick and dog shit separating him from his sister, from his new way of being, which would start tonight, which he would take by force, the same as he would take his sister if he had to. Because he was in control now, would be in control, not tricked any more or hustled or coerced. Would be a man and force his will, dare anyone to stop him. He approached the building now hardly able to breath or walk but still running, slamming into the locked front door of the yellowish five-floor edifice with the force of a carcass falling from the sky. He pounded at the door, clawed at the row of silent buzzers connected by useless wires. He stepped back, his chest pounding, turned up his face to the long face of the building. He opened his mouth and howled, tried to, but his voice vanished weak and tiny into the thick ink of the night. He reeled around the building, staggered, his feet slipping in the debris of the vacant lot, going toward the back stairs now and the door that was never locked. He would be up those five floors in a second and take his sister out of there, no matter what his aunt objected, no matter what his mother did because he needed her, could be better for her than he had been for himself. He pulled open the door. The narrow back stairwell folded above him, stifling and black as an oven. He pulled himself up by the handrail, two steps or three at a time, reaching the landing and turning, going up again blind, wet to his underwear, up bodily, rising in altitude but feeling distinctly the descent, stygian, into chaos. He turned, reaching the third floor landing now, and should have noticed the glow (the little sprig of light alone in that well of darkness), checked or slowed at the movement of shadow in an unused back stairwell in the middle of the night. But when he reached that next landing, the fourth, at full speed, legs and

218

lips quivering, and saw what he saw it was as if there had been no warning, and he had not heard the truck coming, had not detected the velocity and mass behind the blazing headlights.

He could not know or imagine how any of it had come to pass. Could not know the sheer number or weight of events that had needed to converge to kill him at a single moment. He did not know that his sister had been by herself, left alone in that baking apartment with only two windows to breathe because her aunt could not resist the temptation, the opportunity, to visit the shops on Broadway when there was no alarm system, no electronic surveillance device that would serve without wattage to stop her. She had opened the windows and told Anise to stay with one word like a dog, fastening around her neck a tiny flashlight on a rope she had purchased on the train for one dollar. He could not know how many nights the boy had snuck out beneath his frail sleeping grandmother and disconsolate mother and crossed Broadway and come down Kosciusko to stare up at the window where he knew she was sometimes, only partially understanding that she did not actually live there. He had never found her there until tonight, hanging out the dark window frame on her elbows with a tiny light glowing around her neck which he believed was just for him. Neither could Aaron know or believe that his little sister, nine going-on-ten, the only clean thing left, had pulled her pants down to the boy at least six times now in the past two weeks, in that abandoned back stairwell without a door even that locked, most of the time without any prompting. But he knew she had them down now, and knew plainly now too that she had not been forced, coerced, because the little light around her neck shone plainly down on both of them, and on her hands especially, and her little hips, active and seeking, not receptive, benign against the boy, smaller than she was almost, standing there naked too from the waist down.

That moment—when Aaron saw his sister, and she not so much as saw but smelled and felt him there in the dark, just outside her little sphere of light—less like a moment than a lifetime, because everything stopped, all time and breathing and motion, like the hands of the clock frozen at the top of that domed soaring clocktower, and her hands frozen too, horribly frozen on the little honey-colored boy—that moment was the worst of their lives. Until the next one. Because there is always a next; time cannot wait, spins on superbly even when clock hands do not. And when time nudged finally back into motion, temporality, it was to a low growl, beginning deep in Aaron's throat, and the quick shuffling of child-sized clothes being pulled by little arms and legs. Until the limbs stiffened. Realized, felt the blows coming fast and vicious, and bent to cover themselves, making no difference against the brutal sinew and pulsing muscle of an almost-man in total fury. Using even his feet now, kicking in his boots, and the growl growing deeper and louder with the screams, all of that kicking and thudding and howling of children filling up that clapped-out back stairwell, until the very worst moment, when the boy stumbled backward, his legs caught in the pants, and went over the stairs, landing at the bottom with a single expiring squeak like a dog toy.

Then there was silence, sudden and diffused, broken only by the little whimper of Anise hunched over her little light. He looked at her, looked over the stairs at the little crumpled boy, silent there on the landing below, his pants visibly twisted still around his legs, and in that moment had his first inkling, his first sideways glance of the true monster he had become. But before he could think, really think, his feet were moving, down past the little boy, the soles of his boots ringing against the stairs, thudding on the landing, ringing again, down, down now in body and spirit both, down that oven-like back stairwell folding above him in darkness, until he hit the unlockable back door and it flew open before him into even more darkness and more heat, the whole world an oven now, falling to his knees and vomiting again, dry-heaving because there was nothing left.

Then he was on his feet again, moving, where he did not know, past the wheezing pit bulls and chain-link fences and vacant lots, on into the night, letting his feet decide, having no destination except one: oblivion, but he was already there. Unable to breathe or see. Uncertain death was any different, but catapulting towards it nonetheless, because what else was there? *What else was there now?* But how? If he had a gun...But he didn't, and the only person he knew for sure could get one, could get anything, he could not ask, would not, because that person was his downfall. So he went on, or his feet did at least, running like his mind, thinking of the thousand anonymous medicine bottles in the cabinet, the razor blade in the sewing kit, the rat poison under the sink. Wanting more oblivion than this, with its screaming cats and shattering glass and astounded voices too easy, too calm for what was really going on. Cars flew by him, and trees, and stoops peopled with dark faces and waving fans, the too-easy voices coming together into unison like an om, but not calming to him, driving him forward on the contrary, though the moving feet were separate from him, thinking only of the bed sheet around his neck, electricity somehow, a plastic bag over his head. There had to be somewhere, some way to go out of this place without having to enter into another. His feet moved and he hoped they were taking him there, past the overflowing trash cans and piles of brick and dark hanging street lamps on and on out of despair, the exhaust filling up the streets still behind the phantom headlights, rats scuttling one trash heap to the next.

Then he was on Flatbush, his feet still moving, stepping over the broken glass and wasted cigar innards and gutters full of mint green boxes crushed flat against the cement. In his mind he saw his sister crouched, the boy crumpled on the landing. Death deserved him. He craved it. He could not go on in his present form. The streets flew by. Beverly. Cortelyou. Albermarle. Candles flickered in windows. Storefront gates crashed down. *Where was he going?* But it was too late. He was already turning onto Church Avenue, the white belltower moving above him. He was looking for him. Of course he was looking for him. But why? To see him one last time before... No. It was so Sha could see *him*, see his dirty work done and complete, walking on two legs but dead already. The church loomed beside him. The ancient graveyard with its wrought iron belt. The dead Dutchmen purring in their graves beneath the ravished tombstones. His eyes worked now, strained to see in that well of darkness. There was movement, barely discernible, uncertain shapes in the distance. His stomach ached. His head spun. He wanted to vomit again. Then something jumped inside him. Ahead, a tiny red ember rose for a moment in the dark, glowed brighter and fell. He knew it was Sha.

He did not know what he would say. He did not want to say anything. The ember rose again and glowed. He did not take his eyes off it. There were voices, muffled and low. He was close now, and could almost see the thin silhouettes of bodies dimly framed. Then that tiny piece of fire floated up again one last time through the endless sea of black, glowed hard and sailed off into shadow. But in the moment it glowed, it glowed ghastly, illuminating a face stitched together, brutish and quilt-like, from one corner of the mouth almost to the ear. His heart sank, but with relief too, because it was not Sha. He could turn around now and plot his demise. When Sha saw him again it would be too late. His mind had already turned again to the rat poison, the medicine bottles. The voice came: "Come here, son." But he didn't hear it. Did not recognize the voice or any-thing at that moment.

"Eh," the voice said. And then there were footsteps. But he did not hear them either. He felt himself being swung around, was aware of the pressure at his shoulder.

"You don't hear me talkin to you?" Jay Toriace stared at him. Aaron's eyes did not focus or try to. The voice was famil-iar. He had heard it this time, but far off.

"What the fuck is wrong with you, son? You drunk?"

Aaron looked at him finally, recognizing him but not val-idating him in his own mind, as if they were in two different worlds, on two different sides of a television screen, Aaron watch-ing him but not believing in him, keeping him at bay. But Toriace would not let him do it.

222

"Yeah," he said. "You remember me now, don't you?"

Aaron moved his head vaguely.

"You lookin for your boy, ain't you?" Toriace looked at him. "Sha?"

Aaron shook his head. "I ain't lookin for nobody."

"No?" Jay Toriace said. " I am. And when I find him it's gon be problems."

They stared at each other in the dark. Aaron understood his tone but was oblivious to it, impervious to the fear he believed he should feel. He said nothing, turned to leave. But Jay Toriace snatched him back, pulled him around by his shirt. "Don't you never turn your back on me while I'm talkin to you," he growled. "I want to ask you somethin."

Aaron looked at him, startled at his own courage. "You don't have nothin to say to me."

He heard the pop of flesh and knuckle before he felt it in his mouth.

"You got a smart mouth don't you?" Jay Toriace said, rubbing his fist.

Aaron touched his face, again tasted blood in his mouth. "Okay," he said. "What is it?"

Toriace nodded to himself. "It's about your boy. Sha." His arms crossed his chest. "People been tellin me some funny shit about that nigga," he said. "I want to know if it's true."

Aaron's stomach tensed. He was not afraid to die. But he was afraid of this. He looked at Toriace. "I don't know anything about it," he said. "If you want to know something about him, you have to ask him."

"I'm askin *you*." Then: "Let me ask you this. That nigga ever try anything with you?"

Aaron's stomach drew tighter. "What you—?"

"—You know what I mean."

Aaron's mouth opened but there was no sound.

"That nigga never tried none of that faggot shit with you?" Jay looked over his nose. Aaron's stomach turned over and over.

"Yeah, son." Jay Toriace smiled to himself. "That nigga's a homo. Funny ain't it? I bugged out too, when I found out."

Aaron was paralyzed, frozen where he stood.

"You know," Toriace said then, "now that I think about it, that nigga always did have a little bitch in him. Like when he walked. How he always switched his ass a little, like he was sweet." He looked gravely at Aaron. "You ever notice that?"

He knew he must speak, but when he opened his mouth there was not speech, but a thin sound like a creaking floorboard or an unoiled door.

"What?" Jay snapped. "Yo, what the fuck is your problem?" He glared at Aaron. "Son," he said grimly, his brows dropping into each other. "You ain't no homo too, is you?"

Aaron's throat closed. He could not breathe. He had been waiting to deny it his whole life. That is how it seemed to him at that moment. But facing it, and the actual words, was more than he had ever imagined. He stood staring up at him, at Jay Toriace's crooked face, his heart flopping, his breath held. And Jay Toriace's face changed.

"Ah, hell," he said. "Don't tell me you and that nigga…" He looked at him. "Ah hell. Are you fuckin kiddin me? I swear to God, son, that shit is disgusting."

Jay Toriace looked at him another moment, said something over his shoulder. Two thin figures came out of the dark. One of them said something in an accent.

"Can you believe this shit," he said to them. "Where is all these faggots comin from?"

They all stared then, barely seeing each other, their eyes narrowing in their faces. Whatever they wanted to do, Aaron thought, they would have to do it now before one more thing happened, because he would not bear it. Could not bear his skin one second more. He was going to provoke them, make them kill him right now to avoid further insult, but his knees buckled, his eyes rolled in his head. He felt himself slumping forward, being thrust back. He fell to his knees.

"What the fuck is wrong with this mutherfucker?" Jay slapped him, shook him by his shirt. "Get up, son. Get up!"

Aaron felt the blows from far off. *It's not so bad,* he thought. *Not so—*

Then Jay Toriace hit him again, and Aaron thought he opened his eyes. He could hear their voices muffled and the blows muffled too but the outrage beneath it loud and clear and cold and specific *fuckin faggot fuckin faggot.* Aaron felt his ribs shake in his chest. His fists shot out convulsively. He opened his mouth not to scream or cry but to roar that flat unequivocal roar of someone who has simply had enough.

The boys stopped suddenly and looked down at their bloody fists. Aaron exhaled and shut his eyes.

***

Sha had heard it from Flatbush. He did not know what it was, or that is what he told himself, though something in him knew, his feet maybe, because they moved him toward it swiftly over the scorched cement. He had done much to get there. Begged a ride at the Holland Tunnel when the trains would not run. Navigated the driver up the Hudson River when Tunnel service shut down. Crossed the Tappan Zee in darkness, egging the little driver on, across Westchester down into the Bronx. Across the Harlem River then at 137, walking now, twelve miles on foot down the East Side. He had crossed the last bridge onto Flatbush up into the stomach of Brooklyn, and when he heard the howl, the roar, he came towards it down Church, unable suddenly to think. He could only think of Aaron now, though he did not know why, his feet moving, as Aaron's had, outside himself. He came closer and something in him kicked, the roar increasing, and he saw through the wrought iron fence the bodies huddled and something on the ground. He saw Jay Toriace. Saw his foot come back, swing forward into the little thing on the ground. The roar stopped and there was silence and he knew that it was Aaron.

He flew at them, fists square with fury, machine-like but silent under the sheet of darkness. They had not seen him but they felt him: in the windpipe, the ribs, the back of the head, his hands and feet flying wild and methodical, his knuckles crackling as they encountered flesh. Boots scuffed the pavement. A chain clinked to the ground. There were eyes in the darkness surrounding them now, tongues wagging in mouths. Sha swung again; bicuspids clicked, but there were too many of them. They were three. He was one. And by the time he had floored the first and smashed the teeth of the second, the third had got his wits about him and fought back furiously with his own sense of sanctity because the object of his wrath was by definition infinitely less than a man. But Sha was blind with rage, oblivious to any disdain but his own, with lightning reflex to meet the fragile presumptions of his enemy. They fought there toe to toe, matching blows but Sha outpacing him, hitting faster and harder, Aaron curled at his feet. Then the first got up, Jay Toriace, swallowing and holding his throat. He came blood-gulping, smashing with his rings. In a second they had him and he was on the ground, but still fighting, kicking, taking pieces of them. But they took pieces of him too, six hands coming at once—his head, his back, his stomach—until he felt consciousness sliding away, chromatic unconsciousness taking hold, coming down like a curtain. And when his eyes rolled they pulled him, dragged him to the fence, propped him limply up against it. His head lolled on his neck. His eyes began to swell shut. Jay Toriace slapped him hard.

"Wake up," he said. "Wake up." Sha's eyes slit open. Jay hit him again. "What the hell was you thinkin," he said, "comin around here? You think you king of the fags or somethin? Just cause you had everybody fooled?" He hit him a final time viciously in the stomach and blood and vomit fell out of his mouth onto the sidewalk. "Don't let it get on him," Toriace said. "I want his clothes."

They stripped him then, took his boots and his jeans, yanked his shirt over his head. They stood him against the fence, half-conscious in his underwear, his arms wound into the spikes of the fence, supporting him. Jay Toriace bent, picked up something off the sidewalk—a jagged chunk of brick or cement.

"Let this be a lesson to these fuckin perverts." He spit over Sha. He raised the brick then and brought it down hard on Sha's head. Sha's knees gave but he stayed there suspended before the fence, his arms woven between the spikes. Jay Toriace let the brick fall, stood back a moment to consider his work. Something was missing it seemed, because out of his pocket then he drew the black-handled hunting knife that had been folded inside and examined the blade in the dark. He looked at Sha then and spit on the cement. "You fucked up, son," he said. "If you was smart you would a saved yourself." He shoved the knife deftly between Sha's ribs and Sha groaned. He pulled the knife out and blood came behind it. Sha raised his eyes a moment to the sky, whispered something inaudible and died, without terror, having plucked the sting from death.

***

Aaron's eyes had begun to flit, and when he opened them in the dark, and saw the blade shining, and heard the final incomprehensible statement of what he was from Sha, his heart slowed, sped, stopped. Sparks saw it at the same time, coming around the corner from Church. But he kept moving toward them, his heart seizing too in its own way but his hand still going down, down into his pants, coming back with the index finger locked into the trigger, the black Four-Four shining like the knife had from whatever was in the sky. He killed them all, Jay Toriace and the Haitian and the third boy whom he had not even known, and when they fell the only thing he thought was that he hoped he wasn't caught.

Aaron hoped it was a dream, but it was real. He did not get off the ground. He looked at Sha there slumped, his arms still in the fence, and he wailed for himself and for Sha. He wailed for his little sister and the boy dead on the landing. Wailed hard and long for the horror of the tiny room, of Magdalena, of the world without Sha. But his life would go on, though he did not know it; there was still time. Because he would not kill himself. Because the little boy on the landing had not been dead. Because it was not his time. He would go on, grow beautiful as a man, and when he saw love again he would recognize it or he would not, but he would not be afraid because the worst had happened.